RAVENMOCKER

"Beguiling... Jean Hager's novels do for the Cherokee culture what Tony Hillerman has done for the Navajo."
—*San Diego Union-Tribune*

JEAN HAGER

MYSTERIOUS PRESS

$5.99 US / $6.99 CAN.
ISBN 0-446-40107-2
50599>
9 780446 401074
EAN

PRAISE FOR JEAN HAGER AND RAVENMOCKER

"Hager comes closer to justifying the inevitable comparisons to Tony Hillerman than any other writer of Native American mystery novels I have encountered."

—Boston Sunday Globe

"Tightly plotted."

—New York Times Book Review

"Readers of Jean Hager's earlier mysteries will embrace her new sleuth, Cherokee Molley Bearpaw. She's fresh, very appealing, and ready for a long and prosperous series."

—Mostly Murder

"Entertaining . . . Bearpaw is appealing."

—New York Newsday

"Hager writes warmly and vividly about contemporary Native Americans."

—Publishers Weekly

more . . .

"Entertaining and different, this is the first in a promising series featuring the admirable Molly Bearpaw."
—***Booklist***

"Jean Hager's best book yet!"
—***The Armchair Detective***

"Her characters' motives and behavior are convincingly written. . . . The potential appeal is tremendous. A new insight to the traditions of the Charokees has much to offer."
—***Tulsa World***

"A fine and finely crafted tale. . . . Bearpaw is one of the most delightful Spunky-Female P.I.'s to inhabit the pages of a mystery in a long time."
—***Trenton Times***

"Ravenmocker is a suspense-filled tale whose three-dimensional characters and natural dialogue make the book difficult to put down."
—***London Free Press*** (Ontario)

"Molly is an exhilaratingly fresh character."
—Murder Ad Lib

"Jean Hager introduces us to Cherokee life through the experiences of Molly Bearpaw."
—Rocky Mountain News

"Not just a good mystery but a glimpse into the fear and helplessness of the aged. . . . Hager is a fine writer."
—Ocala Star-Banner

"A 'who-dunnit' packed with twists and turns and cultural revelations."
—Bookwatch

"A fine mystery."
—Midwest Book Review

"Molly is a complex and likable heroine, the Cherokee setting is full of interest, and the murder plot quite well worked out. An excellent choice for book-starved Hillerman fans."
—Mystery Lovers Bookshop

RAVENMOCKER

JEAN HAGER

THE MYSTERIOUS PRESS

Published by Warner Books

A Time Warner Company

MYSTERIOUS PRESS EDITION

Cover design and illustration by David Tamura

Mysterious Press Books are published by
Warner Books, Inc.
1271 Avenue of the Americas
New York, NY 10020

Visit our Web site at
http://warnerbooks.com

A Time Warner Company

Printed in the United States of America

Originally published in hardcover by The Mysterious Press.
First Printed in Paperback: April, 1994
10 9 8 7 6 5 4

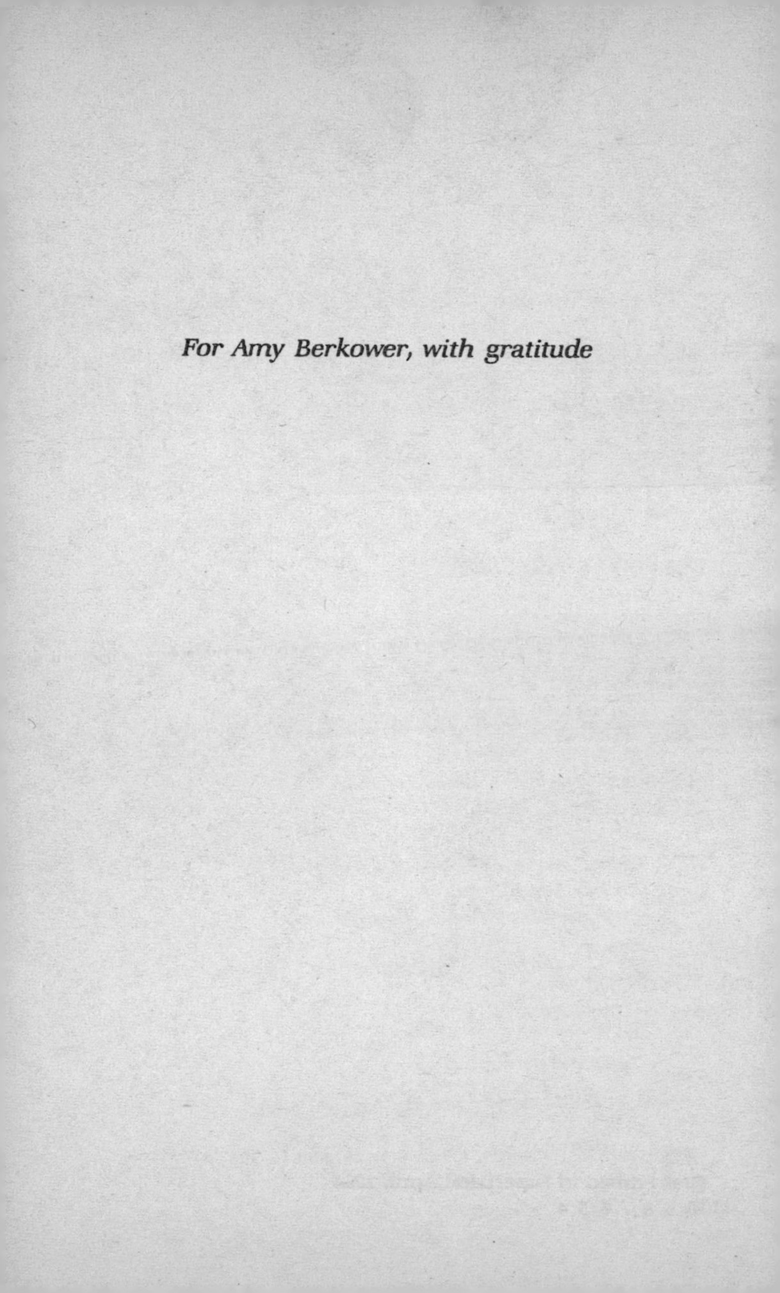

For Amy Berkower, with gratitude

AUTHOR'S NOTE

Although I have tried to be accurate in the description of Tahlequah, Oklahoma, any resemblance between the characters in this book and any person actually living in Tahlequah, Park Hill, or anywhere else in Cherokee County, Oklahoma, is coincidental and unintended. To my knowledge there is not, nor has there ever been, a Country Haven Nursing Home in Tahlequah. It, as well as the Native American Advocacy League, are purely fictitious.

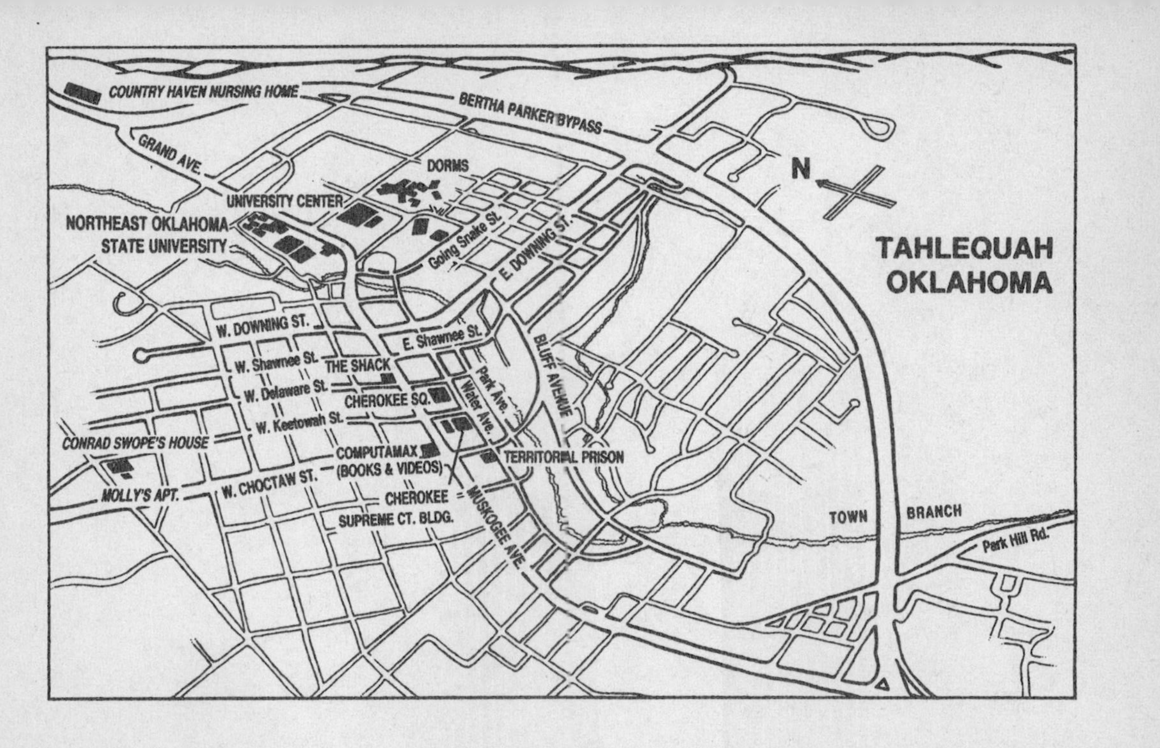
TAHLEQUAH
OKLAHOMA
N
COUNTRY HAVEN NURSING HOME
BERTHA PARKER BYPASS
GRAND AVE.
DORMS
UNIVERSITY CENTER
NORTHEAST OKLAHOMA
STATE UNIVERSITY
Going Snake St.
E. DOWNING ST.
W. DOWNING ST.
E. Shawnee St.
W. Shawnee St.
THE SHACK
W. Delaware St.
CHEROKEE SQ.
Park Ave.
Water Ave.
BLUFF AVENUE
W. Keetowah St.
CONRAD SWOPE'S HOUSE
COMPUTAMAX
(BOOKS & VIDEOS)
TERRITORIAL PRISON
W. CHOCTAW ST.
MOLLY'S APT.
CHEROKEE
SUPREME CT. BLDG.
MUSKOGEE AVE.
TOWN
BRANCH
Park Hill Rd.

OOOOOOOO

1

August heat held northeastern Oklahoma in an iron grip. It hung over the fourteen counties that had been carved, whole or in part, from the Cherokee Nation in 1907. West of the Grand River, dying yellow grass carpeted mile upon mile of gently rolling hills and prairie country. East of the river in the vast wooded areas of the Ozark plateau, hickory trees, native walnuts, elms, and blackjack oaks were already dropping rain-starved leaves. And south of Tahlequah, at the entrance to the tribal office complex, three flags—of the United States of America, the state of Oklahoma, and the Cherokee Nation of Oklahoma—hung limp and unmoving.

On Highway 82, beyond the campus of Northeastern Oklahoma State University, Gable Athletic Field, and Tahlequah's boundary, sweat-drenched workmen toiled feverishly to repair the central air-conditioning unit at the Country Haven Nursing Home. The air conditioning had been off for more than four hours. At nine o'clock in the morning, it was ninety-six degrees in the shade. Inside the nursing home, electric fans circulated the stale air and the windows remained closed, the temperature within the brick walls being fifteen degrees cooler than outside.

In room 105 in A-wing, three men sat watching an elderly Cherokee asleep in a narrow hospital bed, twin to the unoccupied bed against the opposite wall. The sick man was eighty-four-year-old Abner Mouse. He lay on his back, his long braids draped across his shoulders and bony chest, dove gray against the white hospital gown. In repose, his wrinkled brown face could have been a carving in walnut.

Woodrow Mouse, Abner's only son, sat close to the bed, repeatedly wiping Abner's face with a damp washcloth. "He feels a little cooler," Woodrow murmured. He was a tall, lean man dressed in jeans and a blue T-shirt.

Abner's roommate, Mercer Vaughan, who had phoned Woodrow at 6:00 A.M. to say his father had had a bad night, leaned forward in his rocking chair. His hands, the knuckles knotted by arthritis, curled around the crook of a cane. He wore a pair of khaki pants and a plaid cotton shirt. His braided hair wasn't as gray as Abner's, although he was two years older. Mercer's rheumy black eyes monitored the shallow rise and fall of Abner's chest, his expression grim.

The third man, Vann Walkingstick, was a medicine man who had been summoned by Woodrow Mouse. He was heavyset, his straight black hair cropped short and shaved over the ears. An oscillating fan sat on a table at the foot of Abner's bed.

"It's hot enough to cook fry bread out there," said Walkingstick, who had been outside, making preparations for the medicine ceremony. He sighed heavily and mopped his wet brow with a red handkerchief.

Woodrow folded the damp washcloth and laid it on his father's forehead. "Did you see any clouds?"

"No."

"Thunder is mad at us," said Mercer Vaughan in his deep, sorrowful voice. He gazed out the window at a drooping mimosa tree, blinking in a vain attempt to clear his vision. "The son of my father's brother down by Stilwell says they're all mad at us because we forgot the old ways . . . the Apportioner, Thunder, Slanting Eyes, the Red

Man . . . Most of us don't even know what clan we belong to nowadays—the young people, anyway."

In fact, clan descent would be impossible to figure out in most cases because the taboo attached to intermarrying within a clan had been forgotten long ago. Furthermore, if Mercer had voiced his concerns in the hearing of the young members of the tribe, many of them would laugh at him.

In his lifetime, he had witnessed several generations of his people grow up, each becoming more assimilated into the white man's world than their parents' generation. Dwelling on it made him feel hopeless.

Sometimes he thought he had lived too long. He stared at the shrunken body of his roommate, remembering how strong it had been in the old days. Abner was *u-ginay'li,* his friend from boyhood. They had roamed the woods together, snaring birds and animals for family meals. Abner was the best *awi'ayeli'ski,* deer caller, Mercer had ever known. Now Abner was the last link with his boyhood, and Abner was dying.

Woodrow shuffled his feet uneasily. "The doctor's supposed to be on the way." He had stomped out of the room and to the nurse's station a few minutes earlier. "I stood there till that damn nurse called him. She claims she left word for him hours ago. Says he's been in surgery. Who knows? She may just be covering her ass in case Dad is as bad as I've been telling her. If you ask me, she doesn't care."

"Crawford don't like old people," Mercer muttered.

"She shouldn't be working in a nursing home, then," Woodrow said, tapping his foot restlessly. "She acts like Dad's puking up his guts and talking out of his head is nothing to worry about. According to her, it's a virus." Standing, he tugged at the sheet beneath his father to straighten it and smoothed the top sheet across Abner's skeletal rib cage. Dropping into his chair, he added, "He seems to be resting pretty well now."

"That's probably the pill they gave him. It knocked him out," Mercer said. "He's still real bad, though." He expelled a long breath and peered at the backs of his gnarled hands, still curled around his cane.

"I told her half an hour ago he could've had a stroke,"

Woodrow continued. "He was having trouble moving his arms, even before he took the pill. She looked at me like, 'Where did you get your medical education?' But I think she was checking him for paralysis the last time she came in here."

"He already had one stroke," said Mercer, "but it didn't make him puke."

"That was a light one," Woodrow responded, "but if this is another stroke, it's worse, and the nurse says there's not much the doctor can do. I'd sure rather hear it from the doctor, though. I don't think some of them nurses know any more about it than I do."

Walkingstick took a pipe wrapped in a black cloth from his shirt pocket, tucked the cloth more securely around it, and returned the pipe to his pocket. "I'll tell you one thing, that Crawford woman don't want me here. She seen me driving the stakes. Wanted to know what I thought I was doing."

"What'd you tell her?" Woodrow asked.

"I said, 'I think I'm pounding this here stick into the ground. What's it look like to you?' Made her mad. She mumbled something and stomped back inside."

"If a *Ka'lana-ayeli'ski* gets in here," Mercer said, "white man's medicine ain't gonna be worth a damn, doctor or no doctor." His mouth turned down at the corners, a hopeless grimace. "'Course, you can't expect a white woman to understand that."

"That's why I called Vann," Woodrow told the old man, "to keep out the ravenmockers."

A loud moan came from the bed. The three watchers leaned toward the frail old man. Abner frowned in his sleep and his legs beneath the sheet twitched reflexively. His eyes fluttered open briefly. They rolled around but didn't focus. He made no other sound.

"Did you see the way his legs jerked?" Mercer asked. "His stomach's still paining him. He told me last night the cramps in his gut was the worst he ever had." Then to Walkingstick, "How will we know if a ravenmocker gets in here?"

"Them witches can make themselves invisible," Woodrow added.

"If he starts flailing around," Walkingstick told them, "it's a pretty good sign a witch got in and is trying to suck the breath out of him. I have known them to throw a man clear out of bed."

"When are you going to do the medicine?" Woodrow asked.

"In a little while." He patted the pocket containing the pipe. "I been thinking. This nursing home is full of old people."

"Is that supposed to be news or what?" Woodrow asked, a bit irritably. He wished Walkingstick would quit fiddling with that pipe and get on with his medicine.

"Don't climb on your high horse, Woodrow. Maybe your father made some enemies here."

"I don't think so. Dad's not one to get crossways with people."

"Mercer, you know if Abner has any enemies?"

Mercer closed his eyes and worked his mouth like a cow chewing its cud. The others waited. After a moment, the old man squinted at them and shook his head. "I been Abner's roommate for nigh on to two years. He ain't got no enemies among the people here that I know of. He don't like that head nurse, Crawford, but none of us have much use for her. She's the crankiest *young* woman I ever saw. Always yelling at somebody for spilling food or pissing the bed. Makes more work for her. I flat out told her once she wasn't getting paid to read magazines."

"That's for sure," Woodrow agreed.

"Being cranky don't make her a witch," Walkingstick said. "Most ravenmockers are old. That's because every time they kill somebody, they add what's left of the dead person's life on to their own. Some of them are a hundred, even a hundred-fifty years old. My mother's father knew of one that got to be two hundred before he died."

Vaughan and Woodrow exchanged a worried look. "Mercer, think now," Walkingstick went on, "have you ever heard any ravens shrieking around this place at night, or seen a fire in the sky? It would likely have been when somebody was dying."

Mercer shook his head.

"Ever hear a racket at night, like somebody stomping on the roof?"

Mercer looked even more apprehensive. "No."

"Well, that don't prove they haven't been here. Maybe

you were asleep.'' Walkingstick got up and closed the door. ''Just to be sure, I better make medicine in here before I go outside. Woodrow, you stand against the door and don't let anybody in until I'm finished.'' He drew out the pipe and unwrapped it. Then he took a small pouch of tobacco from another pocket and filled the pipe. As soon as Woodrow had phoned him earlier that morning, he had walked half a mile to the branch of the Illinois River—the ''Long Man''—that flowed through Tahlequah. Standing on the riverbank, he had remade the tobacco, invoking Long Man to infuse it with magic power.

Woodrow leaned back against the door, his arms folded across his chest. Mercer moved his rocking chair to a corner of the room, watching the proceedings with eyes squeezed nearly shut, which seemed to make things a little clearer.

Walkingstick produced a match and, after lighting the pipe, closed his eyes and silently reviewed the incantation for killing a ravenmocker. He must invoke the ancient god of the East, the Red Man in ritualized prayers, who had the power to grant success to a supplicant, and the god of the North, Blue Man, who could defeat a witch, called the imprecator in the language of Cherokee ritual. Then with the words fresh in his mind, he chanted in Cherokee:

> Listen!
> Red Man, quickly we two have prepared your arrows for the soul of the imprecator.
> He has them lying along the path.
> Quickly we two will take his soul as we go along.
> Listen! O Blue Man, in the Frigid Land above you repose.
> He has them lying along the path.
> Quickly we two will cut his soul in two.

Walkingstick repeated the incantation four times before blowing smoke toward the window, the door, and into the four corners of the room.

Carefully, he rewound the black cloth around the pipe. ''Now I will go outside and make medicine. I hope nobody's messed with them sticks.''

When he was gone, Mercer said unsteadily, "I never thought about somebody in the nursing home being a witch."

"Me neither," said Woodrow.

Mercer stared morosely out the window, searching for Walkingstick. "You reckon there's anything to it?"

"Don't know, but Dad should be safe as long as he stays in this room," Woodrow said, "and he sure ain't going anywhere today."

Mercer gave him a sidelong look. "Unless the ravenmocker's medicine is stronger than Vann's."

* * *

When Walkingstick stepped outside, sweat immediately beaded his forehead. He had always perspired easily, even before he'd put on sixty excess pounds. Oklahoma's hot, humid summers were truly a trial to a man carrying around that much fat. His wife was always nagging him to go on a diet. To which he routinely responded that he went on diets all the time. The problem was he couldn't seem to stay on one for more than two or three days at a stretch before he started craving his wife's fry bread and fried chicken.

He walked around the nursing home, checking on the sharpened sticks about twenty yards from the four corners, if you could call them corners. This building had the strangest shape Walkingstick had ever seen, flat in front and back with three half-circle extensions on each side. He guessed it was some kind of modern design, but he didn't like it. Looked like one of those spaceships on TV.

The stakes, which he'd earlier driven into the ground, pointed-end up, were still in place. If a witch approached, the nearest stick would shoot up in the air and come down like an arrow on the witch's head. After being hit, he would groan loud enough for those inside the nursing home to hear. The witch would sicken and die within seven days.

The only other way to kill a ravenmocker was to recognize him in his human shape. Again, he would die within seven days after being recognized. Walkingstick had heard of people who had the right medicine to recognize a ravenmocker, but he had never known one personally.

The two repairmen working on the air-conditioning compressor stared curiously at Walkingstick as he passed, and mumbled to each other in low tones. Then he heard one of them laugh.

"*Una-sti-ski,*" Walkingstick muttered to himself. "Crazy man." He ignored the workmen; he didn't want anything but the medicine ceremony in his mind.

Satisfied that all four stakes were as he had left them, he relit the pipe and walked slowly around the building again, repeating, as he went, the incantation he'd said in Abner Mouse's room and puffing smoke in the direction of every trail by which a witch might approach. Sweat poured down his face and stung his eyes. He had to keep wiping it away with his handkerchief.

The workmen watched him cautiously as long as he was on their side of the building, but they couldn't understand what he was saying. Maybe they thought *he* was *una-sti-ski*. Walkingstick didn't worry about that. He concentrated on the Cherokee words of the incantation.

When he finished, he rewrapped the pipe and stuck it in his pocket. Then he shook out his wet handkerchief and ran it over his face. His scalp, face, and arms burned from the sun, which the old people said was the most powerful god of them all, the Apportioner, who lived in *Gulkwa'gine Di'galun'latiyun,* the seventh height immediately below the sky vault. Above *Gulkwa'gine Di'galun'latiyun* and the sky vault was *Galun'lati,* where the animals had lived when all below was water.

It was the Apportioner who, in the dim long-ago, had brought death to the people. Walkingstick wondered if Mercer was right about the ancient Cherokee gods being mad at them. Maybe the Apportioner was thinking up more ways to punish them, even now. He squinted up at the blank blue sky, forgetting for an instant that the Apportioner became very angry when a man didn't look straight at her, but screwed up his face. That was why she had brought death to the people in the first place.

Hastily, Walkingstick looked down and hurried back into the nursing home. If Abner was still alive at dusk, he would return and repeat the medicine ceremony.

He heard the compressor kick in as he entered Abner Mouse's room. "They must have fixed the air conditioner."

"It's about time," said Woodrow. "Maybe it'll make Dad feel better."

Mercer Vaughan didn't think so, but he didn't say it. Leaning on his cane, he pushed himself stiffly to his feet. "I'm going for a walk." He'd missed his early-morning walk around the grounds because he hadn't wanted to leave Abner. Now his joints ached.

The leather soles of his house slippers made slapping noises as he hobbled down the hall past the nurse's station. Beatrice Crawford, the nurse in charge, was talking on the telephone. As Mercer passed, she hung up and said, "Mr. Vaughan, it's too hot to go outside now."

"I'm only going to the end of the hall," he muttered. Damned fool woman. Crawford was even bossier than Irene Robinson, the yellow-haired supervisor who'd been on duty last night at 2:00 A.M. when Abner had awakened him, groaning and doubling over with pain and puking all over his bed. Mercer hadn't bothered to turn on the nurse's signal light near his bed, because sometimes they didn't notice it right away. Mercer suspected the night nurses slept on the job, or they simply ignored the light until they were good and ready to respond.

He had gotten out of bed and found Irene Robinson drinking a Coke in the little room behind the nurse's station. He had been surprised to find her still on duty, since she'd worked the three-to-eleven shift. Evidently she'd had to work double because another nurse had called in sick at the last minute or simply hadn't shown up.

She hadn't heard him approach, and for an instant, he'd watched her press her thumb and forefinger to her closed eyelids, as though her eyeballs hurt. She had frowned and heaved a tired sigh, and when he'd said her name, she'd jumped half out of her chair.

"Good God," she'd snapped. "Don't sneak up on me like that, Mr. Vaughan."

He'd told her Abner was sick. Irene Robinson had changed Abner's sheets and pajamas. And she'd given him something to stop the vomiting, not that it had. She hadn't seemed overly concerned about Abner, saying he must have caught the twenty-four-hour virus that several of the nursing home's residents had had recently. They'd all been sick to their stomachs.

It was the first Mercer had heard of any virus. The nurses rarely told the residents things like that, as though the fact that a contagious illness was making the rounds was none of their business. Mercer could only assume that Robinson had mentioned it so he wouldn't worry about Abner and keep after her to do something. He had worried, anyway.

Having reached the door at the end of the hall with the long, narrow pane of glass beside it, Mercer stopped, leaned on his cane, and looked out across a strip of mowed grass to the field of weeds and scrub brush on the other side of the nursing-home grounds. He thought he saw a movement in the weeds, which were more brown than green now. Probably a rabbit. He suspected the field was full of them, since he often saw one running across the grounds. In the old days, he and Abner would have cleaned them out of there, and his mother would have cooked a big pot of rabbit meat with dumplings. Thinking about it made his mouth water.

He saw no other movement in the weeds. It was so hot that the rabbits would be burrowed down in the coolest place they could find. The August heat sapped the energy from man and animal alike. Back in the old Cherokee country, before the white man stole it and named it North Carolina, Georgia, and Tennessee, this had been the month of the Green Corn Dance, the beginning of the Cherokee year. Mercer wondered if it got as hot there as here.

Waves of heat undulated in the air beyond the pane of glass. Or maybe it was only his failing eyesight. He truly hoped he didn't outlive his eyes. By squinting, he could identify one of Vann Walkingstick's stakes jutting up out of the ground. If Walkingstick's medicine was unnecessary after all, Mercer reasoned, and it really was the virus making Abner sick, he should be improved by tomorrow. Still, it was better to be safe than sorry. He was glad Woodrow had called Walkingstick.

Mercer couldn't help thinking about the dream he'd been having when Abner woke him at 2:00 A.M. He'd been standing under a big cottonwood tree. He didn't know where the tree was except that it was in the country. There hadn't been any houses or other buildings in his dream.

He remembered looking up and seeing dozens of birds lining the tree branches. A gust of wind droned around the tree, swaying the branches. It had raised goose bumps on his arms. That was when he'd realized he was wearing his blue pajamas, and he had no idea how he'd come to be there. He had flailed his arms and yelled at the birds, causing them to take flight. The birds' wings pumping the air made a keening sound like the high, long wail of a coyote. Then he'd been awakened by Abner's groans, and the wailing faded away.

Absently, he rested his forehead against the glass windowpane. It was almost hot enough to sear the skin. He jerked away. Then suddenly, as though the heat from the glass had jolted through his brain, rearranging everything stored there, he remembered something else about the dream. The birds in the cottonwood tree had been ravens.

For a moment, he could see and hear them again. It was as if he'd gone back into the dream somehow. He stood trancelike for a moment with his head down, hearing the low moan of the wind and the sudden, eerie wail as the birds flew away. He shivered and shook off the dream images.

As quickly as his arthritic joints would allow, he hobbled back to his room. "I recollected something just now, Vann. I had a dream last night. A whole flock of ravens were roosted in a cottonwood tree. I yelled at them and scared them off."

"How many ravens?"

"I don't know."

"More than seven?"

"Oh, yes. Too many to count."

"Did you see fire in the sky when they flew away?"

"If I did, I can't remember. Abner's groans woke me up, and I had to get the nurse. I didn't think about the ravens until now."

Woodrow, who had been listening to the exchange with an uneasy expression, abruptly stood and leaned over his father's bed. Abner twisted onto his side and began retching.

Woodrow grabbed a basin and held it under Abner's chin. A little clear liquid ran out, but he'd emptied his stomach hours ago. He didn't seem to be fully awake as his body convulsed with the dry heaves. Then he fell back against the pillow, never having opened his eyes.

Woodrow found the damp washcloth among the sheets and wiped Abner's face. "He looks so weak," he murmured to no one in particular.

"He's lost some weight," Mercer agreed. "But he was feeling good last week. He talked about going out to your place for a visit, but he was afraid it would make more work for Nellie." Actually, Abner had said he could go live with Woodrow if it weren't for his son's wife.

"She's got her hands full with her own mother, and—" Woodrow stopped abruptly and rose from his chair. "Dad," he said urgently. "*Dad!*" He whirled around. "Vann, get the nurse quick! I think he stopped breathing!"

Walkingstick lumbered out of the room. A few moments later, he returned with Beatrice Crawford, followed by Dr. Handley, who evidently had just arrived. Crawford shooed the three men into the hall and closed the door. Almost immediately a young practical nurse appeared, wheeling a defibrillator, and hurried into the room.

"Damn their hides! If he dies, I'm gonna sue their asses," Woodrow vowed. "They should've got another doctor out here when they found out Handley was in surgery."

"You ought to tell them to cut him open," Walkingstick said. "What do they call that?"

"An autopsy," Woodrow said. "I had that in my mind."

"Tell them you want to know what he died of."

"I don't think you can sue them till you know that, anyway," Mercer put in.

"They'll look at all his internal organs," Walkingstick went on, "including his heart—if it's still there."

Woodrow frowned at him. "Don't even think that. Don't you have faith in your own medicine?"

"Yes, but there are some things I don't know. A ravenmocker could have been in the room before I got here. Hiding under the bed, maybe. He could have turned back my medicine. Find out if the heart's still there."

Woodrow gave him a long, thoughtful look, remembering Mercer's suggestion that Walkingstick's medicine might not be as strong as the ravenmocker's. Finally, he nodded. "That's what I'm gonna do, for sure."

Three or four minutes later, the doctor emerged, followed by Beatrice Crawford. The young practical nurse remained inside. "He's gone, Mr. Mouse," Handley said. "I'm sorry I couldn't get here sooner, but I couldn't have saved him, anyway. Abner has failed a great deal in the past few months. The nurses did exactly what I would have done, had I been here."

Which was precious little, Mercer thought, squinting at the doctor's sanctimonious face.

"The nurses thought he had a virus!" Woodrow blurted.

"I'm sure that was part of the problem."

"Would a virus have killed him?"

"There were other compli—"

"I want an autopsy!"

Handley shook his head reproachfully. "Why don't you take a little while to think about that before you decide? Your father was old and in poor health. I can tell you what he died of. A CVA, a cardiovascular accident."

"What's that?" Woodrow asked.

"A stroke. Apparently complicated by an intestinal virus." Handley put a consoling hand on Woodrow's shoulder. "Try to look at it this way, Mr. Mouse. There are things worse than dying. You wouldn't have wanted him to live the way the stroke would have left him. In a persistent vegetative state. An autopsy isn't necessary."

Woodrow frowned and shrugged off the doctor's hand. "It sure as hell is! Don't you have to order an autopsy if the family wants it?"

"You might have to get a lawyer," Walkingstick put in helpfully.

The doctor shot Walkingstick an annoyed look, his lips squeezed together like a tobacco pouch with the drawstring pulled tight, then exchanged a long-suffering glance with the nurse. "If you insist . . ."

"I do," said Woodrow.

"Very well. I'll get in touch with the medical examiner."

OOOOOOOO

2

The noonday sun drew out the patina of age in the dark-red brick facade of the old Cherokee Capitol Building. The sheen seemed to come from deep within the bricks. The building stood, facing Muskogee Avenue, Tahlequah's main street, in the center of Cherokee Square, shaded by sugar-maple trees. Completed in 1870, the two-story structure had been built on the site that had served as the meeting place for the Cherokee government since the tribe's forced removal from east of the Mississippi River to Indian Territory in 1838 and 1839. With Oklahoma statehood in 1907, the building became the Cherokee County Courthouse. In recent years, a new, modern courthouse had been built, as well as a tribal-government office complex south of town.

Presently, the ground floor of the old capitol building housed the Tahlequah Chamber of Commerce, the Cherokee Gift Shop, and, in a tiny corner room, the northeast Oklahoma office of the Native American Advocacy League, a national organization charged with upholding the civil rights of Native Americans. The office was barely large enough to contain a desk, a file cabinet, and two chairs.

Molly Bearpaw, N.A.A.L. investigator and the sole employee of the northeast Oklahoma office, sat at the desk. She was twenty-eight years old and reed thin, a trait she had inherited from Eva Adair, the maternal grandmother who had raised her. Molly's thick black hair fell below her shoulders. It was parted in the middle, pulled back, and confined at the nape of her neck in a leather thong decorated with Indian beadwork. She wore a full, tiered cotton skirt and white gauze blouse, having rejected her usual blue jeans in favor of the skirt, which was cooler. Fortunately, the window air-conditioning unit was doing a fair job of battling the late August heat and humidity.

In spite of the air conditioning, Molly spent as little time as possible in the cramped room, coming by once or twice a day to check the answering machine for messages and to update reports on current cases. When an investigation was concluded, she typed a summary and mailed copies to the principal chief, the deputy principal chief, and the tribal council. Her salary was paid by the tribe, with grant funds from the U.S. Bureau of Indian Affairs.

Occasionally she arranged a meeting in the office with a tribal member who had requested her services. Like Woodrow Mouse, who would be there at 2:00 P.M. She wanted to update the files on two investigations before then.

She opened the Bowman folder. Sherwood Bowman had appeared in her office a couple of months ago, complaining of dizziness and nausea. When she made the obvious suggestion that he see a doctor, he said he already had. He had taken the pills the doctor prescribed, with no noticeable results. Besides, he told Molly, he hadn't come there for medical advice. He wanted her to investigate the Dorman Paint Factory, where he had worked as a delivery-van driver for three months, before he quit. His symptoms had started soon after he went to work at the factory, and he insisted he'd been exposed to some toxic substance there that was making him sick.

Molly had investigated Sherwood Bowman as well as the paint factory. She learned that the factory was in full compliance with OSHA and EPA rules and regulations and, furthermore, that nobody else working there had exhibited the same symptoms as Bowman. As for Sherwood, he had not left his job voluntarily, as he'd led her to believe. He had been fired for delivering the wrong paint to a customer once too often.

She also learned that this wasn't the first time Sherwood had claimed a work-related injury or illness. In fact, he'd drawn workmen's compensation for several months for an injured back, resulting, according to Sherwood, from a fall on the job. A fall that no one else witnessed. Earlier, he had sued a small oil company for firing him, claiming he was a victim of racial discrimination. He had lost the case.

It appeared that Sherwood Bowman was an accident looking for a potentially lucrative place to happen. At any rate, this was the sentiment voiced by the former employers Molly had contacted.

She made notes for the letter to Bowman, which she would type later, along with the case report. The letter would sum up the results of her investigation of the paint factory and suggest that, if he wished to pursue legal action, he should see an attorney.

Probably half of Molly's investigations consisted of gathering information that she had no authority to act on. In those instances, she handed the information over to an attorney or a law-enforcement agency. She wasn't even a licensed private investigator. Sometimes she functioned in a similar way but, as often as not, she undertook assignments that were outside the ken of a licensed P.I. Simply put, her job was to make certain that the Cherokees who requested her services, which were free to enrolled members of the tribe, were not denied their civil rights.

She closed the Bowman file and reached for the one labeled "Gritts." Zeke Gritts was a sixty-year-old man who suffered so badly from emphysema that he could barely walk across a room without running out of breath. Yet his request for disability income had been turned down by the Social Security Administration. A doctor at the local Indian hospital had examined him and reported to the SSA that he was unable to work. Apparently, that hadn't been enough for the bureaucrats.

Molly had arranged appointments with two specialists in

Tulsa, then requested and received money for their fees from tribal funds. After examining Gritts, both specialists had written letters stating unequivocally that he was too disabled to hold a job. In the meantime, Molly had lined up more than a dozen people, from Zeke's last employer to his next-door neighbor, to write letters to the SSA giving examples of the dire state of Zeke's physical condition. They had buried the SSA in paper.

Last week, Gritts had received word that the bureaucrats had reconsidered. Something of a coup in itself, Molly thought. Gritts would soon be receiving disability checks.

Molly wished that all her investigations could be brought to such satisfying conclusions.

As she closed the Gritts folder, her stomach grumbled, reminding her that it was past her usual lunchtime. She placed the two folders in her briefcase and glanced at her wristwatch. If she hurried, she'd have enough time to grab a bite before Woodrow Mouse arrived.

* * *

"My father died this morning," Woodrow Mouse said as soon as he was seated in Molly's office. He had a long, narrow face with a hooked nose, prominent cheekbones, and deep lines around his eyes and mouth.

"I'm sorry," Molly said. "I think I remember him. Abner, wasn't that his name?"

Woodrow nodded.

"Didn't he and your mother live in Park Hill at one time?" Molly's grandmother had moved back to the small community southeast of Tahlequah, her childhood home, after Molly graduated from Tahlequah High School.

"Yes, they lived next door to Nellie and me until Mom died, five years ago. Not long after that, we had to put Dad in the nursing home."

"Which one?"

"Country Haven." Bowing his head, he pressed both hands to his gaunt face, as though trying to compose himself. When he looked up, the hollows around his black eyes seemed deeper and darker than before, as though they'd been gouged out with a dull, dirty instrument. "It was the newest and cleanest of the ones I looked at, but I wonder now if it wasn't a mistake to put him out there. Dad didn't like it, and I felt bad about it from the beginning."

"It's probably natural to feel some guilt when you have to make a decision like that, Mr. Mouse," Molly said reasonably. "I'm sure you did what seemed best at the time."

"All of my sisters live out of state. Suzanne, the oldest, offered to take Dad, but he didn't want to leave Tahlequah." He gazed out the window as he spoke. "He lived in Cherokee County all his life, and if we'd made him leave it would have broken his heart." He glanced sideways at Molly and she nodded encouragingly. "Every once in a while," he went on, "Dad would ask me why he couldn't come and stay at my house. That really tore me up, but we already have my wife's mother living with us. She's got a bad heart and is afraid to stay alone. I couldn't ask Nellie to care for my dad, too, could I?"

Molly made no response; apparently he didn't expect one.

"All six of us kids chipped in to pay the cost of keeping him in Country Haven," he continued. "It's been a real strain on some of us."

"I understand," Molly assured him, knowing that he had to work through the guilt in his own time, and talking about it was therapeutic. "What can I do to help you?"

He turned away from the window, as though returning from a distance. "I'm thinking of suing the nursing home."

"I'm not a lawyer—" Molly began.

"I know. That's not really what I came here to talk to you about. I want you to do something for me. I can't do it myself. I don't think I could handle it. Maybe if it was a stranger, I could do it. But he's my father."

Molly waited, wondering what he was leading up to. He seemed reluctant to get to the point, and she had a distinct feeling that, when he did, she wasn't going to like it.

"You'd feel the same way if it was your father, wouldn't you?"

Apparently it was a rhetorical question, so Molly merely nodded. Actually, her father *was* a stranger, having disappeared when she was four years old. According to Molly's grandmother, he had left a good job with the railroad as well as his family. Her memories of her first four years consisted of vague impressions, a child's adoration of the man who had been her father, and confused feelings of abandonment and betrayal when he was gone. But she wasn't there to burden this man with details of her personal life. He was close to breaking under his own self-imposed load.

"I asked Vann Walkingstick to come to the nursing home and make medicine, but he says we have to be sure his medicine wasn't turned back."

Molly murmured, "I see." As she was growing up, her grandmother had occasionally called upon the services of a medicine man when she or Molly was sick. Eva Adair was a staunch Baptist who saw no conflict in embracing Christianity and praying to Thunder to cure diseases. Molly had been fascinated by the medicine man's ritualized prayers and medicine ceremonies. As a child, she had believed, without question, in the efficacy of such rites. As a university student taking a minor in anthropology, she'd studied several primitive cultures, each of which had its own rituals and ceremonies to deal with the things it could neither control nor understand.

She had been embarrassed by her earlier trust in what she had come to view as mere superstition, but her interest, as an anthropology student, had increased tenfold. She wanted to understand her people's roots. During the following summer, between her junior and senior years, she had read every book on Cherokee culture that she could find. She had begun with disdain and an egotistical confidence in her own superior education and wisdom. She had ended with a new understanding and respect for the old ways. Now, at twenty-eight, she could appreciate the beauty in the ancient concepts and the importance of preserving them for future generations. And she was no longer willing to say categorically that people weren't helped by Cherokee medicine ceremonies. Or harmed, depending on the nature of the ritual.

But she still didn't know what Woodrow Mouse was leading up to. "For one thing," he continued, "I have to know what he died of before I see a lawyer."

"But the doctor must have some idea."

"He said it was a stroke, but he wasn't even there when it happened. He was at the hospital, operating. The nurses did what they could, I guess. Except they should have found another doctor for Dad. I call that negligence, don't you?"

"Well, perhaps, but . . ."

"I'm not gonna let it drop until I know more than I do now. I demanded an autopsy. The doctor didn't like that one damn bit, either. He's probably afraid they'll find out he's wrong about what killed Dad, and he'll look incompetent. He tried to talk me out of the autopsy, but I stood my ground. The medical examiner is going to do it tomorrow morning."

"I see," Molly said again, not seeing at all. What did any of this have to do with her?

"I want you to be there."

"I don't understand. Be where?"

"At the morgue, when they do the autopsy."

Oh, Lord. She had known she wasn't going to like it. Furthermore, it made no sense. The man must be deranged by grief. "I'm afraid," she said soothingly, "this is outside the realm of my responsibilities. I'm here to look into circumstances affecting the civil rights of tribal members."

"Are you trying to tell me that denying my father medical attention when he's sick enough to die isn't trampling on his civil rights? Bull!"

The flare of anger was so quick and unexpected that Molly flinched. But grief often produced anger. That, at least, she could understand. She remained bewildered, however, by what Woodrow Mouse hoped to accomplish in sending her to witness an autopsy. The very thought made her feel faintly nauseated.

She tried a placating tone. "To be frank, I can't see how my witnessing the autopsy has anything to do with your father's civil rights. Regardless of any negligence on the nursing home's part."

"I have to know the cause of death," he said stubbornly.

"So you'll know if you have grounds to sue the nursing home?" Molly asked, wondering if she had another Sherwood Bowman on her hands.

"That's right."

"The medical examiner is quite capable of determining the cause of death without my presence. You can even request a copy of his report," Molly told him, thinking she was off the hook.

"That's not the only reason I want one of us to be there." Molly understood the *us* meant he wanted a Cherokee present.

He had gotten to the point, at last, she realized with a sinking feeling. Maybe she wasn't off the hook, after all. "Mr. Mouse, I know nothing about medicine. Even if I were standing right beside the medical examiner, I wouldn't recognize any physical abnormalities or—"

"You'll know a heart when you see it, won't you?"

Totally bewildered now, Molly said, "Well, yes, of course, but—"

"That's all I want you to do. See if my father's heart is still there and let me know. To tell you the truth, I don't want to ask the medical examiner."

At last Molly understood. Woodrow Mouse feared his father had been killed by a ravenmocker, the most dreaded of Cherokee witches because they attacked when a person was sick and helpless. When a ravenmocker killed someone, he added to his life span by taking out the heart and eating it, leaving no scar. If someone he trusted assured Woodrow that his father's heart was present, he could put that fear to rest and concentrate on the grounds for a lawsuit.

She tried one last time. "I'm not sure the medical examiner will allow it."

"I already talked to him. I said I wanted a family representative to watch the autopsy. I didn't even have to pressure him. He said you could come if you'll keep your mouth shut and stay out of the way."

Molly would have no trouble at all complying with those conditions, particularly staying out of the way. Far, far out of the way.

"Will you do it?"

His black eyes seemed to bore right through her, as though challenging her to do her duty. She could refuse, but if she did, Woodrow Mouse would probably lodge a complaint with the tribal council and she would have to respond in writing. More paperwork.

If she wanted to avoid a hassle, she had little choice. "All right." Maybe after one peek at the heart, so that she could report truthfully to Mouse, she could keep her eyes closed during the remainder of the procedure.

"It's at ten o'clock tomorrow morning. Don't forget."

Fat chance, Molly thought. She probably wouldn't sleep a wink tonight for thinking about what faced her tomorrow.

OOOOOOOO

3

After the meeting with Woodrow Mouse, Molly decided to finish the reports on the Bowman and Gritts cases at home. She had an electric typewriter in the office, but she rarely used it since purchasing a personal computer and dot-matrix printer. There had been no funds for office equipment in the tribal budget, so she had saved for two years and bought the system herself. She kept it at home where she now did most of the paperwork relating to her investigations.

The temperature inside her car felt like 200 degrees. She rolled down the windows until the air conditioner had a chance to cool things down to 150 or so. The radio was tuned to a local station and somebody was reading the weather report. The drought continued across Oklahoma. Temperatures in the county ranged from 101 to 105, and farther west grass fires threatened several rural homes.

Molly switched the dial to a country-music station and listened to a tear-jerking song that was as depressing as the weather report. She turned off the radio and drove her 1979 Honda Civic south on Muskogee Avenue and west on Keetowah

Street. The Civic had one hundred and twenty thousand miles on it, but was still dependable transportation. It needed a new paint job, which she couldn't afford, but it got forty miles to the gallon and it was paid for. She hoped to add another eighty thousand miles before she had to replace it.

It was the only car she'd ever owned. She'd bought it, with forty thousand miles on the odometer, when she'd landed her first job following college graduation, a job it had taken a year of mailing out résumés and pounding the pavement to find. By then, the naive optimism and grandiose plans for saving the world—at least, a small part of it—which had filled her at her college graduation, had been knocked out of her.

She'd lived with her grandmother in Park Hill for those months and felt like the biggest sponge in the world every day of it. A bachelor's degree with a major in psychology and a minor in anthropology, she'd discovered, didn't qualify her for anything but more schooling. When, finally, she'd been offered a job in the Tulsa claims office of an insurance company, she'd grabbed it, feeling pathetically grateful.

For three years, she had spent forty hours a week in an office, typing information for various insurance forms. It was so incredibly boring that, toward the end, she had daily experienced a nearly irresistible urge to scream and throw her computer monitor and keyboard out the nearest window.

Then she'd seen the ad for a Native American Advocacy League investigator in the *Cherokee Advocate*, the tribal newspaper. She had no idea what the job entailed, but she called in sick the next day and drove to Tahlequah. Anything, she was sure, would be better than what she was doing.

It turned out that nobody on the tribal council could tell her exactly what the job entailed, either. She would have to make it up as she went along. That suited Molly fine. As did the variety of requests that came to her and the fact that she wasn't imprisoned in an office all day.

She hadn't fully realized, until she moved back, how alien she'd felt in Tulsa, disconnected from her geographical and biological roots. Her ancestors had come to what was now Cherokee County on the Trail of Tears in the 1830s. It was good to be home.

As she drove toward her apartment, she thought about the day she'd packed everything she owned into the Civic, drove back to Tahlequah, and started hunting for a place to live. Decent apartments were snatched up by students at Tahlequah's Northeastern Oklahoma State University. The university had started as a teacher's normal school, which had grown into a teacher's college. It still drew a lot of future teachers; but it now had more than nine thousand students enrolled in a wide range of undergraduate and graduate majors.

After looking at two filthy, ramshackle places where Molly wouldn't have kenneled an animal, she went to the local newspaper office, hoping to learn of some new rentals before the paper hit the street.

She was in luck. Minutes before, Conrad Swope had phoned in a rental ad for his garage apartment. Molly recognized the name. Although she'd never had a class with him, Dr. Swope had been a professor in the history department at NSU when she was a student there.

She drove to the address on Keetowah Street. The Swope house was an old-fashioned wood structure, painted white. Like most of the houses in the neighborhood, it had wide porches in front and back, where people used to pass the summer evenings in porch swings, while they waited for air conditioning and TV to be invented. The Swope house was in one of the oldest sections of town, and most of the people who lived there were retirees.

Swope, retired himself and widowed, remembered Molly's name, if not her face, from her university days.

The apartment was only one room and a bath over a detached garage. The kitchen consisted of a sink, counter top with cabinets above and beneath, a refrigerator, and apartment-sized electric range on the north wall, all of which could be hidden by closing a set of wooden louvered doors. Beyond that, the apartment was furnished with a sofa bed and matching armchair and a small oak table and four ladder-backed chairs. Dr. Swope had had the apartment painted and new carpeting installed after the previous renters, two college sophomores, moved out.

"This place looked like those boys had been feeding out

hogs up here," he told Molly. "The girls aren't much better, either. I shudder to think what these kids' homes are going to look like when they get out in the real world."

"I guess most people eventually get disgusted with living in squalor."

"Apparently not until later in life. I'll let the apartment sit vacant before I'll rent to any more students. I know it's small, but—"

"It's fine," Molly had said hastily. Small as it was, the apartment was the lap of luxury compared to what she'd already seen. And the modest rent matched her budget. "I'll take it, Dr. Swope."

"Good," he'd said with a grin. "Now that we're to be neighbors, Molly, you must call me Conrad."

Molly had grown quite fond of her landlord. At the age of seventy, he still accepted occasional research jobs, for which he was paid a handsome hourly wage. He said it kept his brain from atrophying. After retiring, he'd knocked down a wall between two rooms in his house and turned the space into a library for the hundreds of volumes he'd collected through the years. As often as not, he could find everything he needed for a research project without leaving his house.

When he wasn't working on an assignment, Conrad took up hobbies, which usually lasted only a few months before his interest was engaged elsewhere. This summer he'd joined a garden club and thrown himself into cultivating vegetables in a backyard plot.

Molly parked next to the single-car garage where Conrad kept his blue Buick. As she got out of the Civic, Conrad called to her from his back porch. "Come on in. I have something I want to give you."

"No more zucchinis, Conrad. Please." Everything else in his garden had withered in the heat and stopped producing weeks ago, but the zucchini plants kept on putting out the long, green squash. It appeared they might do so until the first frost. Molly had eaten them raw, cooked, candied, and as pickles and relishes, which Conrad canned. She never wanted to see another zucchini again.

"All I ask is that you reserve judgment until you see what

I've done with them this time," Conrad said. "Surely you can do that much for a lonely old man."

"What a crock," Molly muttered, but she left her briefcase on the stairs leading to her apartment and followed Conrad into his kitchen. "Don't give me that lonely-old-man line, Conrad. I live in your backyard, remember? I see the neighborhood widow women hanging around here. It's a regular parade."

Conrad dismissed this with a negligent wave of his hand. "Oh, them. They're all in one or another of my clubs. Widowed people have to fill up their time somehow. I've been on committees with most of them. They come here to talk club business. It's all perfectly innocent."

Conrad wasn't that naive. Molly gave him a "yeah, sure" grin. For a man of seventy, he was darned good-looking. Brisk walks had kept him lean and physically fit. He also had a fine Charlton Heston nose and a thin Clark Gable mustache, although Conrad's was silver like his wild shock of hair. But the crème de la crème of Conrad's attributes were his Paul Newman eyes.

"Innocent?" Molly said. "Come on, Conrad. Those ladies are after your bod."

"Tsk, tsk, tsk," he said complacently. "You have a suspicious mind for one so young. And, from what I have observed, little knowledge of such matters."

Conrad frequently suggested that she "find a nice young man" and have some fun. Molly had never confided in her landlord that she had found a nice young man once, or so she had thought. Her relationship with Kurt Williams had lasted for eighteen months, while she lived in Tulsa. They had talked of getting married. In her ignorant bliss, she had shared with Kurt Williams her every thought. She'd handed over her soul. She'd never been happier. Until the day his wife showed up. He'd left her and two kids in California two years previously, and she'd finally tracked him down. She didn't want him back. She wanted a divorce and child support.

Molly no longer wanted him, either. Her illusions had been shattered along with her heart. It had taken a few visits with a shrink to get rid of the resulting pain and anger, or at least to whittle them down to manageable size. She was cautious now. She would never be that vulnerable again.

Molly plopped down in a kitchen chair. "Are you offering to educate me in matters of the heart?"

"Perish the thought, my dear." He studied her for a moment. "But while we're on the subject, whatever happened to D. J. Kennedy?"

"Nothing's happened to D.J., as far as I know." Dennis Jerome Kennedy III, a deputy in the county sheriff's department, had given Molly something of a rush after she'd moved back to town. A couple of times, he'd worn her down and she had accepted his dinner invitations. She liked D.J. But early on she'd realized that having him around could easily become a habit, and she was still licking the wounds left by Kurt.

"I haven't seen him at the apartment in months."

"That's because he hasn't been there."

"I assumed that," Conrad said.

When Molly smiled an enigmatic smile, Conrad gave an exasperated shake of his head and picked up an open pint–fruit jar filled with a pink substance. He set the jar down in front of Molly and handed her a spoon. "Try it."

To humor him, Molly did. The substance was sweet and lumpy with a tart edge. It neither tasted nor looked as though it had even a nodding acquaintance with zucchini. "Not bad. What is it?"

"Zucchini jam," Conrad said proudly.

"It's not green. You're pulling my leg."

"Not at all. I peeled the zucchini, which accounts for the lack of green color."

Molly tried another bite. "What's in here, pineapple?"

"Pineapple and lemon juice and lots of sugar. It's laden with calories, of course. But what isn't, if it's any good? The pink color comes from a package of peach Jello. I found the recipe in one of my wife's cookbooks."

"I never thought I'd say this about anything with a smidgen of zucchini in it, but I like it."

Conrad looked suitably gratified. "You can take that jar with you. Pile lots of it on your breakfast toast. It's wonderful with that raisin bread you brought me last week.

And here's a sealed jar. Keep this one in your freezer until you're ready to open it. I have six more jars in my freezer, so let me know when that's gone and you can have another."

"You're trying to make me fat."

"No, but it would take me two or three years to eat that much jam." He watched Molly pull her damp blouse away from her perspiring chest. "Not that I wouldn't like to see a little more meat on your bones," he said. "You don't eat enough."

"It's true I don't cook many meals at home," Molly agreed. She did bake bread—the kneading was a great tension-reliever—and she was a coffee fanatic. Her apartment was never more appealing to her than when it was filled with the smells of baking bread and brewing coffee. Aside from that, she could put together a decent meal if she had to, although it wasn't among her top-ten favorite things to do. "But," she went on, "that doesn't mean I'm not getting enough to eat. You should see the lunches I shovel in at The Shack. Not to mention the Snickers bar I eat every afternoon. Give it up, Conrad. It's genetic."

"I suppose you're right," he said. "I've seen your grandmother. If only you could bottle those genes. When I think of the number of obese women one sees waddling down the street—well, all I can say is, if you could package your genes in pill form, you'd become a very rich woman." As he talked, Conrad had taken two glasses from the cabinet and filled them with ice cubes. Now he added tea and brought them to the table.

"I have work to do," Molly said in halfhearted protest.

"If there's one thing I've learned in my seventy years, it's that the work will still be there when you get around to it. You can take time to drink this. It'll cool you off. The radio said the heat index today was a hundred and fifteen." He sat down. "What sort of work?"

Molly took a long, cold swallow of tea before replying. "The usual. Writing reports on the investigations I wound up last week."

Conrad said offhandedly, "I understand somebody died out at the Country Haven Nursing Home today, and the family is raising a fuss about it."

"You certainly have your fingers on the pulse of this town," Molly observed. "Where did you hear that?"

"The same place I hear everything that goes on in Tahlequah."

"Super Snoop?"

"Indeed. If I didn't live next door to Florina Fenston, I'd never know anything." Super Snoop was Conrad's name for the widow whose house was immediately east of his. "Florina happened to be visiting a friend in Country Haven this morning, and the friend told her about it. I understand the man who died was a Cherokee."

"Yes. Abner Mouse. His son was in my office this afternoon. He's not satisfied with the treatment his father received. I'm going to the autopsy tomorrow morning."

Conrad's silver brows shot up. "An autopsy? Then there's some question about the cause of death. But why on earth are you going to the autopsy?"

Molly finished her tea. "Don't ask."

"You're being mighty mysterious."

"I don't mean to be, but there's my client's confidentiality to consider."

Conrad nodded, clearly not satisfied.

Molly stood and picked up the jars of zucchini jam. "I could sit here and chat for an hour, but I really need to work. Thanks for the jam and the tea. I'll probably bake later. I'll bring you a loaf."

She glanced over her shoulder as she left the kitchen. Conrad still sat at the table, his chin in his hand. His expression was one of complete absorption. He was obviously trying to figure out why Molly was going to witness Abner Mouse's autopsy. Despite his claims to the contrary, Conrad's curiosity was as sharp as his neighbor's.

If Molly knew her landlord, he would work it out eventually. Conrad's library contained every book available on Cherokee life.

OOOOOOOO

4

Molly's briefcase was no longer on the stairs where she'd left it. Baffled, she looked around, but didn't see the briefcase anywhere. Had someone stolen it? That seemed unlikely—it didn't contain anything a thief would want.

Was it possible she only thought she'd set it on the stairs and had left it in the car instead? As she turned to go back to the car, she heard a soft whine from behind her. She whirled around and saw nothing. When the whine came again, she realized it issued from beneath the stairs. She dropped to her knees and peered into the darkly shaded cubbyhole formed by the garage and the staircase.

A large dog lay in the corner, and her briefcase was on the ground in front of him. His coat was filthy and matted, but he looked like a golden retriever. He gazed at Molly with soulful eyes and his tongue lolled out the side of his mouth, while his tail thumped against the garage wall. But when she started to reach for the case, he growled low in his throat.

"What do you want with my briefcase, boy?" Molly said in as friendly a tone as she could muster.

He whined and his tail thumped harder. He dropped his

head and sniffed at the briefcase. Except for that growl, he didn't seem threatening.

"Are you lost? That's a good boy. . ." Molly kept talking in low tones as she reached in slowly, grasped the case, and pulled it toward her. The handle was covered with teeth marks. The dog stood up and growled again, but made no effort to retrieve the case.

Now that he was on his feet, she saw how thin he was. The poor thing was starving. Judging from the teeth marks, he'd had high hopes that the briefcase was edible. "Don't be afraid, boy. I won't hurt you." She talked to him for another few minutes and finally reached in to pet him. He thrust his wet nose into her hand and sniffed her palm.

"Stay right there," she told him. "I'll get you something to eat."

She ran upstairs. There wasn't much in the refrigerator. She grabbed a chunk of cheddar cheese and found a can of chicken in the cabinet. She took the food out, with water in a large plastic bowl.

The dog was still under the stairs. His tail thumped fiercely when he smelled the food, and he swallowed it in three huge gulps and lapped up half the water. Then he looked up at Molly expectantly. "You better not have any more right now," she told him. "I don't think you've eaten much lately." His ears pricked up and saliva dripped off the end of his tongue. "Where did you come from, fella?"

He took a few cautious steps toward her and, stretching his neck, licked her ear. Molly's heart melted. She loved dogs. "You're a sweetheart," she murmured. He allowed her to pet him again, making soft whining noises. She could feel clumps of matted hair and the outline of his ribs beneath. He wore no collar.

After a few minutes, she went back upstairs, wondering if he'd still be there the next morning. If he was, she'd buy dog food.

She lowered the temperature setting on the window air conditioner and turned the fan on high. She switched on the PC and printer, which sat on a narrow table next to the louvered closet doors, and changed into shorts and a tank top. Then she ground some Swiss chocolate–almond beans and brewed coffee in the Krups. As far as Molly was concerned, it didn't get too hot outside for her to enjoy a good cup of coffee.

With a full mug and a Snickers bar at hand, she wrote and printed out reports on the Bowman and Gritts investigations and a letter to Sherwood Bowman summarizing the results of her investigation into the paint factory. Tomorrow morn ing she'd drop the letter at the post office and run the reports out to the tribal complex before going to the county morgue.

At dusk, she went out to check on the dog. He was gone. Maybe he knew where home was, after all. She hoped so.

Back in the apartment, her thoughts turned to what she had to do the next morning. In an effort to keep her mind occupied with something besides the autopsy, she made two loaves of oatmeal bread, one of them for Conrad. While the bread was still warm, she sliced a thick slab, slathered it with butter, ate it with a fresh peach, and called it dinner.

Her efforts to think about anything but the autopsy looming on the horizon were only semisuccessful. It was like a sore tooth that she couldn't keep from probing with her tongue. But even though she expected to lie awake worrying, she fell asleep within a few minutes after finally going to bed.

Her subconscious must have been working on the dreaded appointment, however, for it was the first thing that popped into her mind upon waking.

* * *

The dog was under the stairs again. He greeted Molly like a long-lost friend. She refilled his water bowl and gave him a second bowl of milk. After delivering the reports and mailing the Bowman letter, she stopped at a grocery store and bought a sack of dry dog food.

She arrived at the county morgue at ten minutes of ten and was ushered into the autopsy room by the M.E. himself, Dr. Pohl. He was amazingly cheerful for a man who was about to cut open a corpse.

A scant twenty minutes later, she left the morgue on legs that trembled, and she dropped down on a bench in the hall outside. In the nick of time. She'd come very close to passing out. Breathing deeply, she bent over until her forehead touched her knees.

The M.E. had spent the first few minutes dictating into a tape machine a medical description of Abner Mouse's physical condition. Molly had been fine until the M.E.'s assistant brought out the scalpels and saw. Then she had started to feel a little queasy but she'd managed to stick it out until Dr. Pohl lifted the heart from the exposed chest cavity. At that point, she'd felt the blood rush from her face to her feet and had known she was going to drop right there on the mustard-colored tile floor if she didn't get out.

The odor of formaldehyde clung to her nostrils as she continued to take deep, steadying breaths. Slowly, the light-headedness passed.

She sat up and, after a few more deep gulps of air, she walked down the hall to a cubbyhole she'd noticed when she entered the building. It contained a coffee urn and a cold-drink machine. She ran a little coffee into a Styrofoam cup. It looked thick enough to stand a spoon on end, so she tossed it, untasted, into a wastebasket. There was nothing better than good coffee, and nothing worse than bad.

After plugging a couple of quarters into the machine, she selected a root beer and took it farther down the hall to another bench, where the medicinal odors wafting from the morgue weren't so strong. She wanted to speak to the medical examiner when he finished the autopsy and wished she'd had the forethought to bring some reading material to pass the time. Resting her head against the plastered wall, she closed her eyes.

She was dozing off some time later when she heard footsteps approaching, and she sat up just as Dr. Pohl reached her. He was a short, pudgy, middle-aged man with a sallow complexion, and his lank brown hair looked in need of shampooing. He blinked at Molly from behind round horn-rimmed glasses, making her think of a groundhog coming out of his burrow after months of hibernation. Smeared across the front of his white lab coat were some very suspicious-looking stains.

"You okay?" he inquired.

"Oh, I'm fine. I just got a little light-headed for a

minute. I should have eaten breakfast." In fact, she had not eaten for fear that she'd embarrass herself by upchucking in the morgue.

He sat down beside her and raked a hand through his hair, leaving wild spikes standing up in all directions. He smelled of disinfectant and death. Molly scooted over.

"Don't be embarrassed," he said cheerfully. "It happens to a lot of people at their first autopsy. You know what they say about riding a horse."

"If you get thrown, you get right back on," Molly murmured.

"Exactly. It's the same with autopsies. I think of the body as a machine that has malfunctioned, and my job is to find the failed part."

"Like a mechanic?"

"Yes. You get used to it."

Not if I can help it, Molly vowed silently.

He peered at her through thick lenses that had a magnifying effect, which made him appear bug-eyed. "Are you Abner Mouse's granddaughter?" Evidently he had assumed a family representative meant blood kin.

"No—a family friend."

"This is a new one, you know—a request for a family representative to witness the autopsy." His expression was quizzical. "Is it some sort of Indian thing?"

"Something like that. Can you tell me what conclusions you've reached?"

"No."

"I guess it's against policy."

"No, it isn't that. I don't know what he died of yet."

"Dr. Handley said it was a stroke."

"It was definitely not a stroke. But I did find congestion and hemorrhages in most of the organs. Very interesting. I haven't done such an intriguing autopsy in a long time. It's a pity you couldn't stay until the end."

A darn shame, Doc, Molly thought. "What do the hemorrhages mean?"

"Oh, the possibilities are numerous. I have a few educated guesses which I prefer to keep to myself for now. In addition to the state of the internal organs, I'm working from what Woodrow Mouse told me about his father's symptoms in the hours before his death. I've asked the lab to do an antigen test . . . and some other procedures. I should have the results later today. Tell Woodrow to call me about four-thirty. I'll at least have narrowed the possibilities by then. It's a bit like working a logic problem, you see." The man was practically rubbing his hands together in anticipation. "Are you a logic-puzzle buff?"

"Not really," Molly said. "I'll pass your message along to Woodrow. Thank you, Dr. Pohl."

"You're quite welcome."

She jumped up, eager to leave the pathologist's odoriferous presence.

"If you ever want to watch another autopsy, I can arrange it."

"Er, thanks . . ."

"I'm at my best when I have an audience."

Molly waved an acknowledgment of the invitation as she hurried down the hall. Were all pathologists a bit ghoulish? she wondered.

* * *

After assuring Woodrow Mouse that she'd seen his father's heart with her own eyes, and passing along Dr. Pohl's message, Molly assumed she was finished with that project—you couldn't really call it an investigation.

The dog came out from under the stairs to greet Molly when she got out of her car that afternoon. "Hey, stop it," she said, laughing, as he tried to lick her face. "Whew, you stink!"

Conrad stepped out on his back porch. "Who's your friend, Molly?"

"I found him under the stairs yesterday."

"I saw him hanging around the neighborhood a couple of days ago. I noticed you'd fed him."

"I didn't have much, but I bought dog food this morning."

Conrad shook his head. "You'll never get rid of him now."

"Maybe he's just lost."

"More likely, somebody driving through dumped him at the edge of town."

"I'll run a newspaper ad," Molly said.

"Looks like a golden retriever."

"He'll be a beautiful dog, once he gets a bath and some flesh on him. You can feel his ribs."

"You could take him to a vet. They'll find a home for him."

"Yeah, I could do that."

Conrad merely looked at her doubtfully.

"I'll try the ad first." She went back to the car for the dog food and filled one of the bowls, then put out fresh water.

Conrad watched her. "Something tells me that dog's already found a home."

* * *

Two days later, there was a message from Woodrow Mouse on the office answering machine, asking Molly to phone him at home.

When she returned the call, Woodrow said, "Dr. Pohl told you to have me call him last Tuesday. Remember that?" He sounded indignant.

She wasn't likely to forget Dr. Pohl or their conversation for some time. "That's what the man said."

"Well, I did and he gave me the runaround."

"That surprises me." Pohl had struck her as being pretty direct, if somewhat strange.

"He *said* he couldn't release any information at that time because he didn't have all the test results in yet."

"He told me that might be the case, but he thought he would have narrowed the possibilities by then."

"He'd narrowed them all right, but he wouldn't admit it. I could tell he was being real cagey about what he said."

"That's odd."

"Wait'll you hear. I finally found out last night what was going on. Pohl called me and apologized for keeping the truth from me for so long. Claims he had no choice. He had to notify the state health department first and wait twenty-four hours before he could tell anybody else." He paused dramatically. "Dad died of food poisoning. Botulism."

"Wow," Molly breathed. "Doesn't sound too good for the nursing home."

"From what I hear, the health-department people were all over the place out at Country Haven yesterday. I guess that's why they told Pohl to wait twenty-four hours. They wanted to get there before the nursing-home people had a chance to do a wholesale cleaning job on their kitchen."

"You may have grounds for a lawsuit, after all."

"I don't know. There's a problem."

"Oh?"

"They took samples of everything edible, leftovers and canned food that hadn't even been opened yet. They didn't find any botulism."

"So . . ." Molly mused, "the nursing home had already thrown out the contaminated food. Wait a minute. Have any other patients been infected?"

"Nope, and that's the big problem."

"As far as grounds for a lawsuit, you mean. Yeah, I can see that. If it was in food prepared in the nursing-home kitchen, your father wouldn't have been the only resident to get sick."

"That's right, but it had to come from that kitchen. Pohl said Dad probably ate the food sometime Sunday. At dinner, he guesses. They serve it at five o'clock. I was there. Dad didn't eat anything from outside at supper or all day Sunday, as far as I know."

"Are you sure?"

"The only visitors he had Sunday, or the week before that, were my wife and me. We didn't take him anything to eat."

"Was he allowed to leave the nursing-home grounds on his own? I'm thinking that he might have gone to a restaurant or a grocery store . . ."

"Dad hasn't been physically able to go out alone for several months."

"Maybe another patient gave him something . . . or one of the employees."

"They say no. Kennedy, the deputy sheriff, came out and helped the health-department people question everybody. If anybody gave Dad something to eat, they wouldn't own up to it."

"Well, it had to come from somewhere. Whoever gave your dad the contaminated food naturally didn't know it was contaminated, and now that they do know, they're probably afraid to admit it."

"That's what I think, too. So I want you to find out who it was."

"That won't be easy. For one thing, the nursing-home management isn't likely to let me wander around asking questions."

"Figure out how to do it behind their backs, then," Woodrow said impatiently. "I can't rest till I get to the bottom of this."

Molly could understand that. Where had the contaminated food come from? It was one of those questions that could drive you crazy until you found the answer.

"Do you know anybody in the nursing home?" Woodrow asked.

"I can't think of anyone at the moment."

"What about Mercer Vaughan? He's been around Cherokee County all his life. Don't you know him?"

"Vaguely. I've heard my grandmother speak of him."

"Maybe you could pay him a visit."

"I'll see what I can do, Mr. Mouse," she said. "I'll get back to you."

* * *

That evening, having received no responses to her ad, Molly gave the dog a bath with shampoo and Conrad's garden hose. Having stopped by a veterinary clinic on the way home to buy a brush and clippers, she spent an hour on his coat, clipping off the tangles that she couldn't brush out. The dog was very patient with her, whining only when she pulled too hard.

"You need a name," Molly told him. She hadn't named him before because that would only make him seem more like hers, and it would hurt worse if somebody took him away. She'd had plenty of experience dealing with the pain of losing loved ones, and she had tried to steel her heart against this abandoned creature. But evidently nobody else wanted him.

Conrad came out to chat while she groomed the dog. "You didn't get any answers to your ad, eh?"

"No. I guess you were right. He was kicked out of a car on the way through town. What kind of person would dump a beautiful animal like this? Or any animal, for that matter?"

"Somebody without a conscience." Conrad watched her scratch behind the dog's ears. "You're glad nobody answered the ad, aren't you?"

"Well not exactly, but I have grown fond of him, even though I've been trying not to. He's so lovable."

"I've never been much of a pet person. My wife once had a crabby little chihuahua who growled at me every time I got close. We had to shut the bedroom door at night or he'd try to root me out of bed. That dog hated my guts, and the feeling was mutual."

"This guy's not like that. Aw, look at that face. Is that sweet or what?" The dog licked her nose. She yelped and moved out of licking range. Conrad was looking at her with a resigned expression.

"What's the matter? Why are you looking at me like that?"

He sighed. "You're going to keep him, aren't you?"

"Do you mind?"

He shook his head. "Just so he doesn't have any accidents in the apartment. You can't get dog urine out of carpets. I know that from past experience."

"Oh, I'll bet he's been house-trained."

"You have no way of knowing that."

"Well, he can stay outside most of the time, and I'll keep a close eye on him whenever I let him in." She clipped out another lump of matted hair. "From the condition of his coat, he must have been on his own for several weeks. Probably eating out of garbage cans." She put down the brush and clippers. "I think I'll call him Homer. He reminds me of a man I worked with in Tulsa, a wet nose and shaggy blond hair."

Conrad threw up his hands and laughed. Then he said, "By the way, I think I know why you went to Abner Mouse's autopsy."

"Oh?"

"The family wanted to be sure everything was still there, inside. Am I warm?"

"You're on fire, Conrad."

He nodded, pleased with himself. "They feared a ravenmocker."

"That's amazing. You know more about the Cherokees than most Cherokees."

"I take it you were able to allay their fears."

"Right, but the mystery has deepened. Abner Mouse died of botulism."

"That's tragic, but not too mysterious."

"Ah, but none of the other residents were sick, and the nursing-home kitchen passed the health-department inspection with flying colors."

He gave her the kind of look then that he probably gave his slowest students at the university. "Obviously Mr. Mouse ate something nobody else had access to. Therefore, it didn't come from the nursing-home kitchen."

"Yeah, only Abner's son says he didn't give his father anything to eat the day before he died, and he's sure Abner didn't have any other visitors."

A silver brow rose fractionally. "Was he with his father every minute of that time?"

"No, of course not. But I gather Abner wasn't able to walk to a store or restaurant on his own, and the other residents and staff deny giving him food. So Woodrow wants me to find out how Abner got his hands on whatever it was that killed him."

"How are you going to do that?"

"I may not be able to, but I'll nose around, see what I can turn up."

ooooooooo

5

Country Haven Nursing Home was operated by a national chain based in Dallas. Six years previously, when the home was built, they had sent in a manager from the head office, who hired the other employees locally. The manager was named David Darwood. Molly had seen the name in the local newspaper in connection with various civic functions, but she'd never met the man and she wasn't particularly interested in doing so now. She wanted to keep a low profile.

She passed Darwood's office as she entered the building at nine o'clock Friday morning. The door was closed.

She went to the nurse's station. The woman behind the desk was youngish, early to mid-thirties, with auburn hair and pale freckles sprinkled across her forehead and nose. The badge pinned to her dress identified her as Beatrice Crawford, R.N.

"May I help you?"

"Which room is Mercer Vaughan's?" Molly asked.

The woman gave her a suspicious once-over. Probably

wondering if she was with the health department. "Our daytime visiting hours are from one to four."

"I'll be tied up this afternoon," Molly told her. "I was hoping I could pop in for a few minutes now."

"Are you a relative?"

"Mr. Vaughan is a friend of my grandmother. I was asked to drop by and see him." If the R.N. chose to connect those two statements, that was her mistake. If she knew the real reason for Molly's presence, Molly suspected, the nurse would give her the runaround.

Beatrice Crawford scrutinized Molly critically for another moment, then said, "He's in A-wing." She pointed down the hall, the direction from which Molly had approached the nurse's station. "Room 105."

The patients were housed in six large semicircular wings clustered around a central hallway where offices, staff lounges, and examining rooms were located. Molly guessed the kitchen and dining room were at the opposite end of the central section from the main entrance. She thanked the nurse and reversed her direction.

Mercer Vaughan's wing contained five rooms. As Molly hesitated, reading room numbers, a young woman in a white uniform came out of 103, her arms full of dirty linens. She stopped short when she saw Molly.

"Why, Molly Bearpaw."

"Hi." Molly recognized her from her high-school days. She'd graduated in Molly's class. "It's Christine, isn't it? Christine Johnson." Christine's brown hair was pompadoured in front, the back done up in an elaborate coil. In high school, she had braided it, winding and pinning the braid at the back of her head. She had pale skin and wore no makeup. She hadn't worn any in high school, either, which had made her look as though she were perpetually recovering from a long illness. Molly had always had an urge to pinch her cheeks and put some color in them.

As Molly recalled, Christine belonged to a church that believed makeup on women was the work of the devil. Apparently they condemned short hair, too. But Molly had never understood why they thought hairdos from the 1940s were holier than modern styles.

"It's Christine Zucker now. I heard you'd moved back to town."

"A couple of years ago."

Christine's gaze raked Molly's knit shirt and khaki shorts. "Gosh, you don't look like you weigh a pound more than you did in high school. All I have to do is *look* at food and it jumps on my hips."

Christine *was* a bit hippy. "You look okay to me," Molly said tactfully. She might need a friend among the nursing-home staff.

Christine groaned. "Yeah, sure. I've put on fifteen pounds since high school. Gained fifty with each of my two kids and never was able to lose it all." She sighed disconsolately. "So, what are you doing here?"

"Visiting Mr. Vaughan in 105. I wasn't sure the nurse was going to let me stay, though. She quizzed me before she'd give me the room number. I didn't know there were no morning visiting hours."

"Oh, nobody pays any attention to visiting hours. People come and go around here all the time. Most of the residents aren't sick, they're just not able to live alone." She leaned closer to Molly. "Between you and me, we had an unexpected visit from some state health-department people Wednesday. Five of them."

"Maybe the nurse is still uptight about it."

Christine nodded. "Everybody is. That's probably why Bea Crawford gave you the third degree. Things should be back to normal in a few days."

"I heard you had a case of food poisoning."

Christine looked glum. "Abner Mouse." Her green eyes widened. "Hey, he was Mr. Vaughan's roommate."

"Really?"

"Yeah. Mr. Vaughan's real down in the mouth about it. He told me he and Mr. Mouse played together when they were boys. Maybe you can cheer him up."

"I hope so."

"I better finish changing my beds or I'll have Bea on my back. Nice seeing you, Molly."

"You, too."

Mercer Vaughan sat in a rocking chair, facing the window. He was so still, he could have been a sculpture. His knobby hands, striped by sunlight tilting between the slats in the window blind, rested on the crook of a walking cane. He didn't hear Molly open the door.

"Mr. Vaughan?"

He turned toward her, squinting. Molly entered the room and closed the door behind her. "I'm Molly Bearpaw." Her name clearly meant nothing to him. "I'm Eva Adair's granddaughter."

He pushed himself slowly to his feet and peered into her face. "I think I can see the resemblance now. Don't tell me Eva's in the nursing home, too."

"Oh, no."

"Good. Nobody ought to be here if they have any place else to go. I outlived my wife and son. That's the only reason I'm here. Besides, Eva must be ten years younger than me."

"She's seventy-five."

"How is she?"

"Very well. Sometimes I think she'll outlast me."

He grinned, rearranging the wrinkles in his face. "I've known Eva since she was seventeen or eighteen. She was full of the devil then." He shuffled his feet, moving away from the rocker. "Would you like to sit down? This is the most comfortable chair."

"No, you sit." He didn't argue. Turning the chair away from the window, he lowered himself into it, using the cane to support his weight.

"Woodrow Mouse asked me to come by and talk to you," Molly said.

He squinted up at her. "You work for the tribe, don't you? Some kind of lawyer or something."

"Investigator," Molly corrected. "Woodrow has asked me to find out where his father got the poisoned food."

"Hmmmph." He worked his mouth cogitatively. "The health department couldn't find out, and they sure tried. What makes Woodrow think you can?"

"He's hoping I'll uncover something they missed, I guess. I told him it wasn't very likely, but he wants me to try. The day before Abner died, can you remember what he ate?"

"Whatever was on his tray," he said, without hesitation.

"Same as I did. Except I left the spinach we had for lunch. Can't stand spinach."

"But other people besides Abner must have eaten it."

"Oh, yes, the health-department people checked into that."

"Then it wasn't the spinach that killed him."

"I reckon not." He considered Molly for a long moment. "It might not have been something he ate, you know. There are things the doctors don't understand."

Molly realized what he was getting at. "I witnessed Mr. Mouse's autopsy. I saw his heart."

His eyes seemed to be judging her sincerity. Finally, he nodded.

"Did Abner have any food in the room Sunday, besides what came from the kitchen?"

"No—at least, I'm pretty sure he didn't. Mostly, people bring us candy or cookies. Abner had a sweet tooth, you see, so we never could keep anything sweet around here, especially candy. My sister's daughter brought a big bag of jelly beans a couple of weeks back. They were gone in two days and I only got one good handful." He sighed and looked philosophical. "They made my teeth hurt, anyway."

"What visitors did you and Mr. Mouse have over the weekend?"

"Just Woodrow and Nellie, Woodrow's wife."

"When were they here?"

"Sunday afternoon. They got here about three, I guess. They stayed till the supper trays came."

"And you're sure they didn't bring in any food?"

"I didn't see any, and the health-department people looked through the closet and every drawer in here. They didn't find anything."

"Were you in the room all the time Woodrow and Nellie were here?"

He frowned. "Why?"

"I need to know who was in this room on Sunday, what time they were here, and if Mr. Mouse was left alone with them."

He looked at her in surprise. "You can't think Woodrow and Nellie gave Abner some poisoned food."

"Of course not," Molly said hastily. "Not intentionally. Nobody thinks the poisoning was deliberate. But isn't it possible they could have given him something contaminated, without knowing it, while you were out of the room—something he ate before you returned?'' Even though Woodrow had said they hadn't, it might have seemed so inconsequential at the time that it slipped his mind.

''Well, let me think . . . I may have gone for a walk down the hall while Woodrow and Nellie were here. I reckon I did. I walk outside early in the mornings and inside every afternoon. If I don't keep my joints limbered up some, I can't get out of bed. It's a painful chore, as it is.''

''How long were you out of the room?''

He shrugged. ''Maybe half an hour. Woodrow came out once, while I was walking, and asked me if I wanted a cold drink. I said no, and he went out to the waiting room and got something from the machine. He drank it before he went back to the room, though. I saw him drop the can in that big wastebasket in the hall outside this wing.''

''How long was Woodrow out of the room?''

''Five minutes, maybe. No more than ten.''

''And his wife stayed in the room with Abner?''

''Far as I know.''

''There were probably nurses and other staff people in here Sunday, too.''

''Sure. The head nurse comes in a couple of times on each shift. Never bothers to knock, either. You could be buck naked, and she'd come on in like she owned the place. We don't have any privacy here at all.''

Molly gave a sympathetic shake of her head. ''Who else was here Sunday?''

He thought for a minute. ''A nurse's aide changes our sheets and helps us get dressed and wash up, if we need help. She's the one who brings in our trays, too. Then there's the cleaning woman. She usually comes right after breakfast.''

Molly pulled a scrap of paper and pen from her pocket. ''Can you give me the names of the staff people who were here Sunday?''

''The nurses were Crawford and Robinson . . . Crawford worked the day shift Sunday. She was griping because the nurse who usually works weekends called at the last minute to say she couldn't come. Crawford is always griping about something. Irene Robinson worked two shifts, three to eleven and eleven to seven. She works seven days lots of weeks—I guess she needs the money—but she usually doesn't work two shifts in a row."

"Yet she did Sunday?"

"Yes. Somebody else must've called in sick or was on vacation, maybe. Either one of the nurses could have come in while I was out walking, I guess. The nurse's aide who works the day shift on weekends is Zelda Kline. I was here every time Zelda came in Sunday, I think—and when the evening-shift aide brought our supper trays. Her name's Nutter. Can't think of her first name right now. I was here when the cleaning woman came Sunday morning, too."

"Her name?"

"Cora something. I don't know her last name. She's only been working here a few weeks. The janitor before that was a young man named Bob. Joking sort of fellow. I liked Bob, but I heard they fired him."

Molly hadn't detected anything suspicious in what he'd told her. "Did Abner Mouse leave this room Sunday, that you know of?"

"We both sat out on the porch for a little while in the morning, but he didn't eat nothing out there, if that's what you're getting at."

Having run out of questions, Molly returned the paper and pen to her pocket. "Thank you, Mr. Vaughan. If you remember anyone else who was here Sunday, will you let me or Woodrow Mouse know?"

He nodded. As Molly opened the door, he said, "Tell Eva hello for me. Ask her if she remembers getting separated from her horse halfway across the creek." He was chuckling as Molly closed the door.

An elderly woman in a wheelchair sat in the center of the semicircular space that joined A-wing to the central hallway. She had a halo of kinky, snow-white hair and glittering blue eyes. She stared hard at Molly as though trying to put a hex on her.

"Don't shoot me," the elderly woman croaked.

"I wouldn't dream of it."

"Are you the cleaning woman?"

"No, ma'am, I'm a visitor."

"Do you have scissors?"

She was plucking at the sheet covering her lower body. For the first time, Molly saw that she was tied to the wheelchair by a white strap around her waist, which also served to keep the sheet in place.

"I'm afraid I don't."

"I want to get out of here," the woman sputtered. "They're going to shoot me!"

"Uh—please don't upset yourself. I'll call a nurse."

"No!" She looked furtively behind her, still plucking frantically at the confining strap at her waist. "They'll shoot me. They're always shooting somebody. They shoot our food, too. I saw them." The woman was fixated on guns. She probably watched too much television.

"Yes, ma'am." Molly looked down the central hall toward the nurse's station. No one was seated there now. She turned back to the pathetic old woman and thought of the grandmother she loved more than anyone in the world. Don't let Eva end up like this, she thought. "Would you like me to take you back to your room?"

"No!" The word escaped with a spray of spittle, sounding like the hiss of a snake, and her eyes filled with terror. "Help me, before they shoot me."

Molly glanced down the hall again and saw Christine Zucker coming out of a room at the far end. She caught Christine's eye and motioned for her to come there.

When Christine saw the old woman, she clucked, "You're a long way from your room, Mrs. Archer. Mercy, what are we going to do with you?" To Molly, she added in low tones, "Every time she gets out of that chair, she runs off. Don't know how she manages it, she's so tottery on her feet. She's energized by fear, I guess. Thinks the Mafia's after her or something. Nutty as a peach-orchard boar, poor old soul."

"I gathered," Molly whispered back.

"Let me out of here!" bellowed Mrs. Archer, straining against the restraint.

"We have to give her a tranquilizer when she gets like this," Christine said out of the corner of her mouth. "She throws a ring-tailed fit when she sees the syringe. There, there, Mrs. Archer. Everything's all right.'' She rolled her eyes at Molly, gripped the handles at the back of the wheelchair, and pushed it toward the hall.

''I don't want to go to my room. Somebody call the police! Hussy! Bitch!'' A stream of shrieked curses echoed off the walls as Christine wheeled the old woman down the hall.

The door to room 102 opened a crack and a woman thrust her head out. Her face was covered with brown age spots. She could have been anywhere from seventy to ninety. ''Sounds like Mrs. Archer's throwing tantrums again,'' she observed.

''Yes,'' Molly said. ''I was visiting Mr. Vaughan and she was here when I came out.''

''She wanders all over the place in that wheelchair,'' the woman said, ''trying to get past the nurses and run away. I don't know where she thinks she's going. Her daughter lives in Nebraska. She brought her all the way down here about six months ago and hasn't shown her face since.'' She opened the door a little wider. ''I'm Estelle Tacker. I don't believe I've seen you here before.''

''This is my first visit. Mr. Vaughan's a friend of my grandmother.''

''Oh.'' The screaming from down the hall stopped abruptly. ''They must have given her a shot. I'm so used to them I hardly notice them anymore. It's a good thing that Archer woman isn't a diabetic, like me, or she'd be carrying on like that twice a day, every day of the week.'' Estelle Tacker shook her head unhappily, retreated, and closed her door.

A wave of sadness swept through Molly. She couldn't blame Mrs. Archer for being angry. She'd been dumped here—like Homer was dumped—and her daughter never came to visit. How terrible to lose all control over your life, even your mind. Molly thought death would be preferable. She hurried down the hall and out of the building, which had begun to feel more like a prison than a nursing home.

* * *

Mercer Vaughan rocked his chair slowly back and forth. He heard the commotion out in the hall, the shrieking and the cursing, and knew that Mrs. Archer was fighting her demons again. It was better to die, like Abner, than to live like Mrs. Archer.

When he was a boy, there had been an old woman who lived in a shack about half a mile from his family's place. She wandered through the woods at night. Sometimes, lying in bed beside his brother, with the window open, he heard the old woman moaning softly as she passed the house. Some folks said old Fleety hadn't been right since her two sons were killed in a car wreck; she was crazed by a great black heartache. But according to a neighborhood midwife, whose grandmother had attended Fleety's mother at the birth, Fleety was destined for a bad end from the beginning. The baby girl had fallen on her face when she was born, a bad omen.

No time should have been lost in taking protective measures. Fleety should have been plunged in the nearest creek with a dark cloth over her head, fished out when the cloth was disengaged, and held over flames, and then a prayer should have been said to the fire. According to the midwife, proper precautions had not been taken.

Crazy or not, cursed or not, Fleety knew things. "Something bad's gonna happen," his father would say the morning after they'd heard Fleety stumbling around outside and wailing pitifully, as though she had partaken of a *skee-nah*, an evil spirit.

Sure enough, a neighbor's calf would be stillborn or a horde of grasshoppers would descend on the garden. Once, after one of Fleety's nocturnal jaunts, Mercer's pet raccoon had fallen into the well and drowned.

Maybe Mrs. Archer's muddled brain also told her things that ordinary people didn't know. Maybe she was a witch.

Mercer shivered and tried to think about other things. He missed Abner and wondered when he would get another roommate. He hoped it would be somebody with enough of his senses left to carry on a conversation.

OOOOOOOO

6

On Saturday, Molly took Homer to the vet for a physical exam. The doctor gave him shots for worms and other common canine maladies. Except for being malnourished, Homer appeared in good health, the vet said. He guessed Homer's age at three or four.

After leaving the veterinary clinic, Molly drove the few miles to Park Hill to visit her grandmother. Eva, who had become the solid, constant center of her life when Molly was four, had been on her mind since her visit to the nursing home. Molly had continued living with her mother after her father's disappearance, but as Josephine's depressions got worse, Molly spent more and more time at Eva's. Even now, it was impossible to imagine a time when Eva wouldn't be there. But she *was* seventy-five, a fact that had borne on Molly's mind since her visit to Country Haven.

Homer stood up on the back seat with his tongue lolling out and his nose pressed against the window, clearly delighted with the passing scenery.

A haze of dust hung over the country road, which was bordered by groves of trees and brush, alternating with cleared spaces that accommodated small homesteads. Park Hill itself was little more than a post office and a few houses clustered somewhat closer together than those along the road. Its glory days had been brief and had ended more than a hundred years ago.

The small community where Molly had spent her preteen years, once called the cultural center of the Cherokee Nation, was the site of the original Cherokee Female Seminary, opened in 1851. But the village declined following the Civil War, which divided the tribe into two hostile factions. In 1887, when the seminary burned to the ground, tribal leaders decided to rebuild it in Tahlequah on the site of what was now Northeastern Oklahoma State University.

In recent decades, however, tourists had begun arriving in droves. In the past several years, the Cherokee National Historical Society opened several tourist attractions in Park Hill—a seventeenth-century Cherokee village, Tsa-La-Gi, featuring tribal members demonstrating the way their ancestors lived and the crafts they practiced; Adams Corner rural village, representative of many settlements in Indian Territory in the late 1800s; an outdoor drama, *The Trail of Tears,* reenacting the bittersweet history of the Oklahoma Cherokees; and a museum. But most of the attractions were only open from June through August, and in the fall the majority of the workers left for homes and jobs elsewhere.

Some new homes had been built in Park Hill in recent years, but Eva Adair did not live in one of them. She lived in a two-story frame farmhouse inherited from her late husband. Originally, the house had belonged to his parents. At one time, they'd owned eighty acres surrounding the house, but eventually they'd sold most of the land for house lots. During the four years she and Molly had lived in Tahlequah, Eva had rented the house to friends, knowing that she would return when Molly started college.

She greeted Molly with a hug, as she did every time Molly visited, and Molly hugged her back with more strength than usual. Eva always said the same thing, too. "Seems like a coon's age since I saw you." Then, as always, she held Molly away from her and gave her a once-over: "Let me look at you. Are you getting enough rest?"

"Plenty, Grandmother. How are you?" Molly was five-feet-seven, the ideal height for a woman, according to a women's magazine article she had once read. But she felt much taller when she was with her grandmother, who had to stretch to measure five feet.

"Fit as a fiddle."

"Honestly?"

Eva cocked her head. "Have I ever lied to you, child?"

"No, but I worry about you being out here without a doctor."

"Nonsense. There are doctors in Tahlequah and plenty of neighbors to take me if I need to go. So you can quit worrying."

Molly smiled and looked around at the familiar surroundings. The living room had changed little since Molly was a child. Same overstuffed sofa and chairs, although some of them had been reupholstered since then. Same bare pine floor with the striped, handwoven area rug in front of the sofa. Same framed photographs on the walls, too. Most of them were of Molly at various ages, but there was one of her grandparents early in their marriage. Her grandfather, a rural mail carrier, had died when Molly was a baby. Another photograph was of Molly's mother, Josephine, taken when she was twenty-five, a few months before she killed herself. A beautiful woman, smiling for the photographer, but the camera had captured the haunting sadness in her eyes.

"Come on in the kitchen," Eva said. "I'm baking a lemon pie for later."

"I wish you wouldn't go to so much trouble, just for me."

"Fiddlesticks. Who else am I going to bake pies for?"

Molly helped herself to ice and tea from the refrigerator. She sat at the kitchen table while her grandmother took the pie from the oven and mixed chicken salad for sandwiches.

"I saw an old friend of yours yesterday," Molly said. "Mercer Vaughan."

Eva turned from mixing the salad to give Molly a puzzled look. "At the nursing home?"

"Yes."

"What on earth were you doing there?"

"Abner Mouse died there last Monday. I guess you heard." Eva nodded and added more mayonnaise to the salad. "Mercer Vaughan was Abner's roommate. Abner had food poisoning."

"Yes, I know," Eva said. "Nellie Mouse told me. Was Mercer sick, too?"

"No. In fact, Abner was the only one in the home who was infected. Woodrow asked me to find out where his father got the contaminated food."

"Did you?"

"Not yet." Molly sipped the cold tea. "Mr. Vaughan wasn't able to help me much. But when I was leaving, he told me to ask you if you remember getting separated from your horse in the middle of the creek."

Eva chuckled. "That Mercer. He always liked to tease me. He and wife lived down the road from us when my folks moved to Park Hill. I was only seventeen, but I thought I was a woman grown."

"What about the horse?"

Eva began piling chicken salad on slices of whole-wheat bread. "I'm kind of ashamed of that escapade now. I went to a stomp dance with a neighbor boy on his horse. That was the night I met your grandfather. He'd been away for about a year, but he knew the boy I was with."

"Was it love at first sight?"

Molly was sure her grandmother blushed, although it wasn't noticeable on her dark skin. "Oh, I don't know about that. I liked him right away, though. Your grandfather was always full of mischief. He thought it would be a good joke if the two of us slipped off and went home on the other boy's horse."

"And you had to cross the creek?"

"Uh-huh. That horse was as gentle as an old dog when I crossed earlier with the other boy, but on the way home, he got to the middle of the creek and took a notion he didn't want to carry us another foot. We had a different idea, but when you're dealing with a mule-headed horse, he's going to have his way. We had to swim to the bank, and the horse turned up the next day about a mile down the creek. You should have heard my father when I walked in with a strange young man, and the both of us sopping wet."

Molly laughed. "Now I understand what Mr. Vaughan meant. He said you were full of the devil when you were young."

"Pshaw." Eva cut the sandwiches in half and arranged them on two plates. "I was the perfect lady compared to today's young people. But I sure got teased about that little escapade with the horse, I can tell you." She brought sandwiches to the table.

The homemade bread was fresh and the chicken salad was crunchy with celery, sweet pickles, and walnuts. Molly began to eat hungrily. "Tell me more about when you were young," she said after several bites. She had heard most of Eva's stories before, but, like most old people, Eva enjoyed recalling past history.

Eva Adair recounted stories for the next two hours, stopping only long enough for Molly to check on Homer a couple of times. She'd left him on the porch. He was stretched out in front of the door when Molly looked out. He appeared to be guarding the door, but in Homer's case Molly thought appearances were probably deceiving. Homer was too friendly to be a good guard dog.

As she was leaving, a little after four, Molly asked, "Where do Woodrow and Nellie Mouse live?"

"You turn left on the first road after you pass the post office," said Eva. "It's a few houses down on the right. The name's on the mailbox."

"I thought I'd stop by and report on my visit with Mr. Vaughan."

"I think Woodrow's working today. He won't be home yet."

"Oh, well, I'll tell his wife." Actually, Molly had hoped Woodrow would be gone. She wanted to talk to Nellie Mouse alone.

* * *

The Mouses lived in a small brick house, one of several similar homes built in Park Hill in the 1970s. The woman who answered Molly's knock was about fifty and on the short side, with a sturdy build. She looked tired.

"Nellie Mouse?"

"Yes."

"I'm Molly Bearpaw. Did your husband tell you he'd asked me to look into his father's death?"

"He mentioned it." She pushed short black bangs off her forehead and studied Molly with narrowed, calculating eyes. "You might as well know, I think Woodrow is making too big a thing out of this. Abner was eighty-four years old and in bad health. He was too weak to fight off disease. People don't usually die of food poisoning."

"Actually, half of them do." Molly had looked it up in Conrad's medical encyclopedia. "I imagine the percentage is even higher among the weak and elderly."

Nellie pushed at her bangs again. "If you say so. Abner simply didn't have the strength to battle the poison. If it hadn't been that, he'd have died of something else."

Nellie certainly wasn't grieving for her father-in-law, Molly thought. "May I ask you a few questions?"

She hesitated, then stepped out on the porch, closing the door behind her. "My mother is taking a nap. I don't want to disturb her." She moved to one of the webbed chairs that sat against the house in the shade. "I been going all day." She sighed as she settled in the chair. She took a pack of cigarettes and lighter from her shirt pocket and lit up. "You about get through taking care of kids and then you have to start on your parents. Can't even smoke in my own house. Mother smoked like a chimney until ten years ago. Now she says other people's smoking makes her choke." She took a deep drag of her cigarette and indicated the chair next to her. "You might as well sit down, get out of the sun."

"Thank you." Molly sat. Heat from the webbing soaked through the back of her shirt. "Sorry to have to bother you, Mrs. Mouse, but I'm trying to interview everybody who was in Abner's room last Sunday. I understand you and your husband were there for a couple of hours that afternoon."

"That's right. We usually go on Sunday because that's the only day I can get my neighbor to stay with Mother."

She watched an old Buick rattle down the street. "I don't mind telling you I didn't look forward to those visits, but it was a chance to get out of the house. And Woodrow was afraid I'd hurt Abner's feelings if I didn't go. Personally, I thought Abner would've been glad if he never saw me again. He never liked me."

Nellie Mouse was into self-pity. No wonder her father-in-law hadn't cared much for her.

"Why?"

She shrugged and tapped her cigarette on the arm of the chair, dislodging ashes. "He'd probably have found something wrong with any woman Woodrow married. When Woodrow and me set up housekeeping, Abner and Woodrow's mother were over here almost every night. Woodrow was the only boy, you see, and they doted on him. Then the house next door went vacant and they moved in there. I couldn't sneeze without them asking if I was taking a cold. I got sick of always having them underfoot, and I guess it showed."

Molly nodded and they watched another car pass. Nellie went on, "It was hard for us to have friends over because Abner and Mazie were always poking their noses in, though I think Mazie would have given us more privacy if Abner had listened to her."

"I can see how that might get tiresome."

"Then Woodrow's mother died and we had to put Abner in the home. That took some doing, believe me. Abner carried on like we were taking him to the gas chamber. And every time we visited, he'd start in nagging Woodrow to let him move in with us. We told him over and over that my mother was here and we didn't have the room. But the next time we went there, we had to go through it all again. He was like a broken record. Then Woodrow would feel guilty and for the rest of the day he'd talk about building on a room for Abner. If I mentioned we didn't have the money to build a birdhouse, much less a room, he'd flare up at me." She cast a look back over her shoulder and seemed to be listening for a sound from inside the house. Turning back to Molly, she asked, "Have you ever felt like you wanted to run away?"

Molly thought of her three years confined to the insurance claims office. "As a matter of fact, I have."

"Then you know how I feel every day of my life." She waved a weary hand. "Since the day I married Woodrow, I've had Abner to contend with, like a weight around my neck."

Molly thought of a cartoon character, walking around with a dark cloud overhead. This was a bitter woman. Poor Woodrow, Molly thought, caught between his father and his wife. "Not anymore."

She shot Molly a swift, sharp look. "That's true, but I still have Mother, don't I?"

Molly wanted to bring the conversation back to the investigation. She said, "The confusing thing about Abner's death is that he was the only one in the nursing home who ate food containing the botulism bacillus, which means he ate something none of the other residents had."

Her eyes narrowed against the smoke from her cigarette. "He got something from outside, you mean. Well, that's what the nursing home would like us to think, but isn't it possible that Abner just ate more of whatever it was than anybody else?"

"Maybe it's remotely possible, but since nobody else had any symptoms, it's almost certain Abner is the only one who ate the contaminated food. Did you or your husband give him anything to eat when you were there?"

She stared at Molly, uncertainty flickering behind her dark eyes. She thrust the cigarette between her lips, inhaled deeply, and blew smoke out the corner of her mouth. "Are you saying Woodrow or me killed Abner?"

Molly forced a smile and kept her voice even. "Of course not."

"Listen, I never denied I dreaded those Sunday visits," she said, her tone almost combative. "And our share of keeping Abner in the home was money we could have spent on other things. A couple of Woodrow's sisters could have paid the full bill and not missed the money, but they didn't offer. We couldn't even afford to get a dishwasher." She took another drag on the cigarette. "But that doesn't mean I wanted Abner dead."

"Nobody said you did. If you gave Abner something to eat, you obviously didn't know it was contaminated."

She flashed Molly a heated look. "We didn't give him one bite of anything," she said tightly. "All he ever wanted was something sweet. He'd have lived on sugar, if we'd have let him. It wasn't good for him, so we stopped taking him sweets."

"And you didn't see anyone else give him something while you were there?"

She shook her head emphatically. "I already told those health-department people. I didn't see any food in that room except for what came in on his supper tray."

A speck of cigarette ash settled on the arm of Molly's chair. She flicked it away with her finger. "If the contaminated food wasn't brought in and it wasn't served by the nursing home, that doesn't leave many options."

"Another patient might have given him something."

"If so, nobody will admit it."

"Not too surprising, is it?" she snorted. "I say, forget it. Abner's dead. Knowing where he got the poisoned food won't change a thing. If you'd convince Woodrow of that, we'd all be a lot better off."

"Aren't you even a little bit curious about where the food came from?"

"No, I don't have time to be curious."

"Well, I won't keep you any longer." Molly stood and extended her hand. "Thank you for talking to me."

Leaving her cigarette hanging out one side of her mouth, she shook Molly's hand without rising.

By the time Molly got back to her car in the shade of an elm tree, Homer had grown tired of waiting for her and was halfway out a lowered window. He was overjoyed to see her. He yelped and licked her face, his tail going full speed. He acted as if he hadn't seen her in a month.

On the drive back to Tahlequah, Molly pondered her interview with Nellie Mouse. The woman had a martyr complex, and she'd gotten pretty defensive when Molly asked if she or Woodrow had taken food to Abner. Molly was certain that, if they had, Nellie Mouse would deny it with her dying breath.

When Molly arrived home, two teenage boys were digging holes for fence posts in Conrad's backyard. A roll of metal fencing wire lay beside the garage. Florina Fenston was hanging over her back fence, her birdlike eyes following their progress. Conrad was supervising the project from the back porch. A pitcher half full of lemonade and two glasses sat on the top porch step, as though the boys had recently taken a break.

Homer leaped out of the car and scrabbled up on the porch, his paws slipping on the smooth wood. Conrad scolded him for jumping on his clean trousers and then scratched behind his ears, taking the sting out of the scolding. "I'm building a pen for Homer," Conrad told Molly.

"So I see."

"Oh, Molly," Florina caroled sweetly, "I don't like to complain, but I caught your dog digging up my peace rose this morning."

Conrad turned away from his neighbor and arched an eyebrow at Molly.

"Florina, I'm sorry," said Molly. As everyone in the neighborhood knew, because she'd told them, Florina's roses were prizewinners. To judge from Florina's conversation, she was prouder of them than of any of her grown children.

"Dear, dear," Florina tutted, "I hate to think what might have been the outcome had I not caught him in the act. I know you're busy, being a career woman and all, but one has a duty to teach pets proper manners."

Molly could only nod and say lightly, "I've had him just a few days."

Florina smiled bravely. "Ah, well, I managed to save my darling peace. I started it from a cutting, you know. Gracious, the lengths I went to, to keep that rose alive in the beginning. It was afflicted by every rose disease known to horticulturists that first year. You remember how I toiled over it, don't you, Conrad?"

"Quite," said Conrad dryly.

"I'm glad you saved it," Molly said. "Of course, I would have replaced it if you hadn't."

Florina gave a sad little shake of her head. Whispy gray hairs fluttered about her round face with the movement. "I'm sure you would have, dear, but it wouldn't be the same. Oh, my, you must think I'm a dotty old woman." She clicked her tongue. "You modern youngsters are so accustomed to instant gratification. Now, don't take that as criticism, Molly. You simply can't understand why anyone would spend hours of time and worry on a poor little rose cutting. You'd go to the nursery and buy a full-grown bush already in bloom. All very sensible, I'm sure, but not nearly as satisfying."

"You would know that better than I, Florina," Molly said tactfully and saw her landlord's lips twitch.

"You see why Homer can't be allowed to run loose," he said.

"I'll pay for the pen, Conrad. In fact, I should have been the one to think of it in the first place."

"Rubbish," Conrad said.

"No, I insist."

He waved her words away. "We'll discuss it later."

Molly turned back to survey the fence-building activity. The boys were digging the last posthole. Having worked their way down four sides, they were back where they'd started. The pen was going to cover about a third of Conrad's big backyard, including the shady place under the stairs.

"He seems a good-natured animal," Florina interjected, "even though he's clearly suffering from a lack of discipline. Conrad tells me he's a stray."

"That's true," said Molly with forced brightness. She always forgot, when she hadn't talked to Florina in a while, how irritatingly persistent the woman could be.

"Have you thought about germs, dear?"

"Not recently," Molly muttered.

"You're to be commended for wanting to give him a home," Florina said patiently, "but there's no telling where he was before he showed up here. One can't be too careful about germs."

"The vet checked him over this morning," Molly said, "and gave him a clean bill of health."

"Oh, well, then . . ." She broke off and sighed. "I do hope he doesn't bark at every sound."

"He's hardly barked at all since he's been here," Molly protested. At which point, Homer decided it was high time somebody paid attention to him and began chasing his tail and barking. Disloyal wretch, Molly thought, frowning at Homer.

Conrad watched the dog, amused. "I got Homer a collar and leash this morning, so he can go with me on my walks. A big dog like this has to be exercised regularly." Homer abruptly stopped chasing his tail and cocked his head at Conrad.

Molly couldn't help laughing. "You're not a pet person, huh?"

"Well, if we're going to keep him, we have to care for him properly."

"True," Molly said, amused at how easily Conrad had slipped into using *we* when discussing Homer. Conrad, it appeared, had a new hobby. Maybe it would take his mind off zucchinis.

As though reading her thoughts, Conrad gazed at what was left of his vegetable garden. "The zucchinis are starting to go mushy. Think I'll get out the Rototiller this evening and plow that plot."

Florina began instructing Conrad on the best way to prepare his garden plot for the winter. Smiling to herself, Molly went to check her mailbox. There were several pieces of junk mail and the letter she'd written to Sherwood Bowman, marked "Moved. Left no forwarding address." She put the letter in the Civic's glove compartment before going upstairs, intending to ask around and see if she could discover where Bowman was living. If she couldn't, she'd have to wait for him to contact her. Which he was bound to do, to see if she'd uncovered anything he could take to an attorney.

OOOOOOOO

7

The phone in Molly's apartment sat on a table next to the sofa bed. It had a particularly shrill ring and there was no way to tone it down. Molly heard the jangling through the layers of the deep sleep she'd fallen into sometime around midnight Monday night. It went on and on as though somebody were blowing a whistle in her right ear. She pulled a pillow over her head to muffle the sound, but that didn't help much. The clanging continued.

She turned over and forced her eyes to squint at her wristwatch. It was 6:29 A.M. Disoriented, she turned her head and saw the window that housed the air conditioner. The sky beyond the upper pane of glass was gray and rain pelted it. She hoped it would rain all day. It would cool things off temporarily. She lowered her gaze to the telephone inches from her head. She reached for it, missed, and knocked a memo pad and ballpoint pens off the table.

"Damn," she muttered, sitting up, and made another grab for the phone. She snatched up the receiver, cutting off the blasted ringing.

"Hu—" She cleared her throat. "Hello."

"Molly Bearpaw?" The gravelly male voice was vaguely familiar.

"Yes."

"I thought you weren't there. The phone has been ringing and ringing." Had it never occurred to him that most people were asleep at this hour?

She flopped down on her back and tucked the receiver between her ear and her shoulder. "Who is this?"

"Didn't I say? It's Mercer Vaughan, out at the nursing home."

Molly was getting her bearings now. She sat up again. Outside, thunder rumbled. "Could you speak up, Mr. Vaughan? I can barely hear you."

"I don't want one of them nosy nurses to know about this call."

Molly pressed the receiver to her ear to hear him better. "Is something wrong, Mr. Vaughan?"

"Something strange is going on here. We had another one die yesterday, and it was food poisoning."

"Are you sure?"

"Yep. I overheard two of the nurses talking late last night. Are you still looking into Abner's death?"

"I thought I'd hit a blank wall, but maybe not. Who was it this time?"

"Estelle Tacker." The name struck a chord in Molly's memory, but she couldn't immediately recall where she'd heard it before. "They rushed her to the hospital yesterday about noon. I thought it was her diabetes. She didn't stay on her diet like she ought."

Now Molly remembered. Estelle Tacker was the woman who'd opened her door when Mrs. Archer was demanding to be let out of her wheelchair and shrieking that people were trying to shoot her. Estelle Tacker's room was near Mercer Vaughan's, in A-wing. "They must have been alert for the symptoms this time. The hospital surely pumped her stomach."

"All I know is, she died, and I heard the nurses say she had that botulism thing."

"Has anybody else been taken to the hospital?"

"I don't think so. They could move somebody from one

of the other wings without me knowing, but word usually gets around fast when one of us has to go to the hospital. Sally Creighton in 101 always knows the latest rumors, and she hasn't heard of anybody but Estelle going. O' course, Sally's half cracked."

Molly climbed out of bed. "I'll be out there right away. It'll take me twenty minutes to shower and dress."

"I don't think they'll let any visitors in this morning. The health-department people are coming again. You may not be able to get in till after supper."

A clap of thunder shook the apartment, and Molly heard Homer whining under the stairs. He should be safe and dry there, she told herself, if only his whining didn't wake Florina Fenston.

She brought her mind back to the conversation, carried the phone over to the window, and looked out at the rain. She considered trying to slip into the nursing home undetected. Could she climb in Mercer's window? She discarded the idea. "Okay. I'll see you then—and, Mr. Vaughan, I think it would be better if nobody else knows I'm there as an N.A.A.L. investigator. I'm merely a friend, visiting."

"Good idea. They might throw you out if they knew. They'll want to cover this up. I'll be waiting. I think I hear somebody coming." He hung up without saying good-bye.

Homer whined pitifully and scratched on the door. Molly opened it and he dashed across the room and crawled under the sofa bed, still whining.

Molly got on her knees and peered under the bed. Homer looked back at her and barked. "We're in trouble if a burglar decides to break in during a thunderstorm." Homer barked again, but he didn't come out.

"You can stay until I leave for work, but then you have to go." He put his head on his paws, sighed, evidently bored with the conversation, and closed his eyes.

The rain lasted less than two hours. By the time Molly left her apartment at eight-thirty, the sun was shining again. You could almost see steam rising from the grass. It was going to be another scorcher.

When she arrived at the nursing home that evening, a sheriff's department car was parked in front. She wondered if it belonged to D. J. Kennedy, but she didn't see any deputies when she entered. A harried-looking blond nurse was at the nurse's station. She glanced up as Molly walked down the hall. Molly smiled and turned into A-wing before reaching the station.

A cart containing three covered dinner trays sat unattended in the center of the semicircular space, where Mrs. Archer had confronted her the first time Molly had visited. Woodrow had said dinner was served at five o'clock, but it was almost six now. At the moment, the aide was evidently in one of the five rooms in A-wing, delivering a tray.

The ranting of a television preacher came from 101. Before Molly reached the door to Mercer Vaughan's room, she heard rubber-soled steps hurrying down the hall. It was the blond nurse. Her name tag read, "Irene Robinson, R.N."

"Miss!"

Molly turned around. "Yes?"

"Where are you going?"

"I'm visiting Mr. Vaughan. He's able to have visitors, isn't he?"

"Oh, yes, Mr. Vaughan's fine."

"I'm relieved to hear it. He's been so depressed since his friend died."

The nurse chewed the inside of her cheek. "I wanted to be sure—I mean, well, we've had a problem with visitors bringing food, usually candy or cookies, to the patients. It's simply gotten out of hand, and we're not allowing any food to come in from outside for the time being."

Prudent move, Molly thought. It appeared the health department had again found no food containing botulism bacilli on the premises, which made it highly suspect that it was being carried in. Very strange, indeed. Molly was relieved the nursing home was prepared to stop food from outside getting to the patients. In fact, she'd feel better if they had somebody posted at the entrance to make sure no one slipped past them, unnoticed.

"I didn't bring any food," Molly said. She was wearing jeans and a cotton shirt, and she wasn't carrying a purse. She'd grabbed a pen and a discarded envelope from her glove compartment in case she needed to make some notes. She pulled them from her jeans pockets to assure the nurse she had nothing edible concealed there.

"All right. I simply wanted to be sure." The nurse returned to the station and Molly tapped on Mercer Vaughan's door.

"Come in."

He was sitting in the rocker, hands on the crook of his cane. Today he was facing the door, rather than the window. As though he were on guard, Molly thought. She closed the door behind her. "I was sure I'd waited long enough for you to have eaten dinner."

His thin hand shook a little as he raised it in greeting. "The trays are late. I reckon they were all busy with the health-department inspectors."

"How are you today, Mr. Vaughan?"

He looked up at her with cloudy black eyes under the wrinkled lids. "Buffaloed, that's what I am. I don't know what's going on around here." He propped his cane against the side of the chair and locked his hands. "If this ain't the work of a *Ka'lana-ayeli'ski,* then somebody else is killing people; but I can't, for the life of me, figure out how they're doing it, or why anybody would want to—if they know what they're doing, that is." He'd had twenty-four hours to imagine the worst, and he was clearly unnerved.

"It could merely be a tragic coincidence."

He looked at her as though he'd already made up his mind it was no coincidence.

"Maybe Mr. Mouse and Mrs. Tacker ate some of the same food," Molly said.

"Where'd they get it?"

She sat on the side of the bed nearest him. "That's the big question, isn't it? I guess one of them could have had it hidden somewhere." Molly thought about that for an instant. "It would have been Mrs. Tacker, since she died after Abner. A week ago Sunday, she could have given some to Abner and kept the rest for herself to eat later."

He looked down at his hands. They were rubbing against each other, as if he were washing them, trying to remove a stubborn stain. "They both loved sweets." He caught one hand in the other to still them. "Either one of them could have stashed some, I reckon. Estelle wasn't supposed to eat sugar, you know, but she did anyway, if she could get it. She said she wasn't getting out of here alive anyway, and she wasn't giving up her sweets in the meantime. The nurses checked her room every night to make sure she hadn't got hold of a candy bar or some dessert from the kitchen. Sometimes, she'd sneak in there and get a handful of cookies or a piece of pie, whatever she could find."

"Well, maybe that's what happened. She got her hands on something poisoned, gave Abner some, and kept the rest for herself."

He scratched his head and peered at her. The whites of his eyes were veined with red. Molly felt sure he had slept very little the previous night. "D. J. Kennedy and the health-department people turned this place upside down and didn't find anything. I guess Estelle could have eaten all of it. But if she gave Abner a sweet more than a week ago, I don't think she'd have waited so long to eat the rest herself."

"And if she did wait," Molly mused, "she'd have to be an idiot to eat it, once she found out what killed Abner."

He shook his head helplessly. "Besides all that, if Estelle had a sweet she wouldn't have shared with anyone. She'd have hoarded it. No, it don't make any kind of sense."

"Do you think the poisonings were deliberate? That somebody gave Abner and Estelle food they knew was contaminated?"

He hesitated. "I don't know. Like I said, if they did, I can't figure out why."

Was there some connection between the two deaths besides the botulism, a love of sweets, and the fact that both the old people had lived in A-wing? A week had elapsed between Abner's death and Estelle Tacker's. It was stretching it to believe the botulism had come from the same food source. On the other hand, it strained the imagination almost as much to think the poisonings resulted from two different, unrelated sources. So, was there another connection? Estelle Tacker hadn't looked Indian, but . . . "I met

Mrs. Tacker, when I was here before. She didn't look Cherokee to me."

He seemed puzzled. "She didn't have no Indian blood a'tall, far as I know."

No connection there, then. "Did Abner know her before he came to the nursing home?"

"Nope."

"Had they become good friends here?"

"He didn't have no more to do with her than with any of the other people here. You see the folks in your own wing more often than others. You pass the time of day with them, but you don't really get to be friends with too many."

Molly hesitated a long moment before she said, "If the poisonings were deliberate—and I'm not convinced they were—there's probably some connection between Abner and Estelle."

"Well, I sure don't know what it is, and I ought to, if anybody does. I knew Abner since we were boys."

They fell silent as they heard footsteps approaching the door. A nurse's aide came in with Mercer's covered tray. She said hello, set the tray on the bedside table, and left.

Molly waited until she heard the aide pushing the cart down the hall before she asked, "Can you give me the names of the visitors Estelle Tacker had the day before she was taken ill?"

He nodded. "I knew you'd be asking that, so I already gave it some thought. Estelle's son was here Sunday. He lives over in Fort Smith, but he came to see her almost every week. I think she gave him money. Doled it out like she was turning loose of her last dollar, but I think she had plenty in the bank."

"Was he here a week ago Sunday, too?"

"Let me think now. . . yes, he was here then. Me and Abner had our door open and he stopped and said hello."

"So Estelle Tacker's son came to see her to get money?"

He scratched his nose with a crooked finger. "I ain't saying that's the only reason, or he wouldn't have stayed so long. Sunday, he was here most of the day. Got here about ten and went to town for lunch around noon. He came back early in the afternoon and stayed till after we had supper.

Estelle had her door open, and I heard her son trying to get her to eat her vegetables.''

Because he'd poisoned them? ''Was he alone?''

''Yes. I think he's divorced. A woman used to come with him, but I ain't seen her in a few months. I heard Estelle talk about a granddaughter, married and living up north somewhere. Michigan, I think. Buster was Estelle's only child, so I know the girl is his.''

''Anybody else?''

''Buster was the only visitor Estelle had all day Sunday.''

''Did you see any other visitors in this wing?''

''Woodrow and Nellie came by to see me, and my sister's daughter was here a few minutes while I was eating supper.'' He waited until Molly jotted down the names and looked up. ''Sally Creighton's niece and the niece's husband and their grown son came to see her Sunday afternoon. The niece comes two or three times a week. I don't know why, because Sally sure gives her a hard time. Like I said, I don't think Sally's got all her marbles. She gets on a subject, and that's all she talks about. Lately, it's been religion.''

It must have been Sally Creighton who was listening to the television preacher. Molly continued to make notes as he talked. ''Do you know the names of Mrs. Creighton's niece and her family?''

He frowned and shook his head. ''I reckon I've heard 'em, but I can't recall right now.''

''Is Mrs. Creighton in 101?''

''Yes, she's right next to Estelle. Room 101 and 102 are private rooms, so they cost more than the others. The rest of us can't afford them.'' He gestured toward the bed where Molly sat. ''I expect I'll be getting another roommate myself pretty soon.''

''Who's in 103 and 104?''

''The Whillocks are in 103. Give me a minute, and I'll think of their names.'' He was rubbing his hands together again. ''Gladys and Ernie—that's it. Quiet sort of people. They keep pretty much to themselves.''

''Did they have visitors Sunday?''

''I heard them talking to somebody—I think it was

sometime after supper—but the door was closed, so I didn't see who it was. Probably one of their sons or the grandson. They all live in town. One of the sons is called Fred, but I can't tell you the other son's name—or the grandson's. He don't come as often as the others. They got a daughter, too, but she lives way off in California. She don't get back here much."

Molly scribbled the Whillocks' names and room number. "And 104?"

"That's Faye Hakey and Lahoma Buckhorn. I don't know if either one of them had any visitors Sunday. I didn't see any, but I had my door closed part of the time. And I walked around a few times to limber up my joints and sat out on the front porch for a spell late in the evening."

Molly finished writing and put the paper and pen back in her jeans pocket. "I'll see what I can find out about these people." She was remembering the car parked out front. "Did somebody from the sheriff's department talk to you today?"

"D. J. Kennedy asked me a few questions, me and everybody else in this wing. The other wings, too, for all I know. He said he'd probably be back."

Maybe she could get D.J. to tell her something. If the other residents of A-wing were as scared as Mercer Vaughan, they weren't likely to answer questions from a stranger who happened to be visiting their neighbor, at least not so soon after Estelle Tacker's death.

Molly got up off the bed. "Aren't you going to eat your dinner?"

"I'll eat some of it, in a while."

She hesitated, then said carefully, "Mr. Vaughan, for the time being, it might be a good idea not to eat anything except what's prepared in the kitchen here."

"Don't worry about that. I wish I didn't have to eat at all, but I have to keep my strength up, and Kennedy told me they don't think the poison came from the kitchen. They'd have to hold me down to feed me anything else till this gets cleared up."

If it gets cleared up, Molly thought. "You call me if something else happens," she said gently.

"If another person dies, you mean?"

Molly nodded. "Or if you hear anything that might throw some light on the poisonings."

He laced his gnarled, bent fingers together and looked away. "I will."

Molly saw nobody in the hall as she left, but when she reached the lobby, D. J. Kennedy was going out the door. "D.J.!" she called.

He turned back and a grin lit his face. Even with exhaustion lining his forehead and either side of his mouth, it was a handsome face. She'd almost forgotten how pleasantly Cherokee and Irish genes had been combined in D.J. "Hi, Molly."

"How are things with you?"

"Can't complain. You leaving?"

She nodded and he held the door open for her and followed her out. "Do you have a relative here?"

"No. I was visiting Mercer Vaughan." As they walked toward their cars, D.J. looked over at her inquisitively. His brown hair and khaki uniform were rumpled, but then D.J. frequently looked rumpled. It gave him a weird kind of charm. It would be easy to fall for D.J. She'd almost forgotten that, too.

Molly stopped walking. "D.J., can I talk to you?"

He stopped, too. "If I don't eat something, I'm going to cave in. Have you had dinner?"

"No—"

"Meet me in town at The Shack." He walked to his squad car and got in without waiting for her reply. By the time Molly reached her car, D.J. was driving away.

* * *

The Shack was on Muskogee Avenue, a block north of Cherokee Square. It had been in that location for as long as Molly could remember. Neither the interior nor the menu had changed much since her high-school days.

When Molly arrived, D.J. was already seated in a front corner booth, his head deep in a menu. She slid in across from him. "D.J., I—"

"Let's order first." He put down the menu and motioned for the waitress.

Molly didn't have to look at the menu. The Shack's cheeseburgers were hard to beat. She ordered one with fries and coffee. D.J. asked for the chicken-fried-steak dinner and iced tea.

"Has Sheriff Hobart turned the nursing-home investigation over to you?" she asked when the waitress left.

"The sheriff doesn't even know about it. He's on vacation, somewhere in Washington or Oregon in his RV. Been gone ten days and he planned to stay a month. He hasn't even called to check on things. Guess he doesn't want to know what's going on, for fear he'll have to come home early." He sat back and covered a yawn with his big hand.

She smiled.

"So," he said, "here we are."

"Yeah, here we are."

"You're looking good, Molly. How's your love life?"

She stirred uncomfortably. "Nonexistent, if you must know," she said and immediately wondered why she'd said it. She hoped it didn't sound as though she wanted him to know she was available, but she did wonder if he was seeing a particular woman at the moment. She wasn't about to ask.

D.J. had been divorced for six years. His ex-wife and ten-year-old daughter, Courtney, lived in Colorado. Because of the distance between them, he only saw his daughter for a few days between Christmas and New Year's and a couple of weeks during the summer.

He didn't comment on Molly's nonexistent love life, but he studied her intently. Reaching for his water glass, he said, "What's your connection to Mercer Vaughan?"

So much for small talk. "He's a friend of my grandmother."

He looked at her over the top of his glass. "And?"

"He was Abner Mouse's roommate and Woodrow Mouse asked me to investigate his father's death."

"I heard he's thinking of suing the nursing home."

"We didn't really discuss that. He just asked me to find out where Abner got the poisoned food."

He set his glass down. ''You do know the health department and I are looking into that?''

''Yes. I guess Woodrow thinks I might pick up on something you miss.''

He gave her a wry look. ''Molly Bearpaw's on the case, eh? Great. Think you can solve it before the sheriff gets back?''

He was going to be difficult. ''I thought—well, I hoped we could share information—compare notes.''

''For old times' sake?''

Molly felt herself blushing. ''What old times?''

''Good point. We go out twice and then you won't give me the time of day. Did I eat my peas with my knife? Forget to put on deodorant? What?''

Molly sighed. ''D.J.—''

''I haven't talked to you in months and, all of a sudden, you want to cozy up to me and pick my brain.''

''I'm not trying to cozy—''

''God, Molly, you might at least have tried to be a little subtle about it.''

''Come on, D.J. Can't we keep this on a professional level?''

''The way I see it, you need me. I don't need you.'' He smiled a wintry smile. ''Professionally speaking.''

At that moment, the waitress appeared with their dinner, giving Molly a few moments to regroup. Apparently D.J. had been more hurt than she'd realized by her decision not to see him again. But that was nearly a year ago, for heaven's sake, and she knew he'd dated other women since then. It must be wounded pride. She tried to come up with an angle that would appeal to him as she sipped her coffee and poured ketchup on her fries. Meantime, D.J. shoveled in steak and potatoes and gravy. Hurt feelings hadn't spoiled his appetite.

The problem was, he was right. She needed him. He could question everybody at the nursing home, including the staff, and the management was in no position to refuse him. She, on the other hand, would get thrown out on her ear if they suspected what she was up to. What did she have to offer him in return for his cooperation? Very little.

"I can usually get people to talk to me," she ventured. "I guess I come across as nonthreatening. I know you have plenty of other things to do in addition to investigating these nursing-home deaths—particularly right now with the sheriff gone."

He gave her a sagacious look.

"I, on the other hand, can devote most of my time to the investigation." She tried a little levity. "You could always deputize me." Good Lord, she was practically begging. "Two heads are better than one, D.J. Between us, we *may* be able to wrap this up before the sheriff returns."

He continued to eat silently, which she decided not to interpret as a flat refusal. "I assume you don't think the botulism was in the nursing-home food," she said.

He buttered a fat roll before he said, "I could get my butt fired for telling you anything." He took a bite of the roll and chewed reflectively. "If that nursing home was a couple hundred yards south of where it is, these deaths would be the city police department's problem instead of ours." He took another bite of roll. "Oh, what the hell. I could use somebody outside the department to bounce ideas off of."

He finished the roll while Molly ate her cheeseburger. It was the one sure way to keep her mouth shut and wait. Finally, her silence paid off. "The inspectors didn't find a trace of botulism. The first time, I figured it was probably in something the kitchen help had already fed the garbage disposal. After that, the cooks were told to dispose of all leftovers after each meal. No exceptions, except for stuff like ice cream and baked goods, like cake, which they can keep covered in the refrigerator for one night only. If they don't use the rest of it the next day, out it goes. And the health-department people went over the proper cooking procedures—how hot the food has to be heated and how long. They swore they'd been doing those things all along. But what else were they going to say?"

"True," Molly murmured.

"I still figured one of the cooks had been in a hurry and had gotten careless, maybe put the last serving of something left out of the refrigerator too long on Mouse's plate and served everybody else from a new batch. But after Abner

Mouse's death, it was certain nobody was going to make that mistake again."

"Then Estelle Tacker died."

"Yeah." He pushed his empty plate back.

"Same story," Molly said. "The inspectors found no botulism in the nursing-home kitchen?"

"You got it. So, the botulism came from somewhere else. It was either in food brought to Mouse and Tacker by a visitor, or an employee carried it in. We didn't find any evidence of food in either room." He sat forward and propped his elbows on the table. "The head of the health-department team is a medical doctor who specializes in this kind of thing. He says the cases of botulism he's investigated generally came from home-canned food, but that wasn't true in every instance. He knew of two babies who got it from honey, for example. Says botulism doesn't need oxygen to grow, and it's odorless and tasteless. The first hint you have that you're infected is the symptoms, which can start as soon as eight hours after eating the contaminated food, or it can take as long as twenty-four hours. Depends a lot on the victim. If he doesn't have much resistance, symptoms will appear sooner. And they can be pretty bizarre."

"I know," Molly said. "You naturally assume there will be nausea and vomiting, but I didn't know victims often have double vision and paralysis, too." At D.J.'s mildly surprised look, she added, "I read the entry on botulism in my landlord's medical encyclopedia. And I talked to the medical examiner who performed Abner Mouse's autopsy. He found hemorrhages in the internal organs. That's what tipped him to what he was dealing with."

D.J. rubbed a finger on the side of his nose. "You have been busy, haven't you?"

"I've talked to Woodrow and Nellie Mouse, too. They were the only visitors Abner had the day before he died. They both deny bringing Abner any food, and Mercer Vaughan confirms that. But he wasn't in the room all the time they were there." She fished the crumpled envelope, on which she'd made notes, out of her pocket. "Mr.

Vaughan says Estelle Tacker's son visited her the day before she died. He doesn't think she had any other visitors."

"Buster Tacker denies giving his mother anything to eat."

"What about the employees?" Molly asked.

"Same song, second verse. They sometimes bring snacks to share with each other, but nobody gave any of the patients food, except for what was prepared in the kitchen. Not on the days before Mouse's and Tacker's deaths, or any other day. It's a company policy."

"Somebody is lying," Molly said.

"Sure looks that way."

"Tell me something, D.J., do you think those two old people were murdered?"

"The idea has crossed my mind," he admitted, "but it seems too fantastic."

"Murder often does."

"Granted, but botulism poisoning is a pretty iffy murder method. Those people could as easily have recovered as died."

"Assume it was murder," Molly said. "If strychnine or some other poison had been used, an autopsy would have made murder obvious. With botulism, there's the possibility it was accidental and that the nursing home would get the blame."

He nodded. "On balance, a killer might think it was worth taking the risk that the victims would recover."

"He could always try again with another kind of poison."

D.J. heaved a tired sigh. "Well, I can't even make a good guess as to whether it was murder until I know who and why."

"And why Mouse and Tacker?" Molly mused. "Mercer Vaughan says they weren't even friends. About the only things they have in common are their love of sweets and living in the same wing."

"Tacker was a diabetic—"

Molly nodded. "She wasn't supposed to eat sugar, but Mr. Vaughan says she did, anyway. The nurses were always trying to catch her eating candy or dessert she'd sneaked from the kitchen." She looked at her notes again. "Since the two victims were old and probably had low resistance, I guess we can assume their symptoms showed up sooner rather than later. The nurses kept telling Woodrow his father had a virus."

"But with Tacker, they were on their toes." D.J. added. "Shipped her to the hospital as soon as she started feeling sick and pumped her stomach. Unfortunately, she died, anyway. Doctor said the strain on her heart was too great."

"At any rate, both victims must have eaten the contaminated food the day before they died. Sunday. Wait . . . that's another thing they have in common. Both ate the contaminated food on a Sunday."

He nodded as though he were way ahead of her. "Most visitors come on the weekend."

Molly smoothed out the wrinkled envelope. "Mr. Vaughan gave me the names of people who visited the patients in A-wing last Sunday. The ones he knew, that is."

"I got some of that information from the patients in that wing today, but a couple of them were too upset to think straight. I'm going to get them all together tomorrow and talk to them."

She looked up quickly. "I'd like to be there."

He looked at her eager face and wondered if he was crazy to even consider it. In the last few minutes, he'd realized that he found her as attractive as he had when they'd gone out on those two dates months ago. He wasn't sure why. Her face was pleasing enough. Smooth, tan complexion. Short straight nose. Wide mouth. Dark-chocolate eyes. Still, it wasn't a face that was likely to stop traffic. She had terrific legs, of course, but she was too thin. When he tried to analyze her features individually, he told himself she was no more attractive than hundreds—thousands—of other women. But there was something about the way all those features were put together in Molly Bearpaw that made her just about the sexiest woman he'd ever known.

"People will wonder what you're doing there," he said. "What am I supposed to tell them?"

Molly had been giving that some thought. "We can say I'm a federal investigator. My salary *is* paid with BIA funds, so it's not an out-and-out lie. Nobody will know what that means, but they won't have the nerve to ask. I hope."

He chuckled. "Molly, Molly." He took out his wallet and extracted money for the check.

Molly laid seven dollars on the table to cover her meal and tip. This was a business meeting. Sort of. "Is that a yes or a no?"

He stuffed his wallet back in his hip pocket. "Okay, you can come; 9:00 A.M. And try not to call attention to yourself." No matter what she did or didn't do, the sheriff was bound to hear about this eventually and, when he did, Claude Hobart would skin him alive.

No doubt about it, D.J. concluded morosely. He *was* crazy.

oooooooo

8

The next morning, Molly arrived early and waited for D.J. in her car. When he drove up, his expression was somber, as though he regretted saying she could come. "Remember," he told her, as they walked toward the building, "let me do most of the talking."

When they entered the lobby, a chubby, middle-aged, worried-looking man in a gray suit came toward them. D.J. introduced him. It was David Darwood, the nursing-home administrator. At Darwood's perplexed frown, D.J. said, "Miss Bearpaw's a federal investigator."

Darwood looked stunned. "I didn't know the federal government was involved in this—this unfortunate set of circumstances. Why is the government interested in two accidental deaths in Tahlequah, Oklahoma?"

D.J. shrugged. "You know the government. They don't tell you anything."

Darwood stared at Molly. She smiled enigmatically. "Sorry, I'm not at liberty to say."

"Are you with the FBI, or aren't you allowed to say that either?"

Molly was tempted to hint at a connection to the bureau, but he might ask to see her ID. D.J. said, "She's with the Bureau of Indian Affairs."

Darwood's expression was blank. "I'm here because of Abner Mouse," Molly added. "He was a member of a federally recognized Native American tribe."

"Oh," Darwood said uncertainly.

"Miss Bearpaw will merely observe and report to her superiors," D.J. told him.

Darwood still did not seem satisfied with this unexpected development, but there wasn't much he could do about it. "The residents of A-wing are waiting for you in the dining room. It's this way."

Six elderly people—Mercer Vaughan, another man, and four women—were seated in molded plastic chairs that had been pulled away from one of the long tables and arranged in a semicircle in a corner of the dining room. There was a lively conversation going on, but it stopped abruptly when they noticed Darwood, D.J., and Molly.

"I believe you've met everybody, Deputy Kennedy," Darwood said.

"Good morning, folks." D.J. waited for Darwood to leave, and when the administrator didn't move, said, "I'd like to talk to them alone, if you don't mind, Mr. Darwood."

Darwood hesitated, miffed. Then he turned on his heel and walked out of the room.

One old woman clung to the hand of the gentleman next to her. Of the six, they were the only ones not in street clothes. They wore matching robes the same shade of gray as their faces and looked enough alike to be twins. Gladys and Ernie Whillock, 103, Molly decided.

"Who's she?" the clinging lady asked.

"This is Molly Bearpaw, Mrs. Whillock," D.J. said. "Molly, Mr. and Mrs. Whillock. You know Mr. Vaughan." Molly smiled at Mercer. He looked as tired and worried as he had yesterday, and his bony fingers kept clenching and unclenching the crook of his cane. "These other ladies are Mrs. Creighton, Mrs. Hakey, and Mrs. Buckhorn."

Sally Creighton, 101, blinked at Molly from behind gold-rimmed spectacles and plucked at her cotton dress, which buttoned down the front, the kind Molly's grandmother called a housedress.

Lahoma Buckhorn, the only other Cherokee in the group besides Mercer Vaughan, shared 104 with Faye Hakey. They had gone to more trouble than the others to prepare for the meeting. Hakey's polyester dress was fire-engine red and she'd painted her cheeks to match. Her blue-rinsed hair looked as though it had seen a curling iron very recently, too.

Buckhorn had on a fake-linen suit and fake pearls. She'd pinned a crumpled, fake white rose in her hair. Hakey and Buckhorn were dressed for a social occasion. Molly figured they didn't have many opportunities for getting dolled up. This was probably the most exciting thing that had happened to them in years.

Lahoma Buckhorn fingered her pearls and peered at Molly. "I know who she is. That granddaughter of Eva Adair's, the one Eva raised."

"That's right, Mrs. Buckhorn," Molly said.

"Are you right with God, young woman?" demanded Sally Creighton.

Faye Hakey's head whipped around. "Shut up, Sally. We're sick and tired of hearing you preach. When did you get ordained, anyway?"

"You don't have to be ordained to warn people that Judgment Day's a'coming," Creighton shot back. "Reverend Teagarden was never ordained, but God called him to preach, anyway."

Hakey snorted. "You mean that shouting, hillbilly TV preacher? Don't lay that off on God."

"Reverend Teagarden had a clear sign," Creighton said triumphantly. "He was plowing a field and giant letters appeared in the sky. GPC. He knew God was calling him to Go Preach Christ."

"Oh, poop! How'd he know God wasn't telling him to go plant cotton?" Hakey said. Buckhorn giggled and earned a furious look from Creighton. "Money," Hakey went on. "That's what called your Reverend Teagarden to preach."

Creighton's eyes spit fire. She rocked forward and backward several times and grabbed the back of Mercer's chair, which was on her right, evidently preparing to get on her feet. "Blasphemy! You take that back, Faye Hakey!"

D.J. cleared his throat. "Ladies, if I might have your attention, please . . ."

Creighton subsided back into her chair. Evidently, getting up was more trouble than it was worth, after all. She shook a finger at her adversary. "God heard you, Faye. Think about that when you say your papist prayers tonight."

"I'll do that," snapped Hakey, "and I'll ask God to strike that Preacher Teagarden dumb, too, before he can delude any more ignoramuses."

" 'When the light in you is darkness, how great is that darkness,' " intoned Creighton.

"Horse hockey!"

Lahoma Buckhorn, who was seated in the line of fire between her roommate and Creighton, said, "I don't know why you don't ignore her, Faye. She likes to get you mad. It's silly to let her rile you."

"Keep your hand off my arm, Lahoma," snapped Hakey. "I'll get riled if I feel like it."

"Remember your blood pressure. You'll work yourself up into a stroke."

"I'll have a stroke if I feel like it, too!"

Buckhorn peered at her roommate closely. "You're as peckish as an old settin' hen this morning. You must be constipated again."

"That's your answer to everything! You're obsessed with bowel movements, Lahoma."

"Mrs. Hakey," D.J. interrupted loudly, "let's get started." He took a small tape recorder from his pocket. "Does anybody object if I record this interview?" Nobody did. "Mrs. Hakey, can you remember if you had any visitors last Sunday?"

"Of course, I can remember! I may be old, young man, but I'm not senile, like some people I could mention."

"Armageddon's coming," muttered Creighton.

"You hear that? Crazy talk. Why, she's going to deed her home to that charlatan. Silly old fool!"

"About last Sunday," D.J. said rather desperately.

Lahoma Buckhorn spoke up. "Her granddaughter came to see her."

"Will you let me speak for myself, Lahoma!" Hakey took out a lace-edged handkerchief and patted the wrinkles around her mouth.

Buckhorn sniffed and picked a bit of lint off her skirt. "Deputy Kennedy wants you to do it today, Faye, not sometime next week."

"What's your granddaughter's name, Mrs. Hakey?" Molly interjected quickly, and six wizened heads swiveled to look at her as though they were watching a tennis match. She was perched on the edge of a table, a little behind and to one side of D.J. Perhaps they had all forgotten she was there.

Hakey patted her blue hair. "Lori. Lori Hakey. My son and his wife moved to Lawton last year, but Lori has a good job at the university, so she stayed here. Such a fine girl. Goes to mass every Sunday."

"What time was Lori here last Sunday?" D.J. asked.

"She came at two o'clock. I looked at my watch. She stayed about two hours."

"It was three o'clock," Buckhorn corrected her. "I told you your watch was an hour slow and you changed it. Don't you remember?"

"That wasn't Sunday. It was Saturday."

"It was Sunday," insisted Buckhorn. "You know I have a good memory for dates."

"You saying I'm forgetful?"

D.J. looked as though he wanted to wring his hands. "It doesn't matter. Did you have any other visitors Sunday, Mrs. Hakey?"

"No."

"What about you, Mrs. Buckhorn?"

"Some people from the Methodist church came by and brought me flowers and a little devotional book. Wasn't that sweet of them?"

"Yes, ma'am. What were their names?"

After some thought, she named four women, adding, "Jane Terry works in the church office. She sends me the church bulletin every week. Now, there is a thoughtful young woman. Do you know Jane, Deputy?"

"I haven't had the pleasure, ma'am. Any other visitors?"

"Not that I recall."

Hakey "hmmmped." "What about that long stringbean of a fellow, Miz Perfect Memory?"

"Oh," Buckhorn fluttered, "you mean Willie George Perkins. He just stepped in to give me the rent money. He wasn't here but a minute Sunday morning. Willie George rents a little house I own in Grove, Deputy. He was a few days late this month, so he brought the money by, instead of mailing a check. He knows I depend on that rent for my spending money."

D.J. turned to Sally Creighton. "I guess it's your turn, Mrs. Creighton. Who visited you Sunday?"

"My niece, Ginny Hulle. Her husband, Bowen, and that son of theirs came too, but they sat out in the lobby and watched a ball game on TV most of the time. Those two can't even spare an hour to visit with me. Ginny told them to go on home and come back for her later, but, no, they had to hang around and keep poking their heads in the door to ask if she wasn't ready to leave."

"They're sick of being preached to, like the rest of us," muttered Hakey.

"They're gonna be a lot sicker when they wake up in the fires of hell. The good Lord knows I've done what I could. I gave Ginny one of Reverend Teagarden's pamphlets weeks ago—"

"The one begging for money?" Hakey inquired.

Creighton raised her voice. "Ginny claims she read it and thought the reverend made some good points."

"That Ginny is a saint," Hakey said to D.J. "Visits two or three times a week and listens patiently to such foolishness as you've heard here today. I've never ever known her to raise her voice to this old crackpot."

"Ginny knows who paid for her college education," Creighton snapped. "If it hadn't of been for me, she'd be waiting tables somewhere. Her parents never had two dimes to rub together. My brother was always as lazy as a hound. Ginny's a hard worker, though. She got that from me. I'm sure she's the one keeps the family business going. Ginny and Bowen own a dry cleaners in Tahlequah and three in other towns. I loaned them the money to get started."

"Charged them exorbitant interest, too, I'll wager," said Hakey.

"I never knew anyone with so many opinions," sniffed Creighton, "on subjects she's totally ignorant of."

Hakey bristled, but settled back when D.J. raised his voice. "What time were they here Sunday, Mrs. Creighton?"

"They got here a little before the supper trays came. Must've been about four forty-five. It was after seven before Bowen got Ginny to leave. Served him right for sitting around out there in the lobby like a bump on a log instead of going on home and coming back. Ginny was reading to me from my Bible when he interrupted her. Psalms. The Psalms are so comforting, don't you think, Deputy?"

"Yes, ma'am."

"King David wrote most of them, you know. Now, there was a great sinner, but he came to his senses in time..."

"You were saying about your niece's husband?"

"Oh, that. Well, Bowen stuck his head in and interrupted Ginny slap dab in the middle of a Psalm. I believe it was the thirty-second... or was it the forty-second?"

"Nobody gives a hoot," said Hakey.

Creighton ignored her. "Bowen said they had to leave right then, smack in the middle of the Psalm. That man is rude. Common. I tried to tell Ginny before she married him, but—"

D.J. turned to Mercer and interrupted Creighton to ask, "Mr. Vaughan, did you have visitors Sunday?"

"My niece and Woodrow and Nellie Mouse came to see me," Mercer said. "I already told you and Molly all about that."

D.J. nodded and moved on to the Whillocks. "The only visitor we had Sunday was our son Fred," Ernie Whillock said. "He lives here in town. He came late in the afternoon and stayed a good while. Our other son lives here, too, but he was out of town on business."

"What time was your son here?"

"Late afternoon," Whillock repeated. "Around four. He must have stayed for a couple of hours. He brought his calculator and helped me get my checkbook balanced. I'm always off. I can't understand it."

"You forget to write down all the checks, Ernie," his wife said hesitantly.

Whillock ignored her. D.J. rubbed his hands together. "We know that Mrs. Tacker's son, Buster, was here Sunday, too. Did any of you see anybody else in your wing?"

Five heads shook in solemn accord. The sixth head, Sally Creighton's, was bent and unmoving. She was absorbed in pulling something from her pocket.

"Then I guess that does it for now." D.J. turned off the recorder. "Thank you for your cooperation."

Mercer pushed himself to his feet and Ernie Whillock helped his wife up. "You *do* forget to write down all the checks, Ernie," Faye Whillock was saying. Whillock mumbled something and led her toward the door. They were followed by the other residents.

D.J. watched them leave. "I wanted to stuff something in those three old ladies' mouths," he muttered.

She grinned. "And get the sheriff's department hauled into court? Actually, I thought it went pretty well."

"I already have a list of the employees who were in A-wing the last two Sundays. Let's blow this joint."

Sally Creighton was waiting in the hall outside the dining room. As they left, she thrust a pamphlet at Molly. "Read this, young woman. It's one of Reverend Teagarden's. It's the most important thing you'll read in your life."

Molly took the pamphlet which had "Where Will You Spend Eternity?" emblazened across the front in red letters. She dropped it in a wastebasket at the other end of the hall on her way out.

As they reached the lobby, a wheelchair blocked their path. It was Mrs. Archer, and she was one irate old lady. Molly was relieved to see, however, that the confused look in her eyes wasn't so noticable today.

"Officer, I want this woman arrested!"

Evidently the look in her eyes was no way to gauge how far out in left field Mrs. Archer was at any given moment. "D.J., this is Mrs. Archer," Molly said.

"I believe we've met."

Mrs. Archer stared at Molly. "Arrest her, Officer!"

"You mean Molly here? Why, what did Molly ever do to you, Mrs. Archer."

"She made them shoot me!"

"Now, you know that isn't true. I came to visit Mr. Vaughan. You saw me when I left his room. Don't you remember?" Molly said, even though she was sure the woman couldn't distinguish truth from the delusions floating around in her brain. She probably didn't even know her own name.

"Don't talk to me like that!"

"Like what?"

"Like I'm retarded. That's how they all talk to me. You're in cahoots with them, aren't you?"

"No—"

"Yes, you are! I would've got clean away if you hadn't called that nurse."

On second thought, maybe she did remember their previous meeting. "I thought you needed help to get back to your room. You were pretty agitated."

"You'd be, too, if people shot at you all the time."

"Mrs. Archer . . ."

"That's what they did, when you called that nurse. Shot me. Are you going to arrest her, Officer?"

D.J. hid a grin with his hand. "I'll take her down to the station and question her, ma'am. See what she has to say for herself when we get her under the lights." He glanced at Molly, a grin still pulling at his mouth. "We may have to use the rubber hose."

"Serve her right."

"Would you like me to take you back to your room now?" D.J. asked.

"Don't need any help." She wheeled past them so fast that Molly had to jump out of the way to keep from being mowed down.

"It's not nice to go around shooting old ladies, Molly," D.J. said as they reached the lobby.

"Poor old soul."

"What really happened to get her so mad at you?"

"She wanted me to help her get out of the wheelchair."

"I noticed they had her strapped in." D.J. held the door open for Molly.

"They have to do that to keep her from running off," Molly said. She asked if I had any scissors, and when I said no, she started ranting about people shooting her. I called a nurse's aide and they gave her an injection to calm her down. Maybe that's what she meant."

"Come again?"

"I assumed all that talk about getting shot was about guns. Christine Zucker, the nurse's aide, said Mrs. Archer thinks the Mafia is after her. But maybe she's referring to the tranquilizer shots they give her when she's upset. Christine said she carries on something awful when she sees the syringe."

"Could be," D.J. said.

They had reached the front walk and stopped to finish their conversation. "Let's get a cup of coffee," Molly suggested.

"Don't have time now. One of the deputies had to check out a report on some rustled cattle, and another one had to take his wife to the doctor."

"Do you want me to transcribe that tape for you?"

He hesitated, then handed it over. "I doubt I'll have time to do it today. I'll come by your office this afternoon when the other deputies get back."

"What time?"

"It'll probably be late."

"I won't be in the office then. I usually work at home after two or three."

"That's even better. I'll try to be there by four."

Better? What did that mean? She wasn't sure of the etiquette of meeting with ex-boyfriends in one's apartment. Not that D.J. had ever been a boyfriend, exactly. Nobody used that term these days, anyway. Dammit, she was letting him fluster her. "Well, okay..."

* * *

It was four-thirty by the time D.J. arrived. His uniform, which had probably been freshly laundered when he put it on that morning, looked wrinkled enough to have been slept in for a week. Molly wondered how he did it.

"You look beat," she said.

"We were busy as bird dogs all day long. Phone never

stopped ringing. This heat has got people frazzled. They call us on the slightest provocation." He went to the sink and downed two glasses of water.

Molly had prepared for their meeting by placing her notes, the tape and typed transcript, a couple of legal pads, and several pens on the kitchen table and brewing a pot of Kona blend. She filled two big mugs, and D.J. pulled out his report on his conversations with nursing-home employees. Combining the information, they made a list of people known to have been in A-wing on the Sundays before the two deaths.

Visitors

Room 101: Sally Creighton
8/11 Ginny, Bowen, and Randy Hulle (Sally's niece and family)
8/18 Ginny, Bowen, and Randy Hulle

Room 102: Estelle Tacker
8/11 Buster Tacker (Estelle's son)
8/18 Buster Tacker

Room 103: Gladys and Ernie Whillock
8/11 Ben and Fred Whillock (the Whillocks' sons)
8/18 Fred Whillock

Room 104: Faye Hakey and Lahoma Buckhorn
8/11 Lori Hakey (Faye's granddaughter)
8/18 Lori Hakey
Methodist-church ladies (B. Guinn, N. Ingles, B. Jefferson, J. Terry)
Willie George Perkins (Buckhorn's renter)

Room 105: Abner Mouse and Mercer Vaughan
8/11 Woodrow and Nellie Mouse (Abner's son and wife)
8/18 Woodrow and Nellie Mouse

		Patsy Pennington (Mercer's niece)
<u>Staff</u>	8/11	7:00 A.M.–3:00 P.M.
		Beatrice Crawford, R.N.
		Zelda Kline, nurse's aide
		Cora D'Angelo, cleaning woman
		3:00–11:00 P.M. Irene Robinson, R.N.
		Mary Sue Nutter, nurse's aide
	8/18	7:00 A.M.–3:00 P.M.
		Regina Smith, R.N.
		Zelda Kline
		Cora D'Angelo
		3:00–11:00 P.M. Irene Robinson, R.N.
		Mary Sue Nutter

They left off the employees who worked the 11:00 P.M. to 7:00 A.M. shift, since the residents had been sleeping during those hours and breakfast wasn't delivered until after the day shift came on.

When they finished, D.J. counted the names and threw down his pen with a groan. "That's twenty-one people. How are we going to deal with that many suspects?" He got up to pour himself more coffee.

Molly glanced down the list of names. "We have to assume the same person is responsible for both deaths."

"We're making a lot of assumptions here, including that this was the premeditated murder of two old people, but we don't *have* to assume anything."

"We do if we're going to get anywhere. So let's assume it was murder for now, and if we assume that, it's reasonable to assume there's only one murderer."

D.J. sighed and brought his coffee back to the table. "Okay. I don't have a better idea."

"We can eliminate anybody who wasn't there on both the eleventh and the eighteenth—for now, anyway." She marked through several names. "That leaves just eight visitors and four employees."

"Just? That's twelve people to check out." He blew on

his coffee before chancing a sip. "Maybe we're coming at this from the wrong angle. Let's think about motives."

"Financial gain is always a biggy."

"Yeah . . ."

They were silent for several moments. D.J. had been involved in only two previous murder investigations during his time with the sheriff's department. In one, the jealous husband was sitting beside the body of his wife, still holding the murder weapon when the deputies arrived. The other, also a shooting, was the culmination of a bar fight witnessed by eleven people. The guilty party had conveniently passed out in his car next to the bar by the time the sheriff and D.J. got there.

In her two years with the league, Molly had never before been asked to look into a death, much less one that was feeling more and more like murder. But she'd read a lot of mystery novels.

"Revenge," she suggested. "Or to keep a secret from coming out."

D.J.'s eyebrows rose. He knew the sort of reading material she favored. "As long as we're flying by the seat of our pants, anyway, there's always your random serial killer. I saw an article in the newspaper a few weeks ago about a male nurse who killed seven old people in a hospital back East before they caught him. He injected them with a medication that made it look like they'd all had heart attacks. Told the police the victims had outlived their usefulness. He was doing the world a favor."

"A maniac," Molly observed. "He probably appeared to be perfectly normal, too. Like these four nursing-home employees." She ran her finger down the list. "Irene Robinson, Zelda Kline, Mary Sue Nutter, Cora D'Angelo. What do you think?"

"I was only half serious. It's a very remote possibility."

"You're right. We'd better concentrate on motives that are at least within the realm of rationality."

D.J. was still thinking about the newspaper article he'd read. "The thing that brings me up short when it comes to the staff—why would you use botulism if you had all those drugs in the nursing home to choose from? And another thing. How would you get your hands on botulism bacilli, anyway? Can you manufacture them by leaving food sitting on the kitchen table for a few days?''

''Presumably.''

''Even then, how could you be sure of what you had?''

''You'd have to have access to a lab, I guess.''

''There's a lab at the nursing home,'' D.J. said thoughtfully. ''They do routine procedures like blood counts and urinalyses. The lab tech only works mornings.''

''So if somebody wanted to use the lab without anyone knowing, it wouldn't be a problem,'' Molly added.

D.J. was frowning. ''The cleaning woman and aides probably wouldn't know how to use the microscope, or what they were looking at if they did.''

''The R.N.s should know.''

He shook his head. ''Let's get back to motives. If it's not some psycho hearing voices, why would anyone murder Mouse and Tacker? Those two in particular, I mean. Whoever might benefit from Mouse's death, wouldn't benefit from Tacker's.''

Molly shrugged. ''Maybe they both knew something the killer didn't want revealed.'' She thought for a moment. ''Or maybe only one of them was the intended victim and the other one was killed to confuse the murder investigation—in case one developed.''

''That's a wild idea.''

''But not impossible.'' It happened frequently in some of the best mystery novels.

''Then we should concentrate on Mouse's and Tacker's visitors. The murderer has to be connected to one of them.''

''Not necessarily.''

''How do you figure?''

''Suppose both of them were cover-ups, and the real victim's still alive.''

''Oh, hell.''

''Exactly.'' She tore a clean page from a legal pad. ''We can't afford to waste any time. Let's split up these names and see what we can find out about them. You'll have better luck with the nursing-home employees.''

''I've already questioned all of them.''

"But you haven't run background checks on them."

He mumbled an agreement and she consulted the list again. "Buster Tacker is the only one who doesn't live in Tahlequah. He's in Fort Smith."

"I'll see if somebody with the police department there can ask around."

"Good. That's five for you. I'll take the others, since I'll have more time to spend on this."

He leaned over Molly's shoulder to scan the list. "Then you'll have the Hulles, Fred Whillock, Woodrow and Nellie Mouse, and Lori Hakey. All average good citizens, as far as I know, except maybe Whillock. He's not the most popular guy in town. Always complaining to the city police about his neighbors being too noisy or not cutting their grass. Not long ago, he ran some kids off his lawn with a shotgun. If you try to question him, he may do the same to you."

She wished he wouldn't lean so close to her. He was making her nervous. "I'll give it a shot—you should pardon the expression." She pushed back her chair and stood. "If he won't talk to me, you may have to take over."

"I'll see what I can find out about all of our suspects' finances."

"Good." She cleared the legal pads and pens off the table.

Watching her, he tilted his chair on its back legs and finished his coffee. He set his mug down. "Why'd you dump me last year, Molly?"

She had her back to him, setting her empty mug in the sink. She didn't turn around. "I didn't dump you. We had two dates, not a relationship."

"Excuse me," he said with a trace of sarcasm. "Okay. After those two dates, you were suddenly busy every time I asked. It took about a dozen turndowns before I got the message. I couldn't believe it. I thought we were good together. Call me dense."

She faced him. "No, you're right. It was fine . . ."

"Fine?" He shook his head. "Talk about the kiss of death."

She decided to be honest. She owed him that. "I had a really bad experience with a man when I lived in Tulsa. When I moved here, I was still—well, I was an emotional mess. I had no business going out with you in the first place."

His smile was tentative. "I wondered if it was something like that. Believe me, I understand. I was a basket case the first year after my divorce. Gloria and I brought out the worst in each other, and I knew it wasn't going to get any better. We'd been to counselors and all that. But I'd invested five years in the marriage and I hated admitting defeat. Mainly, it was Courtney, though. Gloria wanted to take her to Denver. To be honest, that's what really tore me up, knowing I wasn't going to be there to help raise my daughter."

Molly had no idea what to say.

"As soon as I could think about it sanely, I knew the divorce had been inevitable." He let the chair's front legs fall to the floor with a thump, as though putting a great big period to the past. "What happened to the guy in Tulsa?"

"I have no idea. I don't really care."

"You're over him?"

"Oh, sure. The problem was, I thought I knew him, but I didn't have the vaguest idea who he was. I felt conned."

"Funny how that can happen..."

"I think that's what hurt the most. Knowing how easily I'd been duped. It was humiliating."

He weighed her words for an instant. "It's a good thing you found out before you married the guy, though."

"Yeah." She took his mug to the sink. "But afterward I was no longer sure of my instincts when it came to men."

"I know what you mean, but what else is there?"

She shrugged.

After a moment, D.J. asked, "So, you want to go out Saturday night?"

She hesitated, taken by surprise. Seeing her hesitation, he picked up the tape and transcript and stood. "I don't mean to hustle you." He went to the door, opened it.

"No, it's all right, but I need to think about it."

"We'll be talking before then. Let me know."

OOOOOOOO

9

Molly found addresses in the phone book for all the people on her list. First, she decided to tackle Lori Hakey, who lived on the west side of town on Mission Avenue. She waited until six-thirty, giving Lori plenty of time to get home from work.

The house was small, at the back of the lot behind a larger house—a detached garage or storage shed converted to rental property. Molly parked at the curb and walked down the driveway. It didn't look as though anybody was home. There was no car in the drive, and only Molly's in the street out front. She was already trying to decide whether to wait or come back later as she knocked.

At her touch, the door moved inward slightly. Molly waited a minute, then nudged the door open wider and called, "Miss Hakey?"

"Yo!" She heard movement inside, and then footsteps approached. The door opened wider and glazed blue eyes made a valiant effort to focus on her face.

The sweet smell of marijuana wafted through the open doorway. "Is this where Lori Hakey lives?"

"Yo, mama." He propped a bare shoulder against the doorjamb and gave her a moronic grin. He was barefoot and shirtless. Faded, beltless jeans rode well below his naval, anchored precariously by sharp hipbones. Lank, sandy hair was pulled back and tied in a ponytail at the nape of his neck. Molly guessed his age in the late twenties. "Is Lori here?"

He seemed to find it a difficult question. He gave it some thought, a tough exercise in his zoned-out state. "I think she's gone to the grocery store."

"Will she be back soon?"

He shrugged. "I ain't her keeper. Like, I'm just her main man."

"I need to talk to her. I'm Molly Bearpaw."

He gave her another slack-jawed grin. "Bearpaw? Cool. That's some righteous name. I'm Robert Perrone. You probably heard Lori talk about me."

"Actually, I don't know Lori. I got her name from her grandmother."

"Old lizard butt? That ain't exactly a four-star recommendation, know what I mean?" He scratched at his scraggly chest hair and grinned some more. Everything was fine, mama, just fine. "You wanta come in and wait?" Molly hesitated. "Hey, like stand out there in the yard and broil. Suit yourself, mama." He was already drifting away from the door.

Molly went in, leaving the door ajar. An electric fan sat on the floor, directed toward a sagging brown couch. He flopped on the couch, where the draft from the fan hit his face. An open plastic bag containing a few shreds of marijuana lay on the coffee table. Molly wondered how much the bag had contained when Perrone started on it. "This heat's a bummer. Air conditioner konked out this afternoon. Does it about every two weeks."

"Hmmm," Molly murmured.

"Repairman's supposed to come fix it. Landlady's too cheap to buy a new one."

Molly took the chair facing the couch. It gave her a view of the tiny kitchen, where several empty beer cans were scattered on the floor. Perrone had evidently been aiming at the wastebasket in a corner of the kitchen—one's aim is bound to be off when one can't focus. Perrone was lolling back against the couch now, his eyes closed, humming tunelessly.

"You know Lori's grandmother?" Molly asked.

"Old lizard butt? Yeah."

"Do you go with Lori to visit her?"

He opened a bleary eye and squinted in her general direction. "Me? I look bugs to you? Besides, I ain't invited. Lori don't want the old bitch to know she's tight with me, know what I mean?"

Molly didn't blame her. Grandma's blood pressure might shoot right off the scale if she knew what kind of company her good little Lori was keeping.

"What'd you say you wanted to see Lori about?"

"I didn't. I'm a federal investigator—"

Both eyes flew open and he jerked upright, his glance going unerringly to the bag of marijuana. He could focus when he had to, it seemed. "A friend was here earlier. Brought the weed with him and smoked most of it."

And I'm Princess Di, Molly thought. "I'm not a narc. I'm working with the sheriff's department on the deaths of two residents of Country Haven Nursing Home."

He gazed at her warily. "Old people die all the time. It's a bummer, but I never knew the federal government gave a shit." He frowned, trying to figure it out. "You sure you ain't a narc?"

"Honest."

They heard a car pull into the drive and he grabbed the bag and pushed it out of sight, under a cushion. "Lori's back," he said, still eyeing Molly with suspicion.

A young woman carrying a grocery sack came in. She was looking at Perrone and didn't see Molly. "Did you call about that job?"

"No answer," he mumbled.

She walked past Molly without noticing her and into the kitchen. "God, Bob. This place is a pit." She kicked a beer can furiously and set the groceries on the table. "I'm up to here with this crap!"

"Chill out, babe. You got company."

She came out of the kitchen. Molly rose and extended her hand. "Hi. I'm Molly Bearpaw."

"She like works for you," Perrone said, as Lori shook Molly's hand, looking bewildered. "Your taxes pay her salary. She's a fed fuzz." Perrone tittered, pleased with the turn of phrase.

"What do you want with me?" Lori asked.

"Guess she thinks you know something about those old people who died at the nursing home," Perrone told her. "Maybe old lizard butt killed 'em. Wouldn't that be a hoot?"

"I didn't say anyone killed them," Molly put in.

Perrone blinked at her. Lori said, "Go put on a shirt, Bob. I'll talk to her." He shrugged and got up reluctantly, stubbing his toe on a leg of the coffee table. He cursed loudly and limped into the bedroom. "And clean up the kitchen," Lori yelled, turning back to Molly. "Let's go outside."

They stood in the shade of a sickly hackberry tree next to the driveway. "I'm sorry the place is such a mess," Lori said. "He promised he'd have it cleaned up before I got back. I work all day. You'd think—"

"You don't have to apologize to me."

A grasshopper jumped out of the grass and landed near Molly's foot. Lori folded her arms and stared back at the small house. "I knew I shouldn't have let him move in with me. He went through a rehab program about eight months ago, and he swore he wasn't using again. I guess I wanted to believe him, and I felt sorry for him. He lost his job and they repossessed his car." She sighed. "Now it's going to take a bulldozer to get him out."

Molly moved her foot and the grasshopper jumped a couple of feet and disappeared beneath a scraggly shrub. "If he won't leave, the police will be glad to assist him."

"He'd be back." Lori raked a hand through her brown hair. Her nails were bitten into the quick. "He's not even looking for a job . . . I may call his—the person who helped him get the last job. Maybe she can find another one. If she hasn't washed her hands of him . . ."

A blip rippled across the screen of Molly's memory, but she couldn't bring it into the light. "Miss Hakey—Lori."

Lori brought her gaze back to Molly. "I'm sorry. Bob's not your problem. Are you a detective?"

"Not exactly. I'm a federal investigator. I'm talking to

everyone who visited A-wing of the nursing home on the past two Sundays. You do know that two residents of that wing died recently, don't you?"

"Yes, my grandmother told me. But I don't see what it has to do with me."

"They died of food poisoning. From the evidence, the contaminated food doesn't appear to have come from the nursing-home kitchen, which means somebody brought it in."

Lori stared at her. Her jaw was too long and her hazel eyes set too close together for prettiness. But there was shrewd intelligence in those eyes. "I didn't even know those people."

"What time were you at the nursing home the past two Sundays?"

"It was late in the afternoon. I usually put it off as long as possible. I'm not sure exactly what time it was, though."

"Did you see any food in any of the rooms in A-wing?"

She chewed on a thumbnail. "Well, last Sunday I stayed while my grandmother and her roommate had supper, but that's the only food I saw."

"Did they eat everything on their trays?"

She stuffed her hands into the pockets of her cotton skirt, as though to keep herself from biting her nails. "Mrs. Buckhorn sent her vegetables back, but Grandmother didn't leave a crumb. I remember saying something about her healthy appetite. God, she'll probably live forever." She frowned. "I thought you said the poisoned food came from somewhere else."

"That's what we think."

"You aren't positive?"

"We're ninety-nine-percent sure. The one percent still worries me, but I'm more worried about the possibility of contaminated food being brought in. We have to trace the source, to make absolutely sure it doesn't happen again."

"Do you think somebody's poisoning those old people on purpose?"

"I'm not suggesting that at all."

She raked both hands through her hair, then pressed them against her cheeks. "That would be too bizarre for words."

"Yes," said Molly.

She dropped her hands. "I hate that place," she said with sudden vehemence. "Sometimes, you know, I think about leaving Tahlequah. I'm the only relative here, so I'm expected to visit every Sunday. When my mother calls, she wants to know if I've seen Grandmother that week, and if I say I missed a Sunday, she gives me a lecture about how selfish I am." The day's last rays of sunlight turned the sky behind Lori orange.

"Mothers," Molly observed, as though she knew what she was talking about.

"Yeah. And Grandmother's worse. She never forgets to quiz me about whether I've been to mass. If I told her I hadn't been in months, she'd flip out. It's easier to lie." She made a sour face. "It would be simpler all around to get an unlisted number, I guess," she went on. "Then neither one of them could phone me." She shook her head. "I'm a coward, and I know it, and I don't know why I'm telling you all this. I guess I shouldn't begrudge Grandmother an hour on Sundays. It's all those old people . . . and the smell. I can't believe most of them wouldn't rather be dead than have to live like that." She shuddered. "It's so depressing."

"Country Haven's pretty nice, as nursing homes go. It must cost a mint to keep your grandmother there."

"I don't know what it costs. Grandmother doesn't have any savings, but she gets enough with her pension from the company where she worked for thirty years, plus her Social Security, to pay her own way."

Scratch financial gain, Molly thought. Unless Faye Hakey had named her granddaughter the beneficiary of an insurance policy. "Does your grandmother have life insurance?"

Lori's eyes sharpened and she lifted her chin. "You'll have to ask Grandmother about that."

"Are you saying you don't know?"

"I'm saying you'll have to ask Grandmother. Look, I have to go in now. I'm sure Bob didn't phone about that job advertised in the paper, but I'm going to make him if I have to threaten to kick him out."

"Good luck, and thanks for talking to me."

Molly returned to her car, having learned nothing very helpful, although there had been that faint signal from her subconscious. But she didn't know what it meant, and she couldn't remember now what Lori had said to set it off.

After what D.J. had told her about Fred Whillock, she dreaded the interview and wanted to get it over with. From Lori Hakey's house, she drove to the Whillock address; it was on the other side of town, out past the Highway 82 bypass near the city hospital. It was after seven, but it wouldn't be dark for an hour or more.

The house was a neat brick ranch with a meticulously manicured lawn and well-tended flower beds bordering the front walk. A balding man in baggy, grass-stained trousers and a ribbed undershirt knelt on the walk near the front steps. He was pinching off the old blossoms from the begonias and dropping them into a plastic bucket.

"Mr. Whillock?"

He whirled around. His face was fiery red from the heat, and sweat streaked his eyeglasses. He snatched them off and glared at Molly. "You scared the bejesus out of me. What the hell do you want?"

"To talk to you, if you're Fred Whillock."

He tried to find a dry spot on his undershirt to wipe his glasses, cursed, and pulled a handkerchief from his pocket. He polished the glasses and went back to pinching begonias before he responded.

"Who wants to know?"

"Molly Bearpaw, sir. I'm a federal investigator, working with the sheriff's department in the investigation of the nursing-home deaths."

"Bearpaw, eh? My father said you were out there with Kennedy when he questioned them. I'm not impressed by that federal investigator shit. I called around. You work for the Cherokees right here in Tahlequah." Still on his knees, he set the bucket farther away from him on the walk and moved down a few feet.

Molly followed. "My territory is northeast Oklahoma, but my salary is paid from federal funds. I'm involved because one of the botulism victims was an enrolled Cherokee."

His tongue snaked out and licked the perspiration on his

upper lip. "Words. Typical bureaucratic bullshit. Abner Mouse was nothing to me. Never even met the old injun."

"I understand you were in A-wing on Sunday, August eleventh, and also on the eighteenth."

"Oh, you do, do you?"

She saw a curtain on a front window twitch. Somebody was watching them from inside. Whillock's wife? Molly plowed on. "You may have seen something that would help us find the source of the contaminated food."

He snorted and knee-walked to the next clump of begonias. "Look, Harelip or Hareclaw, or whatever your name is. Don't take me for a fool. You and I and everybody else knows where that food poisoning came from. The nursing-home kitchen."

"The health department didn't find any trace of it."

"Hell, that's not too hard to figure out. I thought you were some kind of investigator. They threw it away before the health department got there. Covering their fat asses. If it'd been my folks who got it, I'd bankrupt that place with lawsuits."

A lot of people had litigation on the brain these days. "You'd have to prove it. At this point, we suspect the botulism was in food prepared elsewhere and delivered to the home by a visitor. Did you have anything edible with you when you went to see your parents on the eleventh and eighteenth?"

"Dammit! You've got a nerve!" he growled and grabbed hold of the rim of the bucket to lever himself to his feet. The gardening trousers hung low beneath a pot belly. He hitched them up with both hands. "I don't have to put up with this badgering. I don't give a rat's ass who pays your salary. You're nothing but a skinny squaw to me."

"It isn't necessary to be insulting," Molly began.

"My father already told a sheriff's deputy I didn't bring any food." He was shaking, either from forcing his out-of-shape body into a cramped position for so long or from fury. Molly was betting on fury. Whillock definitely had a short fuse. "You're hell-bent on clearing the nursing home, aren't you? How much are they paying you under the table?"

Molly wasn't about to let him put her on the defensive. "Did you see or hear anything that made you think another visitor might have brought food?"

"What I saw and heard is none of your damned business! Get off my property." He pointed at her car parked at the curb.

Molly retreated a few steps. "Do your parents have life insurance, Mr. Whillock?"

"Git!" he bellowed.

She walked to her car, opened the door. "Mr. Whillock," she said loudly enough for the neighbors to hear, if they were listening, "we have ways of finding out these things."

As a parting shot, it was pretty feeble, but the best she could come up with on the spur of the moment. Whillock seethed but didn't say anything.

Molly got in her car and drove to the Hulle address. Nobody was home. She waited for half an hour in front of the Hulle house, using the time to make notes on the interviews with Lori Hakey and Fred Whillock. The Hulles didn't return. It was almost eight-thirty by now, and she still hadn't eaten dinner. She could phone the Hulles later from the apartment, but she preferred being face to face with people when she questioned them. She'd try their place of business tomorrow.

She pulled into one of the many fast-food restaurants on Downing Street and went in. Ten minutes later she came out, after eating two pieces of greasy fried chicken and baked beans and slaw. She went home and brewed some decaffeinated Irish-creme coffee to cleanse her palate.

Sitting at the kitchen table, she wrote down what she'd learned from the interviews with Lori Hakey and Fred Whillock. Neither of them had liked the question about life insurance. Of course, Whillock hadn't liked much of anything she'd said, but Lori had been forthcoming until Molly posed that particular query.

She made a note to remind D.J. to find out if the Whillocks or Faye Hakey had life insurance and, if so, whom they'd named as beneficiaries.

OOOOOOOO

10

Hulle Dry Cleaners was housed in a narrow stone building, located on a side street a block off Muskogee Avenue. The few parking slots in front were taken, so Molly drove down the alley and parked behind the building, between a late-model Olds and an old tank truck, the kind used to transport petroleum and other industrial liquids.

She walked around to the front entrance. The windows were covered with bright green letters announcing: "Shirts, folded or on hangers, $1.25"; "One-day service on request"; "Three days for alterations"; "Added fee for pickup and delivery"; "Two ID's for personal checks"; "No out-of-town checks accepted."

The woman behind the counter was fortyish and obese, the kind of female who'd been chubby all her life, fought it valiantly as an adolescent, a little less enthusiastically in her twenties, and about the age of thirty waved the white flag and retired from the battlefield.

Alerted by the bell above the door, she looked up from the magazine she was reading. Even her nose was fat. It was also shiny and red—allergies, probably. Unless she'd been weeping over the movie fan magazine she'd been reading. Her lips curved up in an automatic may-I-help-you? smile that didn't reach her eyes. It made her cheeks pouch out, as though she were storing food for the winter.

"I'd like to speak to one of the Hulles."

The smile disappeared. "They're in the office," she said, bored. "In back." She returned to her magazine, which was open to a full-page photograph of a current male movie idol who'd recently starred in a steamy romantic comedy. Molly recognized the star's face but couldn't recall his name.

She thanked the woman and, skirting the counter, walked down a short, dimly lighted hallway. Near the end, a door stood open. Inside, a middle-aged woman sat behind a desk with a stack of bills in front of her. She was using a calculator with great efficiency. A man lounged on an orange plastic couch, sipping a canned cold drink. His red-and-green Hawaiian print shirt clashed mightily with the couch.

"I'm looking for the Hulles," Molly said. "The girl out front told me to come on back."

"I'm Ginny Hulle." Her brown hair was sprinkled with gray, jaw-length and thin, parted in the middle, pulled back and secured with rhinestone-studded combs at her temples. She wore a plain gold blouse, a bad choice of color for her sallow complexion. Both these people could use a color analysis, Molly thought.

From Ginny Hulle's appearance, though, she had more pressing concerns on her mind than worrying about whether she was a "winter" or a "summer." There were circles under her eyes, and her voice was flat and tired.

"I'm working with the sheriff's department on the investigation of the botulism deaths at Country Haven Nursing Home. May I have a word with you?"

She gazed at Molly wearily—a this-too-shall-pass look—and then glanced at the man, as though for rescue.

"What about?" he asked.

"You're Mr. Hulle?"

"That's me." He sat forward abruptly, tossing the empty cola can into a wastebasket. He was probably in his early fifties, stout without being flabby, with a hairline that had receded to the dome of his head. Strands of long dark hair were combed across his skull from back to front, but they didn't begin to cover the bald spot. Molly always wondered why men did that. It made them appear pathetically vain.

Since no one seemed inclined to offer her a seat, Molly helped herself to the plastic-covered chair next to the door. "I gather you've heard that the deaths resulted from food poisoning."

Ginny Hulle nodded. "My aunt called a couple of days ago to tell me about Mrs. Tacker. We already knew about Mr. Mouse. We visit my Aunt Sally—Sally Creighton—two or three times a week."

"Both of you?"

Bowen Hulle's eyes slid over Molly curiously. "My son and I usually go with Ginny on Sundays. Once a week is about as much of Aunt Sally as we can take. Did you say you're with the sheriff's department?"

"Actually, I'm employed by the federal government. We're working with the local authorities on this." With practice, Molly was learning to say it with a confidence that seemed to make people hesitant to question her credentials further. Fred Whillock might have been unimpressed, but it appeared to work with the Hulles. "Mrs. Creighton may have told you we're having trouble tracing the source of the contaminated food."

"No," said Ginny, "we assumed the nursing home was at fault."

"That was our first assumption, too, but we haven't been able to prove it. In fact, all the evidence the health department has gathered seems to prove otherwise. Naturally, we have to consider the possibility that food was carried in from outside. In particular, we're interested in any food brought in the past two Sundays."

Ginny's expression flickered with uncertainty. "Well, I didn't take any."

Bowen gave Molly an easy smile. "You got me. I guess I might as well own up. Last Sunday, I had a package of M&M's in my pocket."

"Did you share them with any of the residents?"

He cocked a brow. "Let them buy their own M&M's. My

son and I ate them while we were in the lobby, waiting for Ginny to finish visiting with her Aunt Sally."

"Did you enter Mrs. Creighton's room at any time?"

"Pardon?"

"I'd like to know how many people were actually in each of the rooms in A-wing last Sunday, or the Sunday before."

"Bowen and Randy always go in to say hello as soon as we get there," Ginny said.

"We clear out after a few minutes and wait for Ginny in the lobby, then we go back to say good-bye. That old lady will drive you nuts if you have to listen to her very long. I don't know how Ginny puts up with her. On Sundays, Randy or I usually have to go back and remind her when it's time to leave. Personally, I don't think it's necessary to traipse out there two or three times a week, the way Ginny does."

"She doesn't have anyone else, Bowen," Ginny said irritably, as if this were a long-standing bone of contention between them.

"Whose fault is that?"

"She's the way she is, that's all. But I'll always be grateful to her for putting me through college and helping us get started in business. Where would we be right now, if not for her?"

"We'd have made it somehow," Bowen said, with some irritation. "And we've paid her back with interest, but she expects you to keep on paying for the rest of your life by dropping what you're doing and running out there whenever she calls."

"She wasn't always like that. She's old now." Ginny sighed and restacked the bills in front of her.

"Mean as a bobcat, too," Bowen said, "not to mention out-and-out crazy."

"Oh, Bowen . . ."

"Mrs. Hulle, did you notice any food in your aunt's room Sunday?"

"She ate her dinner while I was there."

"Did she eat everything on her tray?"

"I think so." She hesitated. "Actually, I left the room a couple of times, once to talk to the nurse and once to go to the rest room. They took the trays away while I was in the rest room."

"So you can't say for sure that she ate everything."

"I guess not. I know she didn't eat her cake while I was there. She saved it to eat later. I noticed it on her bedside table as I was leaving." She frowned slightly. "I didn't actually see her eat it, of course, but even if Aunt Sally ended up throwing her cake out, some of the other residents must have eaten theirs."

"I never heard of anybody getting food poisoning from cake," Bowen observed.

"Regardless," Ginny went on, "it must not have been anything served at dinner that killed Mrs. Tacker. I'm beginning to see the problem. They all eat the same meals, and I haven't heard that anyone else was taken ill. I hadn't thought of that before."

"Yet Mrs. Tacker's son says she ate nothing but the nursing-home food Sunday."

"How strange."

"It certainly is," Molly agreed.

Ginny's eyes clouded. "Those old people must be scared to eat *anything* now."

"They're uneasy," Molly admitted. "I talked to some of them earlier in the week. Including your aunt."

"I'll bet that was fascinating," snorted Bowen.

"She's very religious-minded, isn't she?" Molly asked.

Bowen humphed.

"That's a recent development," Ginny said. "I think the thought of dying scares her. Before she went to the nursing home, she never belonged to a church. She always said charity begins at home and I was her charity project."

"Can you imagine telling that to a kid?" Bowen wanted to know.

Molly couldn't. "Did being described as a charity project bother you, Mrs. Hulle?"

"A little, when I was a teenager. But it was just her way."

"So this religious bent developed since she's been at the home?"

"About a year ago. Aunt Sally started reading her Bible and sending money to a television evangelist."

"Shyster," Bowen muttered.

"Naturally"—Ginny frowned at him and went on—"she can spend her money any way she wants, but I'm concerned that she's no longer competent to make rational decisions."

"That's putting it mildly," Bowen interjected, ignoring his wife's frown.

Molly wanted to be careful how she framed her next question. "I understand, from her neighbors, that she talks of little else but this TV evangelist. Mrs. Hakey told me your aunt has deeded her property to him. Is that true?"

Ginny hesitated before she answered. "She's thinking about it. Her attorney's on vacation. I'm going to discuss it with him when he gets back."

"Are you planning to have her declared incompetent?" Molly asked.

She hesitated again. "I don't know . . . I hate to have to do something like that. It's so demeaning, but she doesn't have much money left in the bank, and Social Security plus her pension only pay about two-thirds of the nursing-home bill. It would help, if she'd agree to a roommate, but she insists on a private room."

"Let her insist—" Bowen began.

Ginny went on talking, raising her voice to override his. "As I was saying, we may need to sell her house and land to keep up with the nursing-home payments."

Bowen snorted. 'That'll last five or six months, at best. I'd be surprised if that place is worth five thousand, lock, stock, and barrel."

Ginny glanced at him helplessly. "It would give us a little breathing space, while I try to find another nursing home with lower rates. If I can't, or she refuses to move, I guess we'll eventually have to pick up the difference ourselves. We can afford it."

"That's not really the point, Ginny. It's the idea that she'd give away her last asset, with no thought to how it might affect us."

"I know. I guess that's what gets to me, too, but I can't help but believe she's not herself now."

"Where is Mrs. Creighton's home?" Molly asked.

"East of town a few miles, on Highway 51." Ginny

chewed her lip. "The house was vandalized recently. I think teenagers have been going out there to have beer parties. There was a pile of Coors cans in a corner of the living room."

"Ginny broke down and cried," Bowen said.

"It made me sick to see it like that. I loved that place when I lived there with Aunt Sally. Bowen and I and our son spent all day a couple of weeks ago cleaning up the trash. Randy hauled off three or four loads of trash in his pickup. We had to rent storage for the few pieces of furniture that were worth salvaging."

"She doesn't have anything that would bring a hundred dollars at auction," Bowen complained, glaring at Molly as though it were her fault. "Guess who's getting stuck with the storage bill. Ginny refuses to ask her aunt to pay it."

"It isn't that much, Bowen. I don't want Aunt Sally to know her home was vandalized. There's no point in her getting all worked up about it when there's not a thing she can do."

"Good God, no," he exploded, "let's don't get Aunt Sally upset." Ginny looked at him, her eyes suddenly welling with tears. He was immediately contrite. "Aw, Gin, I'm sorry. You know I don't care about the piddling storage bill. It's just seeing the way she treats you, like an indentured servant. You're always so worn out and your nerves are frazzled, crying if anybody looks at you cross-eyed. It hurts me to see you like this."

Ginny pulled a tissue from the box on her desk and pressed it to her eyes. "She used to be so strong." There was a tremor in her voice. "When I was sixteen years old, she told my parents she was going to take me to live with her. She said I had a brain in my head, but she wasn't sure I'd learn to use it if she didn't get me out of there. She was right, too. If not for Aunt Sally, I'd probably be on welfare, like my sisters."

"Didn't your parents object to her taking you?"

She blew her nose, recovering her composure. "Not really. They had three other kids, and my father was out of work most of the time. He was an alcoholic."

"Did you want to go and live with your aunt?"

"I wanted to get away from home, even though her gruff manner scared the pants off me at first. But I'd never had a bedroom all to myself before, and everything was so clean. Aunt Sally was a perfectionist with her housekeeping."

"You always felt like you couldn't sit down, for fear you'd leave a stain on something," Bowen interjected.

"As soon as I went there," Ginny went on, her eyes taking on a distant look, "she started brainwashing me. 'You're smart, Ginny,' she'd say. 'You can be anything you want to be if you make up your mind to it.' She must have told me that every day for the next two years. Then she sent me to the University of Texas because she thought they had the best business school in the region, even though it would have been a lot less expensive for me to stay here and go to NSU. When I graduated from the university, Aunt Sally was the single member of my family who cared enough to be there. She and Bowen were the only ones who came to see me get my degree."

"That's when I met Aunt Sally," Bowen put in. "She almost blew a gasket when Ginny told her we were getting married. She wanted Ginny to marry a doctor—or at least a lawyer—and I'd dropped out of school to go to work several years earlier. She said if Ginny married me, she'd be throwing away all that expensive education."

"Well, she was wrong," Ginny said.

Bowen nodded emphatically. "You got that right, honey. My wife is the business head in this operation, Ms. Bearpaw. I'm just the brawn."

"Bowen is too modest," Ginny amended. "He's much better with people than I am, and in the early days we couldn't afford to hire any help. We did everything ourselves. I kept all the records and Bowen worked up front. He chatted with the customers, asked about their kids or whatever was going on with them. People appreciate that kind of thing. We built the business together, and now it supports us and our son and his wife very well."

"Your son and his wife work here, too?"

There was a short silence, during which the tired little lines at the corners of Ginny's mouth were suddenly very noticeable and dislike flickered in her eyes. For her son's wife? Molly wondered. Ginny wouldn't be the first woman to have an aversion to her daughter-in-law.

"Randy works here with us two days a week, but he spends three days at the cleaning establishments we own in other towns," Ginny said, leaving Randy's wife unmentioned. "He gets along so well with our employees."

"Everybody likes that boy," Bowen added.

Ginny smiled. "He inherited Bowen's way with people. I guess you can tell we're awfully proud of Randy."

Molly wondered if they were a bit too intent on convincing her that everything was hunky-dory with them, both professionally and personally. "Do you have other children?"

"No," Ginny said. "We had to spend so many hours working in the early days that we decided it wouldn't be fair to the children to have more."

"By the way," Molly said, as though it were an afterthought, "do you know if your aunt has life insurance, Mrs. Hulle?"

Ginny pursed her lips. "I don't think so." Molly couldn't read Bowen's expression.

She stood. "You've been very patient, and I'm sure you both have work to do." She held out her hand to Ginny Hulle. "Thanks for talking to me."

Bowen got to his feet and shook Molly's hand. His grip was solid, his flesh warm. "Is it all right if I go out the back?" Molly asked. "I had to park behind the building."

"The door's at the end of the hall," Bowen said.

"Thanks again."

When Molly reached her car, a red pickup was pulling in next to the tank truck. A young man with longish hair that covered his ears and collar in back got out. A younger version of Bowen Hulle, with hair. He looked at Molly inquisitively.

"Are you Randy Hulle?"

"Yes, ma'am," he said with an easy grin. "You looking for me?"

"I've been talking to your parents, about the nursing-home deaths. I'm Molly Bearpaw. I'm working with the sheriff's department on the case."

He leaned back against the hood of Molly's car and looked her over doubtfully. "Sure 'nuff?"

"You can check with D. J. Kennedy if you like."

He hesitated, then grinned. "I'll take your word for it."

"I wonder if I might ask you a few questions."

"Me?" He placed his hand flat against his chest. His blue eyes were so pale they were almost transparent. "Why?"

"I'm talking to everybody who visited a resident in any of the five rooms in Country Haven's A-wing on the past two Sundays. Both victims lived in that wing. I understand you were there with your parents."

Bracing himself, he spread his long fingers out on the car hood. "It's my weekly duty call. My wife washes her hair and does her nails on Sunday afternoons, so she doesn't nag me about being gone, and it keeps Mom off my back."

"I understand your mother is Mrs. Creighton's heir," Molly said, as if it were common knowledge.

He focused on her, apparently perplexed. "What's that got to do with anything?"

"Probably nothing," Molly replied with ease, "but I've met Mrs. Creighton, and she seems quite fond of your mother."

He chuckled. "I'm not sure Aunt Sally's fond of anyone. She drove everybody else in her family away years ago. Mom's a lot more tolerant than most people, and she lets Aunt Sally put a guilt trip on her. The old lady is always reminding her that she plucked her out of poverty and sent her to the University of Texas. Hell, you'd think it was Oxford, the way she goes on about it sometimes."

"How long has Mrs. Creighton been in Country Haven?"

"Three or four years."

"Has she always had a private room?"

"Oh, yeah. She insists on her privacy. Besides, I don't think anybody would room with her. Not for long, anyway."

"She must be well off, then," Molly said smoothly. "Nursing homes are expensive."

"I guess she was at one time, but from what Mom and Dad say, most of what she had has been spent on medical bills and keeping her at Country Haven. She still has a house and ten acres west of town, but she wants to give it to some church. It's where she lived when Mom moved in with her. Mom has a sentimental attachment to the old place."

"If she's strapped for cash, surely her attorney will try to talk her out of giving it away."

"Benson? Maybe, but nobody talks Aunt Sally out of anything when she gets her head set."

Molly gave silent thanks for the gift of the attorney's name. A direct question might have stopped the stream of information. Molly had a nodding acquaintance with Felix Benson. She knew his secretary much better. She'd give Moira a call when she got to the office.

She gave Randy Hulle the same spiel she'd given the others she'd questioned, asking if he'd taken any food with him when he visited Mrs. Creighton or if he'd seen any food in A-wing that hadn't come from the kitchen on the trays. His answer to both questions was negative. He went on talking, though, while Molly took mental notes. He had a lot to say about his great-aunt, none of it very complimentary. He agreed with his father that she was a cross-tempered old lady but, contrary to what his mother had said, he couldn't remember Mrs. Creighton ever being any other way.

"Of course, I didn't know her when she was younger, but my grandfather, my mother's old man, once told me Aunt Sally was born cranky. She's an old maid, you know. Not hard to understand why no man wanted to marry her. It'd be like crawling in bed with a grizzly bear."

"Apparently she's trying to mend her ways now. Your mother says she reads her Bible regularly."

"Oh, yeah, she's gone off on a religious kick." He twirled his index finger beside his temple. "It's hard for me to keep a straight face, some of the weird things she says. My wife swears I make them up." Molly got the feeling he and his wife had a good laugh when he returned from the nursing home and recounted Aunt Sally's latest craziness. "She's as selfish as she ever was, though, and just as demanding. Dad or I could run out there with some of the stuff she thinks up for Mom to bring her. Last week it was corn plasters, can you believe it? I offered to drop them off, but Aunt Sally wanted Mom. She always wants Mom, and my mother will do anything to avoid a fuss."

"Mrs. Creighton is fortunate to have such a devoted niece."

"She sure is. To compensate a little, I try to give Mom some relief in the office when she'll let me."

"Your mother says you're a big help to them in the family business."

Randy nodded immodestly. "They made me a full partner last year. I earned it, too. I started working in the business summers and after school when I was fourteen." He paused slightly. "At the time, I thought my folks were slave drivers. All the other kids got to hang out after school, but I had to go to work. Later, I appreciated Mom and Dad. I learned every aspect of the business by the time I graduated from high school and went to work full time."

"I gather you're out of town several days a week," Molly asked. He acknowledged this. "I keep track of the operations at our other plants. Mom does the paperwork. Dad supervises the plant operation here, orders all our supplies, and keeps up with when the vats need to be cleaned and stuff like that."

"Sounds as though you have a successful business."

He pulled at his chin. "It's a living. We're lucky. *I'm* lucky, I guess I should say. Mom and Dad got where they are through hard labor, not luck. They worked night and day to get the first plant going and pay off a business loan; then they started plowing the profits into expanding. By the time I was old enough to help out, they were able to hire a few people, so they no longer had to do everything themselves."

"I guess you and your wife will run the business together someday."

He held both hands out, palms up. "If the damned IRS and EPA don't tax and regulate us into bankruptcy." He pushed away from Molly's car. "I better get to work."

"You've been a big help," Molly said.

He shrugged. "Don't see how."

To be honest, Molly didn't either. If Sally Creighton's assets were as depleted as the Hulles said, there was no financial-gain motive here.

She had some work to do at the office first, but later, out of curiosity, she might drive out Highway 51 and see if she could locate Mrs. Creighton's property.

OOOOOOOO

11

Felix Benson's law office, a one-man operation, occupied space above a dress shop on Muskogee Avenue. It consisted of three rooms—the reception area where Moira Pack sat at her desk, Benson's private office, and a small conference room. Molly decided on the spur of the moment to stop and ply Moira for information before going to her office, on the theory that it would be harder for Moira to turn her down face to face.

She'd had some classes with Moira at NSU and they'd become friends, often studying together. When she'd moved back to town, she'd looked up Moira. Since then they met for lunch every month or two.

On previous visits, a haze of smoke had hung in the reception area, and if Molly stayed long, she always left with a pounding headache. Today the air was clear and the reception room smelled of pine air freshener. A No Smoking sign had been taped to the wall facing the entry door.

Moira sat at the desk, a sack of jelly beans and a giant thermal cold-drink jug at hand. Moira was nearing thirty, unmarried but oft-engaged. Men always wanted to marry

Moira, and judging from the number of times she'd said yes, Moira was taken with the idea, but as each wedding date approached she got cold feet.

After one of Moira's broken engagements, Molly had asked her if she actually knew what she was looking for in a man. Moira hadn't hesitated. "You bet. Kevin Costner," she'd said. Since Kevin Costner wasn't likely to stop over in Tahlequah, Oklahoma, Moira made do with substitutes, of which there seemed to be a copious supply.

Molly was pleased to see that Moira was alone. "You cut your hair," she said.

Moira combed elegant, red-tipped fingers through a cap of short blond tresses that had been shoulder length the last time Molly saw her. The new style was sleek and sophisticated, the kind that required minimal care.

"I got tired of spending an hour blow-drying that thick mop. What do you think?"

"It suits you. Makes you look like an ambitious career woman on the way up."

"I wish." She grimaced and reached for a jelly bean. "Anyway, I'm changing my image."

Molly dropped into a chair. "Quit smoking again, huh?" Moira had quit half-a-dozen times since Molly had known her.

She munched another jelly bean. "I'm really serious this time."

"How long has it been?"

"A week. I decided to do it while Felix was out of town so I'd have my nerves under control by the time he gets back." She reached automatically for another jelly bean but, when her hand was halfway to her mouth, she frowned and put it back, sipping from the thermal jug instead.

"Diet Coke," she said. "I've been drinking four of these a day. All I do is pee. I've put on a couple of pounds, too, but I'm trying not to worry about that now or whether so much artificial sweetener can cause cancer."

"You know for a fact that cigarettes can, so it's not a bad trade-off."

"Yeah, and I figure I can only deal with one problem at a

time. I can cut back on the candy and Cokes when I get a handle on being a nonsmoker."

"Are you seeing a new man, or what?"

"You don't think I'd put myself through this for a man, do you?"

Molly grinned. "Na-aw."

"I am seeing a couple of guys, but nobody special. We didn't have a lunch date, did we?" She consulted her wristwatch. "It's too early for lunch, anyway."

"I need some information on one of Felix's clients."

Moira leaned back in her secretary's chair. "Who?"

"Sally Creighton."

"What do you want to know?"

"The terms of her will."

Moira's mouth turned down. "Does this have something to do with one of your investigations?"

Molly explained her interest in the nursing-home deaths. "At this point, we can't prove the poisonings were accidental. Or that they were deliberate, for that matter, but we want to know who would gain by their deaths and how much. It's only a working theory, and you have to promise to keep it under your hat."

She picked a pencil up and tapped the eraser against the desk. "I don't get it. Do you have some reason to think that both the people who died left money to the same person, and that person is Mrs. Creighton's heir, too?"

"No, we don't. In fact, I'm sure we'll discover it's not true. We haven't found anyone who was related to or even friendly with both Abner Mouse and Estelle Tacker."

Molly didn't bother explaining her theory that the death of one of the victims could be a smoke screen to cover the murder of the other. Or that both deaths could be a smoke screen in preparation for killing a third victim.

Molly didn't know what she thought anymore. The possibilities kept going round and round in her head. First, she'd convince herself the two deaths were nothing but freak accidents. Then she'd get an attack of panic, of terror almost, and she'd be sure a murderer was watching her and D.J. sort through a tangled mass of threads, searching for a loose end to pull. And waiting for the opportunity to kill again.

"We're gathering all the evidence that might be connected in some way to the deaths, that's all."

"Get real, Molly. Murder's pretty preposterous." She tapped the pencil again. "Those old people aren't long for this world, anyway. Why would anybody kill them, when all they have to do is wait a while?" She laid the pencil down. "That job is turning you into a suspicious woman."

"A good investigator doesn't exclude any possibility without evidence. Right now, we're pursuing the murder theory because every other trail has come to a dead end."

Moira thought about it for a moment and shrugged. "I'm no detective, that's for sure. I've never even dated one, come to think of it, so what do I know?"

"Mrs. Creighton is in the same wing where Tacker and Mouse lived. If Mrs. Tacker and Mr. Mouse were murdered, there's somebody out there who might have reason to want another one of the old people in that wing dead. We simply don't know."

Moira's carefully plucked brows rose. "You keep saying *we*."

"D. J. Kennedy and I are cooperating on the investigation."

She drummed glossy red fingernails on the desk top. "D.J. still have a thing for you?"

"We haven't discussed it," Molly said with elaborate casualness. "About Mrs. Creighton's will—"

"You're asking me to betray client confidence. And she's not even my client. I'm just the peon who works here. Besides, Felix would kill me."

"Felix never has to know."

Moira looked out the window.

"All I'm asking," Molly said, "is that you take a peek at Creighton's file and tell me what assets are listed and who inherits. I swear no one will ever know where the information came from, not even D.J."

"I can't believe I'm even considering it. I must be bored. This is the most interesting conversation that's taken place in this office since Felix left." She took another pull on her Coke. "Something tells me I'll live to regret this." She pushed away from the desk. "You wait here." She went into Felix's office, shutting the door behind her.

A few minutes later, Moira came out with a file folder. She looked around to make sure they were still alone before she said, "Mrs. Creighton doesn't have a lot of assets, so it's a simple will. She has checking and savings accounts in a local bank and owns ten acres and a house west of town free and clear."

"That's it?"

"Nothing else listed here. Ginny Hulle gets whatever's left when Mrs. Creighton dies."

"That's her niece," Molly said. "Has she called here recently, asking for Felix?"

Moira opened a desk drawer and went through a stack of phone-message slips. "Yes, here it is. She wants Felix to call her when he gets back. She didn't say what it was about. Mrs. Creighton called, too. Same message."

"Creighton wants to change her will and leave the real estate to a TV preacher."

Moira cocked a brow, intrigued in spite of herself. "Wonder how much the place is worth."

"About five thousand dollars, according to Ginny Hulle's husband."

"Surely you aren't thinking the Hulles are planning to kill Mrs. Creighton before she changes her will. Why kill two other people first? Trial runs? Or maybe they're real bumblers at this murder business and keep killing the wrong people? It's unbelievable, Molly."

Molly agreed with her. "Creighton's inheritance doesn't sound like a motive for murder, either. Have you any idea how much is in those bank accounts?"

"No, but Felix gets copies of some of his clients' bank statements. I'll see if Mrs. Creighton is one of them." She was back in a few minutes. "As of July 31, the balance in her checking account was four thousand and a few dollars. She has another ten thousand in savings."

"That plus the land comes to less than twenty thousand," Molly mused.

"If Mrs. Creighton dies, the Hulles have got the funeral expenses and probate costs. They'd be lucky to net out eight or ten thou. That would be peanuts to the Hulles. They're not poor people, from what I hear. I'm not saying they're rich, but they're comfortable."

"Would life-insurance policies be listed in a will?"

"Not necessarily. Generally, insurance proceeds don't have to go through probate before they're paid out. They're sent directly to the beneficiary. And before you ask, I don't know whether Mrs. Creighton has life insurance or even how to find out."

"Well, thanks for the information." Molly wondered how far she could push her luck and decided to go for it. "Felix wouldn't, by chance, have any other clients in A-wing of Country Haven Nursing Home, would he? Gladys and Ernie Whillock, Mercer Vaughan, Faye Hakey, Lahoma Buckhorn . . ."

Moira gave her a speculative look. "You are one pushy broad."

"I'm sort of desperate here."

She sat down at her desk. "The Whillocks are Felix's clients. I don't even have to look up their will. They left everything split three ways among their two sons and a daughter. As I recall, most of what they have is in CD's. I have no idea how much is involved."

Molly sighed and got to her feet. "I have to go to the office. You've been a big help, Moira. I appreciate it."

"You owe me. I'll collect one of these days."

"Anytime."

"Let's have lunch next week," Moira suggested. "Is Monday good for you?"

"Sure. Where?"

"Meet me at noon at Oak Hill. I feel like treating myself."

"Sounds good," Molly agreed.

"Hey, I met a sweet guy the other night, but I was with somebody else. How about I fix you up and we double?"

"I appreciate the thought, Moira, but I'm really not interested."

"How are you ever going to get interested, if you won't give men a chance? That's not normal, Molly."

"I never claimed to be normal."

"Molly—" Her eyes narrowed calculatingly. "You're sweet on D.J., aren't you?"

"Good-bye, Moira."

* * *

It was after eleven by the time Molly got to the office. There were three messages on the machine. The first was from Woodrow Mouse, wanting to know what was happening in her investigation of his father's death. The second was from Zeke Gritts, saying he'd received his first disability check and thanking her for her help.

The third was from D.J.: "Haven't heard from you about Saturday night. Why don't you come over to my place and I'll throw a couple steaks on the grill. About seven? I've got some information on you-know-what, but I don't know if it means anything. I'm running out of tape here. If I don't hear from you, I'll see you Saturday at seven."

D.J. was no fool; that bit about the information he'd gathered was bait. Molly would much prefer a neutral location for the exchange of information. But it had taken some talking to get him to combine their investigations; if she turned down his dinner invitation, he might not be so cooperative. And maybe Moira was right. If she wasn't sweet on D.J., going to his house wouldn't be a problem, would it? She pushed the uncomfortable question aside. Today was Thursday. She didn't have to decide right now about the dinner invitation.

She spent an hour completing her notes on the interviews she'd conducted that week and put them in a file that she labeled Country Haven. Then she made a note to herself to call Woodrow Mouse that evening after work. Before going to lunch, she looked up Randy Hulle's home address in the phone book. Until today, she hadn't known he was married and had assumed he lived with his parents. She added the address to the file.

It seemed a good idea to confirm with Randy's wife some of the information her husband and in-laws had given Molly. All three of the Hulles had seemed truthful in their answers, but it didn't pay to take anything for granted.

After gulping down a steak sandwich and fries at The Shack, Molly went to Randy Hulle's home address. Nobody had said anything about children, so there probably weren't any. Which meant his wife probably worked. She'd check it out, anyway.

She got lucky. A late-model foreign job sat in the driveway.

The woman who came to the door could have been a *Playboy* centerfold. Glossy black hair, bedroom eyes—the color of smoke, fringed by black lashes—flawless ivory complexion, pouty mouth. And a voluptuous body—tiny waist and size-forty boobs that were about to fall out of the plunging neckline of the shirt she wore with tight white shorts. She made Molly feel like a stick.

Life was not fair.

"Mrs. Hulle?"

"Yes?"

"I'm Molly Bearpaw. I'm working with the sheriff's department on those nursing-home deaths."

She looked totally at sea for an instant. "Oh, you mean the home where Randy's great-aunt, Sally Creighton, lives?"

"That's right. I've already spoken to your husband and his parents. I was wondering if you'd mind answering a few questions for me."

She tossed back her hair. "I didn't know the people who died. I hardly know Aunt Sally." She wrinkled her pretty nose. "Randy visits her, but I usually stay home."

"Have you gone with him in the past couple of weeks?"

"No."

"Does Randy ever take food to her?"

"Food? I don't think so. I'm sure they feed them well at the home. Randy says Aunt Sally spills her food down the front of her clothes, but she won't tie a towel around her neck. She says she's not a baby who needs a bib."

"I guess it's a matter of pride."

She propped a hip against the door facing. "Sure, but Randy says everything she has is stained from the food she spills. Some of the people in Country Haven are even worse. Have to be spoon-fed every bite." She grimaced as though she had a bad taste in her mouth. "That's *one* place

I'd never work. Old people are so depressing, don't you think?"

"Some of them."

She giggled. "Aunt Sally is, for sure. I think she's getting senile." She pushed away from the door facing. "You might as well come on in. I've been trying on clothes. Maybe you can help me decide which ones I should keep."

Molly followed her inside. Dresses, skirts, slacks, and blouses, with the tags of an expensive women's-clothing store still attached, were spread over most of the furniture. "The new fall collections are in, and I got sort of crazy. Here." She scooped up a couple of dresses from a chair and threw them on the couch. "Sit down. Would you like some iced tea or a Pepsi?"

"No, thanks. I just had lunch."

She picked up one of the dresses and held it against her. "I don't eat lunch. I really have to count calories or I'll gain weight just like that." She smoothed the dress down over her breasts, an oddly caressing gesture. This woman was in love with her body. "I've had this dress on four times and I still can't decide. What do you think?"

Molly felt a sympathetic pang. She seemed lonely for another young woman to talk to. "Mauve's a good color for you."

"You don't think it's too plain?"

"No, it's very elegant."

She tossed the dress aside, chose one with a lot of ruffles and bows and held it up, looking at Molly for an opinion. "That's nice, too," Molly said, "but I like the other one better."

"I could model them for you."

Maybe she wasn't lonely for companionship, after all. Maybe she needed an audience. "Thanks, but I really don't have time, Mrs. Hulle."

She dropped the dress on the pile on the couch, pushed it over, and sat down. "Call me Lucinda. 'Mrs Hulle' sounds like Randy's mother."

"I really didn't expect to find anyone here. You don't work in the family business?"

"I tried it for a while, when Randy and I were first

married. I was bored out of my skull, and that cleaners' smell made me sick. It was sort of fun, talking to the customers who came in, but Bowen accused me of flirting with the men.'' She flipped a careless hand. ''Then Ginny tried to teach me bookkeeping, but numbers are Greek to me. After that, I worked as a receptionist for an insurance agent, but Randy made me quit.'' She smiled. ''He thought my boss was too friendly.'' Her well-manicured hands fluttered. ''Oh, well. Randy makes good money, so I don't really have to work.''

Randy would have to make plenty to pay for all those clothes, Molly thought. What she could see of the furniture looked expensive, too, and the price tag on that car in the drive was in the mid-five figures. Lucinda Hulle definitely had good taste.

''You know,'' she said, sighing, ''sometimes I get awfully restless, staying home. There's not enough to do, and I can't stand women's clubs.'' Molly would have given odds on that. Women like Lucinda Hulle preferred to be surrounded by admiring males, and other women saw them as a threat. Probably with good reason. ''Randy likes to pamper me,'' she was saying. ''Every time I mention that I want to look for another job, he buys me something, like he's trying to prove I don't have to work. I've told him that's beside the point. I wish I could find something interesting to *do*. Something Randy wouldn't get his nose out of joint about. I'll bet being a detective, like you, is never boring.''

Molly didn't bother correcting her. Explanations about being an N.A.A.L. investigator were sometimes more confusing than helpful. ''Actually, it can be pretty monotonous at times, but every job has its drawbacks.''

''I guess,'' she said doubtfully.

''Lucinda, have you been out to Sally Creighton's place, west of town?''

She fingered a dress button in the pile beside her. ''Once, before Randy and I got married. We took a picnic lunch and ate in the woods. Randy said it would be romantic. What a laugh. We had ants and all kinds of bugs crawling on the food.'' She shuddered. ''I couldn't eat a bite. I guess I'm not the outdoor type.''

"I gather it's not a valuable property."

"*I* wouldn't have it as a gift."

"I wonder," Molly said, "if it would be worth more split up into building lots."

"Who'd want to live way out there?"

"You've never heard Randy or his parents mention having an offer from a builder or anything like that?"

"No." Her smoke-colored eyes were guileless.

Nor did Molly know of any new home construction being considered on Highway 51 outside the city limits. It had been a shot in the dark. "I've been told that Mrs. Creighton is going to give the property to a charity."

"So I hear. To this hick preacher on TV. Isn't that just the limit? Bowen was really ticked off when they heard about it, 'cause Ginny loves that place. Don't ask me why. It's just ten acres of old blackjack oaks and a house that's falling in. Ginny used to talk about building a summer cabin out there someday. I don't think Bowen was ever too hot on the idea, though."

"Do you know if Mrs. Creighton has life insurance?"

Her brow furrowed. This was a new thought. "I never heard anything about it if she does. Between you and me, I think she's too selfish to pay for life insurance that another person would spend when she's dead."

There was always the possibility, Molly thought, that somebody else was paying for insurance on Mrs. Creighton's life. She must find out somehow.

Lucinda fluffed her thick, glossy hair and her glance drifted to the clothes on the couch. "I have to get this stuff back to the store before Randy comes home. You know how men are about women and shopping. They don't understand."

"Uh-huh," Molly said, although she didn't understand it herself. She'd never been very interested in clothes, and shopping for them was way down there with taking a dose of castor oil on her scale of fun things to do. Right above witnessing autopsies.

Lucinda was holding a silk blouse up for inspection. Before she insisted on putting on a full-scale fashion show, Molly rose to her feet. "I'll get out of your way now."

Lucinda got that lonely-little-girl look on her face again.

It probably sent men scurrying for whatever might please her. "Oh, do you really have to go? Can't you stay long enough for a Pepsi?"

"No, thanks. But tell me something. If you keep any of these, won't Randy know you've been shopping?"

She giggled. Molly could tell the giggles would grate on her nerves if she saw much of Lucinda. "I'll put them at the back of my closet," Lucinda said. "When I get around to wearing them, he'll say, 'Isn't that new?' And I'll say, 'This old thing? I've had it for months.' It works every time. Men are so gullible."

Molly flashed on Kurt Williams. Men didn't have the market cornered on gullibility, she thought. Remembering Ginny Hulle's reaction to the mention of her daughter-in-law, though, Molly felt sure Ginny was one woman who wasn't as gullible as her son. Did Ginny see Lucinda as a lazy spendthrift, bent on spending Randy into the poorhouse?

"Keep the mauve one," Molly said as she opened the door.

"You really think it's elegant?"

"Like something out of *Vogue*." Molly had no idea what was in *Vogue*, but anybody could see that with Lucinda's body, she didn't need ruffles and bows.

She smiled. "Okay, you convinced me."

OOOOOOOO

12

Molly drove out Highway 51 in search of Sally Creighton's acreage early that evening. Conrad thought he knew where it was, so he and Homer, sporting his new red collar and leash, went along. Conrad sat beside Molly, Homer in back with his nose stuck between the front seats and his tongue lolling out, a big dog grin.

Molly was glad for their company. She'd finally told Conrad about the investigation and he was fascinated. He was also intrigued by the fact that Molly was working with D.J. He hadn't been home when D.J. came to the apartment, and clearly none of the neighbors had mentioned it to him. Molly didn't either. Apparently even Super Snoop had missed that juicy tidbit. Florina was definitely slipping.

"I think it's a little farther out," Conrad said, as she slowed down to read the names on mailboxes. "Couldn't swear to it, though."

"Hey!" Molly braked and pulled off the highway. "That last mailbox said 'Sherwood Bowman.' "

"Who's Sherwood Bowman?"

"A client," Molly said. She backed the Civic into a

graveled road and turned around. "My report to him was returned because he'd moved. It's in the glove compartment. See if you can find it, will you?"

She turned into the lane next to the mailbox as Conrad sifted through the compartment. He made a face and held up a Snickers wrapper filled with mush. "Molly, this candy bar has melted."

"I forgot I left it in there. Put it back and I'll throw it out later."

He pulled out the envelope addressed to Bowman. "It says Route 2. Isn't that where we are?"

"Maybe he moved to another place on the same route." Molly took the letter, got out of the car, and walked up to a small frame house. It had an untended look, and the grass around the house was knee-high in places. She knocked on the door. Nothing. She walked around back and found an uncovered window. The room she peered into was probably a bedroom, but there was no furniture. Apparently this was where Bowman had lived before he moved, and nobody else had moved in to change the name on the box.

Disappointed, Molly returned to the car. "It's vacant." She stuffed the envelope in the glove compartment and backed out, stopping to look inside the mailbox. Nothing but bulk-mail advertising, addressed to Occupant at Rural Route 2.

"Have you checked the utility companies for a new address?"

"I haven't gotten around to it—I've had my head in this nursing-home thing. Frankly, I expected he'd be in touch with me before now. I'll try to run him down tomorrow so I can get that report to him."

They passed another clearly deserted house and, a quarter of a mile farther along, Conrad said, "Turn here. I think this is it." There was no mailbox beside the highway, and Molly couldn't see a house until they were a couple of hundred yards down a sloping graveled driveway.

The house sat in a shallow, bowl-shaped depression in the land, surrounded by trees. A sagging wire fence enclosed the yard, which was overgrown with weeds. A rusty iron gate had been removed or had fallen from its hinges and lay to one side of the cobbled walk.

"This is it, all right," Conrad said. "I came here once eight or ten years ago to speak to a ladies' study club. It's certainly gone to seed since then."

"Doesn't look as though anybody has lived here since Mrs. Creighton went to the nursing home."

"It's a crime to let a place go downhill like this," Conrad lamented.

They got out and Molly grabbed hold of Homer's leash. He was wriggling all over with excitement and sniffing the air, raring to explore, but she was afraid he wouldn't come when she called him.

"You'll have to travel at my speed, Homer." She tugged back on the leash. "I don't want to spend an hour looking for you when I'm ready to go."

"I'll bet this is a breeding ground for ticks," Conrad observed, glancing around at the weeds and the woods behind the house. Many of the trees were blackjack oaks, as Lucinda Hulle had said, but there were also numerous silver maples, black walnuts, hickories, and several elms that were afflicted with webworms.

Boards had been nailed over the front windows of the house where panes were broken, probably by the vandals Ginny Hulle had mentioned. There was a new dead bolt on the front door. They picked their way around the house through tall grass. The back door had no dead bolt, but was locked. Molly jiggled the knob and pushed hard. The door gave only fractionally. Homer looked up at her and whined, then scratched on the door.

She gave the door a good kick, startling Homer, but it wouldn't budge. "I wish I were the sort of woman who carried a nail file," she muttered.

"Breaking and entering is against the law, Molly," Conrad said mildly.

"Do you have a credit card?"

Silver eyebrows shot up, but he got out his wallet and extracted a card. "I hope D.J. will bail us out if we get arrested."

Molly handed him the leash and slipped the card into the

crack between the door and jamb. A little careful positioning, and the flimsy lock gave. Molly was amazed at how easy it was. So was Conrad. "You sure you haven't had some practice at this?" he asked, as he and Homer followed Molly inside.

"No, must be an inborn talent."

Conrad removed Homer's leash and the dog raced through the rooms, sniffing corners and snuffling in closets. The house smelled dusty, even though it had obviously been swept and cleaned recently. Nothing in the kitchen cabinets. The broom closet contained a broom, sponge mop, and plastic bucket. Old wallpaper hung loose in a couple of places in the living room, and there was evidence of a leaking roof in one of the three bedrooms.

A few pieces of broken or severely soiled furniture were scattered throughout the house, clearly judged not worth storing by the Hulles. Molly had to agree with them. What must once have been beautiful oak floors were scarred and stained, and there was a warped spot beneath a front window where rain had blown in before the windows were boarded up.

"Sally Creighton would be fit to be tied if she could see this," Conrad said, sounding angry. "Look at these floors. That looks like cigarette burns over there."

"I think teenagers have been using the house for partying."

"Still, the Hulles have made no effort at all to repair anything."

"I got the idea they didn't think the expense was justified. Bowen Hulle says the house and ten acres aren't worth much more than five thousand."

Conrad sighed. "He's probably right."

"Let's walk around outside a little."

They put Homer back on the leash and made sure the back door locked behind them. Homer tugged on the leash, straining toward a clump of tall weeds. He barked excitedly and Molly let him have his head. He parted the weeds and sniffed at a cellar door lying almost level with the ground.

"Maybe there's an animal in there," Conrad remarked.

Homer looked at him and barked. Conrad bent down and

pulled up on the door, letting it fall back on the ground. Steps descended into shadow.

"You hold Homer," Molly said, handing him the leash. "I'll have a look. If an animal's trapped down there, maybe I can scare him out."

"I hope it's not a skunk," Conrad said.

Molly hesitated. "Pleasant thought." She bent over the opening and sniffed. No skunk odor reached her, so she started down.

"Be careful."

There was enough dusky light from the open doorway for Molly to see where she was going. She made her way slowly down the stairs, swiping a cobweb out of her way at the bottom. The cellar was small, with shelves around three sides. Except for a couple of kerosene lamps and an old kerosene lantern, the shelves were empty, marked by dark stains and rings where fruit jars had once sat. Sally Creighton must have done a lot of home canning at one time.

There was no dead animal scent, only a musty, closed-up odor. Molly peered into the corners, but no bright animal eyes stared back at her. She climbed back to ground level. "Nothing down there now." Homer sniffed her legs and seemed satisfied.

Conrad shut the cellar door and they followed a rutted lane from the house through the woods. Conrad and Homer led the way. "Looks as though there have been cars through here recently," Conrad called over his shoulder.

"Let's follow their tracks."

Homer made a snatch for a butterfly and missed, and they walked in silence for a few moments. Much of the land was covered with dense woods, no good for farming or grazing cattle. Not good for anything much that Molly could think of, except to hold the world together, as Eva would have said. "Could there be oil on this property?"

"I doubt it. There was never much production around here. In the early eighties, when oil prices were sky-high, speculators lost their common sense and started sinking holes everywhere, even in Cherokee County. The prospect of big money makes them more reckless gamblers than they usually are. Several wells were drilled nearby, but they didn't find any oil."

The rutted lane led to a small, treeless, circular space where rotting boards lay over a hole in the ground. Homer sniffed at the boards, then backed off, whining. Molly laughed. "I won't let you fall in, Homer." The dog was a wimp, but a lovable wimp, she thought.

"It's an abandoned well," Conrad said, "a dry hole."

"One of those drilled in the eighties?"

"Or even earlier. There was an oil boom in the seventies, too."

About a dozen Budweiser cans had been tossed into the weeds at the edge of the well site. Molly kicked at one idly. "This explains the tire tracks. Some of those teenagers drove out here. Probably afraid their cars might be spotted around the house."

"I have to agree with the Hulles," Conrad said. "Land like this will bring less than three hundred dollars an acre in today's market. Add another two thousand, tops, for the house."

They walked back through the woods as darkness fell. The trees shut out the moonlight and they proceeded cautiously, letting Homer lead them around trees they otherwise could have bumped into before seeing.

The late-summer heat had abated little with nightfall, and somehow the darkness made it seem more oppressive. Molly felt an uneasy prickling down her spine. She rarely felt claustrophobic, but she sensed the woods closing in on her now and was very glad she wasn't alone.

Beyond the trees, the sloping, graveled drive shone eerily white in the moonlight. As they reached the Civic, Molly said, "There's nothing here worth committing murder for. This was a useless trip."

"Depends on your point of view," Conrad told her. "Homer had a good time, but we better check him for ticks when we get home."

On the drive back to town, Molly turned her mind to nonfinancial motives, hoping to come up with a new idea. Absorbed in thought, she didn't notice that an oncoming truck barreling toward her had two wheels over the center line until it was almost too late to veer onto the shoulder of the road. She slammed her palm down on the horn and muttered an oath, then steered slowly back on the road. Conrad had both hands braced against the dashboard.

"Sorry," she said, "I was wool-gathering."

They passed a tank truck, but this one kept well to its side of the highway. Conrad sat back in the seat. "This road gets a lot of truck traffic since they built that waste dump across the state line in Arkansas."

Molly realized she was gripping the steering wheel hard and relaxed her fingers, still shaken by the close call. "Next thing, we'll have our taxes raised to pay for the upkeep."

"Be happy they didn't build it in Cherokee County," Conrad advised.

OOOOOOOO

13

After vacillating all day Friday, Molly finally convinced herself that her reluctance to go to D.J.'s house for dinner Saturday night was silly. It was as suitable a place as any to discuss the investigation, and more private than most. There would be no chance of being overheard, which couldn't be said for any public place she might have suggested as an alternative.

To keep from feeling like a guest, however, she decided to make a contribution to dinner. After simmering a pot of pinto beans with a ham hock all Saturday morning, she made bean bread from her grandmother's recipe. Later, while the loaves cooled on racks, she went to the grocery store and bought fresh peaches, apples, bananas, cantaloupe, and honeydew melon, which she combined with frozen blueberries and coconut in a summer salad.

Later, she stood at her open closet and scanned her wardrobe. As she was about to reach for the nearest pair of jeans, a flash of hot pink caught her eye. The dress was jammed in at the far end of the closet with the other bright, feminine dresses given to her by her grandmother on various birthdays and Christmases. She wouldn't have felt comfortable wearing any of them to work, and her sparse social life provided few occasions for such attire. To make her grandmother happy, she usually wore them to Eva's house a couple of times before consigning them to the back of the closet.

Eva seemed oblivious to the fact that most of them were too frilly for Molly's taste. The pink one, however, was a simple affair with a scoop neck, elasticized waist, and wide hem banded by a dozen pin tucks. Without questioning the impulse, she put it on and slid her bare feet into white sandals. It was but another moment's work to brush out her long black hair and slip on a white headband.

When she arrived at D.J.'s, he was standing over a gas grill on the deck, in shorts and a sleeveless knit shirt, checking the glowing charcoal with a long fork. Plates, silverware, and paper napkins were laid out on a redwood picnic table.

D.J. had lived in the house for about nine years. He had scraped together half the equity at the time of the divorce so that he could keep the house he and his ex-wife had bought when Courtney was a baby. "So Courtney will always have her old home to come back to," he'd once told Molly. It was too bad Courtney spent so little time there with her father.

"I brought bread and a fruit salad," Molly said, setting her contributions on the table.

"Good," he replied, his eyes crinkling in a smile, "I'll go get the steaks."

He was back in a minute with two thick T-bones and potatoes wrapped in foil. "The potatoes are done," he said, forking the steaks onto the grill. He set the wrapped potatoes at the edge of the grill to keep warm. "How do you like your steak?"

"Medium well." Molly sat down at the table.

"What's up?"

"I've been busy." She went on to recount her interviews with Lori Hakey, Fred Whillock, and the Hulles. "Unless they're the beneficiaries of big life-insurance policies, I think we can eliminate financial gain as a motive for anybody wanting Hakey or Creighton dead."

"Creighton, for sure. Ginny Hulle is her only heir."

"I discovered that too," Molly said.

"Well, I happen to know the Hulles' business does quite well, so they don't need money."

"Nobody gains financially by Abner Mouse's death, either. He didn't have any assets. His six kids were chipping in to pay for the nursing home, so it probably wasn't a great amount for any one of the six. Two or three hundred dollars, I'd guess. Of course . . ."

D.J. turned from the grill. "What are you thinking?"

"A few hundred could seem like a fortune if you don't have it to spare, which I gather is the case with Woodrow and Nellie. Not having to contribute their part of the nursing-home payment is probably a big relief. From what Nellie said, it put them in a bind and she resented it." Molly shook her head. "Somehow, though, I don't think they did it. Not Woodrow, anyway. He seemed pretty torn up over his father's death, and I don't think it was an act." She reflected for a moment. "Nellie, maybe . . . she told me she'd had Abner around her neck since the day she and Woodrow married."

"People reach the end of their rope, no telling what they might do."

"Mmmm. Nellie and Woodrow were in the nursing home the day before Tacker died, too," Molly said. "Of course, they've known Mercer Vaughan all their lives, but Nellie didn't like going there to see her father-in-law . . ."

"So why would she go to visit somebody she wasn't related to?"

Molly nodded. "Good question. As for the Whillocks, they have money in CD's, but I couldn't find out how much."

"Three hundred thousand," D.J. said.

"What?"

"I ran some names past a local banker. The Whillocks have three hundred thousand in CD's and another fifty thousand in a money-market account, and they don't even spend all the interest. Ernie Whillock gets a nice pension, enough to pay their room and board at Country Haven. Their three children are their beneficiaries.''

''The daughter lives out of state,'' Molly observed thoughtfully. She did a quick calculation. ''Fred Whillock and his brother and sister will inherit about a hundred and fifteen thousand each.''

''Both the old people have to die before the kids get a dime. The CD's are in joint accounts. If only one of them dies, the surviving spouse gets it all.''

They sat absorbed in speculation for a moment. Finally, Molly asked, ''Are you thinking what I'm thinking?''

''Probably. If both the Whillocks had died of food poisoning in the beginning, the finger of suspicion would have pointed right at Fred and his brother, once we got around to thinking about murder. But killing Mouse and Tacker first would throw us off the scent, and if the Whillocks died later, we'd be totally confused. That could be the assumption, anyway.''

''Since Fred is the only one of the brothers who visited his parents prior to both Mouse's and Tacker's deaths . . .''

''Yeah,'' D.J. added.

''I wonder if Fred needs the money.''

''I haven't heard any rumors to that effect,'' D.J. told her. ''Seems Fred and his wife have always been frugal. The banker says they paid off the mortgage on their house several years ago and they have about sixty thousand in his bank. They also have a safe-deposit box. The banker thinks Fred has quite a few corporate-bond certificates in it. It would take a court order to find out for sure.''

''Maybe Fred is greedy. No matter how much that kind has, it's never enough. I can really see that guy as a killer.''

D.J. grinned. ''Gave you a hard time, eh?''

''He ordered me off his property. He was furious, D.J., not to mention insulting. I think he was mad enough to hit me if I'd refused to go.''

''I warned you.'' He cut a small slit in one of the steaks. ''Perfect,'' he pronounced. ''Hand me the plates. Then you can get the sour cream and butter out of the refrigerator.''

Molly brought out the condiments, including a bottle of steak sauce she'd noticed on the kitchen table. After forking the steaks and potatoes onto the plates, D.J. set them on the table and went to the kitchen for iced tea.

Molly's steak was cooked just the way she liked it and tender enough to cut with a fork. "I didn't know you could cook, D.J."

He wiggled his eyebrows. "Stick around, woman. I have many talents you have yet to discover."

Molly eyed him askance. "Uh-huh." She buttered a piece of bean bread.

"Want to know what I learned about Buster Tacker?"

She shot him a swift look. "You already got information on him? Why didn't you say so, for heaven's sake?"

"I was waiting for you to finish your report."

"Well, I'm finished. Talk."

"Buster has a terrible credit rating. He's behind on his car payments, and a couple of credit-card bills have been turned over to collectors. My contact in Fort Smith reported that Buster works as a security guard. He lives alone, so he makes enough for one person to get by on, if he has no monthly bills except the basics. But Buster is in debt up to his gullet. There's no way he could keep up all his debt payments on his wages."

"Mr. Vaughan told me his mother gave him money when he visited her."

"It wasn't enough to keep him solvent," D.J. said, "but he should be able to get caught up now. His mother left him something over four hundred and fifty thousand. The funeral was Tuesday afternoon, by the way. Buster didn't waste any time putting Mom in the ground."

She blew out a breath. "Four hundred and fifty thousand. Wow. Buster just moved ahead of Fred Whillock on my suspect list."

"I like him, too. You up for a trip to Fort Smith tomorrow afternoon?"

"Sure. We need to get a reading on Buster, eyeball to eyeball. But we can't be hasty in narrowing the list of suspects. We have to find out about life-insurance policies on the people in A-wing. Lori Hakey sure clammed up when I asked if her grandmother had insurance. When I asked Fred Whillock that question, he got so red I thought he was going to rupture a couple of blood vessels."

"I've already asked the new deputy to check on life insurance," D.J. said. "He should have something for me by Tuesday or Wednesday."

"What about the nursing-home employees?"

D.J. shrugged. "I didn't turn up anything that sent up a red flag in my mind. Zelda Kline and Mary Sue Nutter, the nurse's aides on the two shifts when food was served, seem like ordinary working wives and mothers. They need two paychecks to make ends meet. Kline has two kids, Nutter, three, all elementary-school age. Kline and her husband are big workers in the Presbyterian church. Both women do their jobs and get along well with their co-workers."

"Nutter and Kline don't sound much like murder candidates."

"Neither do Cora D'Angelo, the cleaning woman, and the nurse, Irene Robinson. D'Angelo's only worked at Country Haven a few weeks. Darwood says she's the best cleaner he ever had. She doesn't linger in the residents' rooms, shooting the breeze or watching soap operas. Evidently that's been a problem with some of the previous people in that job, and they had to let one guy go for coming to work under the influence. D'Angelo's widowed and has a couple of grown daughters living in Oklahoma City. The other employees describe her as cheerful and a willing worker."

"Robinson?"

"A good nurse, according to Darwood. Some of the residents say she gets cranky with them sometimes, but she's not as apt to lose her patience as the day nurse, Beatrice Crawford."

". . . who wasn't there on either of the Sundays in question," Molly murmured.

"Right. A couple of the employees on Robinson's shift did mention that she'd seemed a little preoccupied lately. Christine Zucker, who usually doesn't work Robinson's shift but did one day a couple of weeks ago, said she got the impression Robinson was worried about something. When she asked if she could help, Robinson said no, that she was concerned about a personal problem. She didn't get any more specific than that."

His words connected with something at the back of Molly's mind, a connection she would have to explore later. "I can't believe it's an employee, anyway. There's just no sane motive."

"And those four women strike me as perfectly normal, whatever that means," D.J. said.

"So, we're back to Buster Tacker and Fred Whillock."

"Looks that way, unless the new deputy uncovers a big life-insurance policy naming somebody else on our list as the beneficiary."

Molly sighed. "Well, we've covered a lot of ground this week, even if it all turns out to be wasted effort."

"That's what most investigative work is—wasted effort."

"Tell me about it," Molly agreed. They fell into a companionable silence, as they finished the meal. Molly ate until she felt stuffed and wished she had room for more. Pushing her plate back and cupping her chin in her hand, she asked, "Have you seen Courtney this summer?"

He scooted his chair away from the table and slid down in it with his legs stretched out. "She was here for ten days in June. I took my vacation and we went up to Branson. She loved Silver Dollar City and the country music shows. We had a good time."

"Too bad you can't see her more often."

He propped his elbows on the chair arms and tented his fingers. "I'm going up there in December and take her skiing while Gloria is on her honeymoon."

Molly couldn't discern a clue to his feelings in his tone. "I didn't know Gloria was getting married again," she said cautiously.

"No reason you should."

"Does that bother you?"

He looked startled by the question. "Hell, no. What bothers me is Courtney having another father figure in her life, one who's going to be around all the time."

She was surprised by her desire to reach out and touch him in a comforting way. First the hot-pink dress and now this. What had got into her tonight? Fortunately she came to her senses in time to keep her hands to herself. "I'm sorry, D.J."

He straightened, as though shaking off the depressing thought of Courtney with Gloria's new husband. "Hey, that's the breaks."

"You didn't want Gloria to take her out of the state in the first place. It's not right." It occurred to her that she'd had more than one occasion recently to reflect upon the unfairness of life.

She leaned over, reaching for the foil with which she'd covered the salad bowl. She smoothed the foil back in place around the bowl's rim. The tilt of her head sent her long dark hair swinging.

When she looked up, D.J. was staring at her with a tender expression. He shifted in his chair and cleared his throat. "*Right* doesn't come into it," he murmured. "Life hasn't covered you up with good luck, either. You never asked to be left an orphan at the age of six."

Whatever had passed through his mind as he stared at her, she was sure it had more to do with now than with her childhood. "Fortunately, I had my grandmother." She rested her chin in her hand again. "She was wonderful, even if she would never admit the truth about my mother."

"You mean the suicide?"

Molly nodded, already wishing she hadn't brought up the painful subject. "Grandmother always said that Mother had had a little too much to drink that one time, and the gun went off by accident. Maybe she believed it, or maybe she wanted me to believe it. She should have realized that I'd hear other people talking about how Josephine always drank too much, and she got worse after my father left. Several people heard her threaten suicide when she was drunk. I guess they didn't take it seriously." Molly had, though. She could remember thinking there must be something wrong with her to make both her parents want to go away.

"Do you remember your father at all?"

"A few flashes. One is of him laughing and throwing me up in the air and catching me. Or maybe it was only a dream." She stared into the gathering darkness beyond the deck. Her father had become little more than a dream image for her. She wasn't sure whether the mental picture she had of him was accurate or something conjured up in a child's mind. The love she'd felt for him had been real, though. And the crushing unhappiness after he was gone, that was real, too. "I can also remember running to meet him when he came home from work, and how frightened I was that day when he didn't come home."

D.J. made a sympathetic sound. "What else do you remember?"

"Not much more about my father. I remember my mother having hysterics after he'd gone—not just once, but again and again as time went on and he didn't get in touch with her. She'd cry and scream and say she didn't want to live without him." She paused, then added with an air of moving away from dangerous ground, "So, she didn't."

It was the first time she'd talked to him, or anyone, about her parents in years. It hadn't gotten easier with time. How could things that happened so long ago still hurt so much? She drew a deep, steadying breath and turned her back on the memories.

He seemed to sense it was time to drop the subject. He stirred and slapped his arm. "The mosquitoes are coming out. Let's go inside."

"I need to get home." It sounded like the weak excuse it was. She retrieved the fruit-salad bowl.

"It's not late."

The conversation had left her feeling too emotionally vulnerable to stay any longer. "I know, but I really do have things to do at home."

"Whatever you say. I'll see you to your car."

They walked around the house to the front without touching. "Thanks for dinner," she said when they were standing beside the Civic.

"You're welcome."

His eyes moved over her face. Suddenly, he turned her to him, lifted her chin with his fingers, and placed a tender kiss on her startled lips. A shock went through Molly and, for an instant, she kissed him back. Then she pulled away and dropped her eyes.

Flustered, she fumbled with the car door until D.J. reached around her and opened it.

She got in. "Good night." Her tone was brittle-bright. She started the engine.

"See you tomorrow, Molly," he said softly.

She managed a smile. Should she mention the kiss? Or pretend it wasn't worth mentioning? Silence was the better part of wisdom, she decided. She didn't want to sound like a twit, even if she did feel like one.

She waved and drove away with little aftershocks rippling in the pit of her stomach.

ooooooooo

14

At home, she roamed her single room restlessly, her thoughts returning, again and again, to D.J.'s kiss. Dismayed by such an adolescent reaction, she took a long shower, adjusting the stream of water until it was cool enough to raise gooseflesh on her skin. She warmed up by rubbing herself briskly with a towel until her skin felt raw.

When an errant thought of D.J. flitted across her mind she pushed it firmly away. She was still talking sense to herself as she climbed into bed and buried her damp head under her pillow. She put herself to sleep by mentally lining up the suspects in the nursing-home investigation and going back over the information gathered thus far, trying to find a pattern in all the data. No pattern emerged. Maybe, she thought drowsily, it's like one of those kids' drawings with objects concealed among a plethora of lines. You had to keep turning those drawings, viewing them from different angles in order to find the hidden objects. A thought worth pursuing when she wasn't so sleepy, she decided as she dropped off.

The next morning, she returned the hot-pink dress to its

dark corner, donned her oldest jeans and a simple cotton shirt, and plaited her hair in a single, no-nonsense braid.

At midmorning, she dialed Muskogee information to request a number for Sherwood Bowman. When she'd checked with the electric company on Friday, the woman who'd taken her call said Bowman had left an address in Muskogee where the remainder of his deposit could be returned after final charges were deducted.

Molly had jotted down the address but had forgotten to put the report in the mail. It had been so long now that she decided a phone call explaining the delay was in order.

"Hold for the number, please."

Molly wrote it down, then dialed. Bowman must have been sitting beside the phone. He picked up on the first ring.

"Hullo."

"Is Sherwood Bowman there, please?"

"Speaking. Who's this?"

"Molly Bearpaw. I've been trying to run you down. I've completed my investigation, but the report I mailed you was returned."

"Oh, that. I moved, but you obviously figured that out. Did you dig up any dirt on the paint factory?"

"Not a speck. Nothing to base a lawsuit on, certainly."

"I've decided to drop that idea, anyway." He didn't sound particularly reluctant to let it go, which surprised Molly. Had she—and a number of other people—misjudged him? "I'm feeling a lot better now," he said. "Must have been some kind of bug that kept hanging on. A virus, I guess."

"Could be. I'm glad to hear you're better."

"I like my new job much more than the old one, too."

"That's good. I'll put the report in the mail, anyway. You may want it later."

"Okay. Do you have my address?"

"The electric company gave it to me."

Molly was about to hang up when he said, "It's strange, though."

"What is?"

"I lived there two months and didn't feel up to par most of the time. That's a long while to have a virus."

"Maybe not. It could have been a particularly virulent strain."

"If so, it seems odd I'd get over it, all of a sudden, after I moved."

"What are you getting at, Mr. Bowman?"

He expelled a breath. "Look, I know you think I just want somebody to sue."

"I never said that."

"You didn't have to. It was your attitude when I came to your office. You wanted to give me the brush-off."

He'd read her pretty well. Must have been her body language. She would have to watch that. "I'm very sorry if I gave you that impression."

There was a silence before he said magnanimously, "That's okay. Here's what I've been wondering, see. Sometimes the water in that place smelled funny. Do you think there could've been something in it that made me sick?"

Here we go again, Molly thought. "I assume the house had its own water well?"

"That's right."

"Is there an outside faucet?"

"Yes, at the back of the house."

"I happen to know the house is still vacant. If you really think there's something wrong with the water, Mr. Bowman, why don't you collect a sample and have it tested."

"I don't know when I could drive over there. I've been working twelve-hour shifts, and I'm beat when I get off. I wouldn't want to run into the landlord, either. We didn't part on the best of terms. He wouldn't return my deposit. He said he'd have to paint the whole interior; claimed it was fine when I moved in. That was a lie and I—well, I kind of told Whillock where he could go."

Whillock? The name came out of nowhere and rattled Molly. "What did you say?"

"Which part?"

"Your landlord's name. I thought you said Whillock."

"Yeah. Fred Whillock. You know him?"

"I've met him." Molly chewed her lip and tried to figure

out what it meant. If anything. "Tell you what, Mr. Bowman. I'll get a sample of the water and have the county agent test it."

"You will? I appreciate that. It would put my mind at rest if I knew it wasn't the water. I feel like I owe it to whoever moves in that house."

Sherwood Bowman, humanitarian and all-around good citizen? Molly had a little trouble swallowing that. "I understand, Mr. Bowman. I'll send you the results of the test."

Molly hung up. She dropped into a chair, closed her eyes, and stared at blackness. Fred Whillock owned the house on Highway 51 where Sherwood Bowman had lived. Two people involved in two entirely separate investigations. What a bizarre coincidence. Or was it?

Something stirred in her mind. Some memory she couldn't quite place had been roused by her conversation with Bowman. She racked her brain, but she was adrift on a sea of bewildering recollections, and she couldn't dredge up the memory she was looking for.

She gave up and addressed a new envelope to Sherwood Bowman. After transferring the report and sealing it, she propped it against the table lamp where she'd see it Monday morning when she left for the office.

She ate a bowl of soup with a couple of slices of bean bread, then decided to do her laundry in the time remaining before D.J. was due to pick her up. About a year ago, when Conrad had purchased a new washer and dryer for his house, he'd installed the old ones in the garage downstairs for Molly's use. Before that, she'd gone to the Laundromat.

Clouds were gathering overhead when she carried her laundry down. Homer was stretched out in his favorite corner under the stairs and was too lazy to get up when she spoke to him, contenting himself with a wag of his tail.

Rain didn't appear imminent, but maybe the clouds would build and there would be rain later. She was sure Conrad would allow Homer in his house if a storm developed. In fact, Molly had seen him let the dog in for short periods on clear, sunny days. For someone who wasn't a pet person, Conrad was a pushover.

Molly gave the clouds a final inspection before entering the garage. It had been a typical Oklahoma summer; they'd had only a couple of brief showers since early June. Today's clouds were probably a false alarm. On the other hand, autumn was the rainy season, and she could always hope that it would come early this year.

While the washer and dryer did their thing, Molly went back upstairs and got out the list of suspects she and D.J. had made. Her eyes stopped on Cora D'Angelo's name and she recalled the connection her mind had made when D.J. reported what he'd learned about the cleaning woman. She thought back over the interviews she'd had.

Abner Mouse had mentioned a janitor named Bob who'd been employed at the home until a few weeks ago, when he'd been fired and Cora D'Angelo had been hired.

Her gaze slid down to Lori Hakey's name. Lori's pot-smoking friend was named Bob, and Lori had mentioned someone—a woman—who'd helped him get his last job. Put it all together, and what did she have? Alas, nothing concrete. Merely a feeling that there was a connection in these seemingly unrelated details.

Could Bob Perrone be the janitor who was fired? And was it another employee who'd helped him get the job, perhaps a relative?

She considered stopping by the nursing home Monday and talking to Christine Zucker. But it might be difficult to question Christine privately while she was working. Molly reached for the phone book. Only one Zucker was listed. A man answered and called Christine to the phone.

"It's Molly Bearpaw, Christine."

"Hi, Molly. How are you?"

"Very well. I hope I'm not interrupting anything."

"Oh, no. I just put the kids down for their naps, so I can talk. I heard you came out to the nursing home with D.J. Kennedy when he questioned the residents of A-wing. Mr. Darwood told all the employees to let him know if you contacted us. He seemed really worried about something."

Maybe Darwood hadn't bought her story and still thought she was with the FBI. "You're not at work now, so you don't have to tell him about this call, do you?"

She hesitated. "I guess not."

"Not that it would matter," Molly said. "I only called you at home because I need a couple of things confirmed today."

"What?" She sounded leery.

"Wasn't Bob Perrone once employed as a janitor at Country Haven?"

There was a pause before Christine said, "That's no secret. Bob was the janitor for several months."

"What happened?"

Another hesitation. Then, "All I know is what I heard. One day I went to work and Mr. Darwood had fired Bob. The janitor goes to work at six in the morning, and I don't have to be there until seven, so it was all over before I arrived."

"What did you hear about it when you got there?"

"One of the night aides told me that Bob showed up drunk or high on drugs that morning." There was no hesitation this time. She must have decided that what she said and to whom on her own time was nobody else's business. "She said his eyes looked funny and his words were slurred. Somebody called Mr. Darwood. He usually doesn't arrive until after eight. But he was there in a few minutes, saw the shape Bob was in, and told him to clear out. Said he could come back for his last paycheck when he sobered up, and after that he never wanted to see his face around there again."

"Have you seen Bob there lately?"

"No. He wouldn't dare come after what Darwood told him."

"I understand Bob was pretty close to somebody on the staff out there, a relative." It was a wild thought, but nothing ventured . . . Irene Robinson *had* said she was worried about a "personal problem" following Bob Perrone's dismissal. Coincidence? "It was one of the nurses, I think. How did she react to Darwood's firing Bob?"

"A nurse?" Christine asked blankly.

"Maybe it's one of the aides."

"I can't imagine where you got the idea Bob was related to another employee. They don't hire relatives at Country

Haven. It's a company policy. They won't even hire first cousins."

Oh, well, it had been a nebulous idea at best. "Were any of the employees particularly friendly with Perrone?"

"Irene Robinson did kind of take him under her wing."

"Is she married?"

"Divorced. But it wasn't a romance with Bob, nothing like that. She felt sorry for him, for some reason."

"I see," Molly mused. "How long has Irene Robinson been employed at Country Haven?"

"She was hired several months before I got on out there, and that was eighteen months ago. Bob was hired later, so, like I said, I know he can't be related to Irene. Why are you so interested in her?"

"I'm not, really. Listen, you've cleared up a few things. I appreciate it."

"Any of the employees could have told you everything I did."

"Thanks a lot, Christine."

OOOOOOOO

15

While Molly waited for D.J., she thought about Bob Perrone as a suspect in the poisonings. He conceivably might want to make Darwood and the nursing home look bad, but where would he have gotten the botulism bacilli? She supposed that wasn't an impossible task if one was determined, but nobody had mentioned seeing him at Country Haven on the days in question. Which didn't prove conclusively that he wasn't there.

Perrone had been friendly with Irene Robinson. The nursing employees were there five days a week, Irene Robinson sometimes six or seven days, according to Christine. Were botulism bacilli cultured by companies who supplied them for research projects? Nurses would probably know about such places, and Irene Robinson had been Perrone's friend. Maybe she was in love with him, in spite of what Christine Zucker thought on the subject.

Molly sighed. Even she found it hard to believe in a romance between Robinson and Perrone. Robinson was several years older than Perrone, for one thing, but mainly

Molly couldn't imagine a sensible, attractive woman falling for a loser like Bob Perrone.

They could be very good friends, though. Suppose she'd been so angry about his dismissal she'd decided to take revenge. The botulism poisonings certainly weren't helping the nursing home's reputation.

Molly gave herself a mental shake. Talk about grasping at straws!

She consulted her notes again. Lori Hakey had mentioned phoning somebody who'd helped Bob get his last job. Could that person be Irene Robinson? She had to find out and, from the way Lori had skipped quickly over the subject, she doubted Lori would identify the person. That was odd, come to think of it. Why would Lori want to keep the person's identity a secret?

* * *

D.J. arrived at ten after two. His hair was still damp from the shower. He had on a plaid cotton sport shirt and tan trousers that had a crease and everything. He hardly looked rumpled at all.

"I can't go," he said, when Molly answered his knock.

"Oh." She was deeply disappointed. The sooner they talked to Tacker, the better. Her disappointment had nothing to do with the fact that plans for spending the afternoon with D.J. had been thwarted, she told herself.

"There's been a bad car wreck south of town. One dead and two others in critical condition. I have to get to the hospital right away and talk to the survivors. I'm sorry, Molly."

"It can't be helped."

"I called Tacker this morning to let him know I was coming. He didn't sound thrilled to hear from me. Kept asking what I wanted to talk to him about."

"What did you tell him?"

"That I was tying up loose ends."

"With him trussed up inside," Molly said.

"We can dream. I'd like to have somebody trussed up before the sheriff gets back."

"Or before another person dies. I'm still not convinced the poisoner's finished."

"If it's Tacker, he is. He's gotten what he wanted, so why would he risk doing it a third time?"

"He might if he thinks he's a prime suspect and panics."

"We better make sure he doesn't, then. I'll phone him from the hospital and say I can't make it today."

"No, don't do that," Molly said quickly. "I'll go alone."

"It doesn't have to be done today, Molly."

"I want to, really."

His expression was troubled. "I'm not crazy about you going by yourself. We don't know enough about this guy. What if he *is* a killer? If he thinks you suspect him . . ."

"I'll make sure he doesn't."

He shook his head. "If he's guilty, he'll be on the defensive. Wait. I can probably go with you tomorrow."

"I have this feeling that time's running out, D.J."

He studied her. "I can't talk you out of it, can I?"

She shook her head. "I'll be careful. And don't call him. Did you mention you'd have somebody with you?"

"No."

"Good. He'll be expecting to see you, and maybe I can take him off guard."

D.J. finally agreed, but he didn't like it. He gave her a piece of paper on which he'd written Tacker's address and told her to call him as soon as she got back.

The clouds overhead were darker and a few raindrops splattered the Civic's windshield as Molly drove out of town. Recalling the analogy she'd made last night, comparing the investigation to a kids' drawing, she thought about the case all the way to Fort Smith, but didn't come up with any brilliant new insights.

It rained, off and on, during the drive, but the sky was clearing by the time she reached Buster Tacker's place of residence, a battered trailer house on a bare patch of ground in the middle of a seedy trailer park.

An old Plymouth with four flat tires was parked next to the trailer. This couldn't be the car on which Tacker had let the payments lapse. Maybe the finance company had repossessed that one. Or Tacker parked it elsewhere to guard against that possibility.

Concrete blocks were stacked in three narrow steps up to the door. Tacker answered Molly's knock immediately. "I'm expecting a visitor and saw you coming up the walk. If you're selling something—"

"I'm not."

"What can I do for you, then?"

"D.J. Kennedy asked me to come," Molly said. "Something came up that kept him in Tahlequah. My name's Molly Bearpaw, Mr. Tacker."

He gave her a quick once-over as he shook her hand.

"May I come in?"

He stood back for her to enter a small, shabby room with an open gas heater in one corner and threadbare carpet of indeterminate hue on the floor. Several large cardboard boxes sat against the wall, taking up most of the available floor space. A few books and a stack of folded shirts and jeans were piled next to the boxes.

"Moving?" Molly asked.

"Not right away, but probably in the near future," Tacker said. "I'm boxing up what I won't be needing so I'll have less to do later." After he had the inheritance in his hot little hands, Molly thought.

He was wiry, blond and mustachioed, with eyes that kept shifting away from direct contact with Molly's gaze.

"How long have you been with the sheriff's department?"

"Not long." It seemed wise not to disabuse him of his false assumption. He couldn't very well refuse an interview with a sheriff's deputy, even one from another state. For a man who was supposedly concerned with getting at the truth of his mother's death, it would look bad.

"Sit down," Tacker said briskly. "Would you like coffee? I only have instant."

Molly declined. She would as soon drink hot water poured over pulverized rocks. When they were seated, Molly smiled at him and asked, "Are you planning to leave Fort Smith?"

Tacker stared at her for a second before his gaze moved to a picture on the wall depicting hunting dogs on point and a covey of quail flying out of the brush in front of them. The glass was cracked. "I haven't decided. There's really nothing to keep me in this area"—he looked down at his hands—"now that mother's—gone."

"You're giving up your job?"

He fidgeted. "I'll find something else." He jerked to his feet. "I'm going to have some coffee. Sure you won't join me?"

Molly shook her head and he headed for the kitchen. He was definitely nervous, like a man with a guilty conscience. If he did have something to hide, asking the wrong questions could be dangerous. She didn't need D.J. to tell her that, and she'd really meant to keep her promise to D.J. and avoid anything that might arouse Tacker's suspicions.

But now she reconsidered. Tacker wouldn't do anything to her in his own house, surely, and this was the perfect time to mention the inheritance while he was unnerved and concentrating on trying to appear calm and cooperative. He might let something slip.

He came back carrying a chipped cup, placed it on the arm of the couch, and sat down. "I have an appointment later." While in the kitchen, he had evidently decided to get rid of her as quickly as possible.

"I won't keep you long," Molly said, smiling benignly. "I just need to ask you a few questions about your last two Sunday visits to your mother before her death."

"I already went over it in detail with Deputy Kennedy."

"I know. We're checking back with everyone who was in A-wing on those days to see if they've remembered something they forgot to tell us."

"Like what?"

"Anything that struck you as unusual. I know you spent several hours on Sundays with your mother, so you had more opportunity than most visitors to notice any change in the regular routine."

He was ill at ease and appeared affected by her words, but shook his head and mumbled, "I was there to please my mother, and she wasn't the easiest person in the world to please. I didn't pay any attention to anything else."

"I know elderly people can be a trial sometimes. You're

to be commended for spending so much time with your mother. You wouldn't believe the number of people in that nursing home whose children never come to visit."

"I'd believe it," he said grimly. "Every Sunday when I walked up to the front door, I wanted more than anything to run like hell in the opposite direction."

"But you didn't."

He glanced at her. "You think that was out of some sense of duty or devotion?"

"She *was* your mother."

"I wasn't about to forget that. She used it all my life to beat me into submission."

"There was the inheritance to think about, too."

His eyes widened with shock and then his face seemed to crumble. He struggled to pull himself together. "I didn't have to agree to see you in the first place. Now I want you to leave."

Molly didn't move. "We know all about the inheritance, Mr. Tacker. Close to half a million, isn't it? I'm not suggesting that's the only reason you spent your Sundays trying to please your mother, but it wasn't something you'd lose sight of, either."

"So?" he asked belligerently.

"When do you expect to get the money?"

Tacker threw her a hot glance, and as swiftly looked away. But there had been time enough for Molly to see a flash of something unpleasant. "The sooner the better. I've waited long enough." The words seemed to crowd past Tacker's ability to restrain them. A bright flush suffused his cheeks. "I don't expect you to believe me, but I wasn't thinking about the inheritance when I went to visit Mother. With my luck, I expected her to live forever. What I was hoping for was that she'd realize I could use a little of that money immediately. She wasn't about to spend any of it on herself, that's for sure. My mother squeezed every penny until it squealed." He squared his shoulders as though gathering a cloak of bravado around himself. "I've had some financial difficulties lately, and she had money she hadn't touched in years."

"You asked her for a loan," Molly said, fixing her eyes

on him. Tacker was already on the defensive, so there seemed little point in holding back now. "You were overheard," she lied.

"So that's what this is about." He cleared his throat and managed to hold Molly's stare for several seconds this time. His eyes darkened ominously. "Yes, I asked for enough to get me on my feet. The money was sitting in the bank, not doing anybody any good. I told her so."

"I gather she didn't see it that way."

"Hardly. You know what she did? Opened her purse and took out a wad of money that would choke a horse. She always kept some hidden behind the purse lining. It was seven hundred dollars, to be exact. The nursing home turned over Mother's purse to me along with her other belongings. That alone was enough to get the bank off my case about my back car payments for a while."

"She gave you some of it the day before she died?"

"She peeled off one bill and handed it to me." He laughed but there was no humor in it. "Twenty dollars, and it hurt as much as if she'd stripped off a piece of skin." His face had drained of color.

Molly waited.

"I could say I'm sorry she's dead, but I'm not. She didn't care enough about her only child to help me out of serious financial problems. I can't even pay the funeral home until I get the money from the estate." He stared at the floor. "I keep imagining her, watching me spend that money, once I get my hands on it." He reached for his cup with an unsteady hand, blew on it, and drank it in one gulp. "God, what I wouldn't give to be sure she'll know!"

"Do you expect to get it soon?"

"The lawyer promised he'd try to hurry the probate proceedings along. Two or three months, I'd guess."

Whenever it was—Molly glanced at the packing cartons—Buster Tacker would be out of this tacky little trailer. In his place, she'd do the same.

She went through the questions she'd asked the other interviewees, questions that were becoming automatic by now. Had he taken his mother anything to eat on the past two Sundays? Had he seen any food in her room besides what was delivered from the nursing-home kitchen? Had he noticed any food from outside in *any* of the rooms in A-wing? The answer was no, to all three questions.

Aside from employees and residents, had he noticed other people in A-wing on the past two Sundays?

An Indian couple had visited Mercer Vaughan, and four women went into 104 while he was there the previous Sunday. That would be the Methodist church ladies who had visited Lahoma Buckhorn. Aside from those six people, Tacker hadn't seen anyone.

Now that they'd gotten off the subject of his mother and the inheritance, he appeared more in command of himself. "I'm going to have to leave now—that appointment I mentioned."

Molly knew the appointment was fictitious, but there was no point in prolonging the interview. Whatever advantage she'd had because of his nervousness and surprise at being questioned by a woman instead of D.J. was gone.

"Thank you for being so candid," she said as she left.

On the drive back to Tahlequah, she kept remembering that one brief, unpleasant flash she'd seen in his eyes. Bitterness? Fear? She couldn't quite pin it down.

But when she talked to D.J. on the telephone that evening, it came to her. "He literally hated his mother, D.J. I think she was pretty domineering. She used the fact that she was his mother to make him feel obligated to do whatever she wanted."

"Hogwash. I'll bet it was the money that kept him at her beck and call."

"That, too. At any rate, his resentment had been building for years. I saw it in his eyes. He's glad she's dead."

"He actually said that?"

"In so many words. And you should have heard the way he talked about her when I mentioned the inheritance, how stingy she was with her money, how she refused to help her only child get out of debt."

"*You* mentioned it? Dammit, Molly, I thought you weren't going to arouse his suspicions."

"He was nervous, and my showing up instead of you threw him. It was too good an opportunity to pass up."

"I should be shot for letting you go there alone," D.J. grumbled.

She didn't like his proprietary attitude. "You didn't *let* me do anything, D.J. I went."

"Bad choice of words, but—"

"The thought was in your mind, or you wouldn't have said it." She added a terse good-bye and hung up.

OOOOOOOO

16

Later, she wondered if she'd been a bit too defensive, but when D.J. called her Monday morning from the station, he didn't mention the abrupt end to their previous conversation. In fact, his first words might have been merely a continuation of it. "Didn't you forget to mention something?"

"When?"

"The last time we talked."

"If you're asking for an apology—"

"For what?"

She had put him in his place and he hadn't even noticed. "Never mind," she mumbled.

"I'm referring to the fact that you told Buster Tacker you were a sheriff's deputy."

"I didn't tell him that."

"He sure as hell got the impression," D.J. said. "I guess that means the thought was in your mind, or he wouldn't have reached that conclusion."

Wise ass, using her own argument against her. Molly managed not to grind her teeth. "He assumed it when I said I'd come in your place. I wasn't about to set him straight. He might not have been so open with me. Besides, how did you find out about it?"

"After you left, Tacker got to thinking."

"He was worried because he'd said too much, you mean."

"Whatever. He called the office early this morning and asked if Deputy Molly Bearpaw was on duty today. I wasn't in yet. The new deputy took the call."

"Huh-oh."

"Yeah. I haven't exactly spread it around the department that we've been working together on this."

"So he told Tacker the department had no deputy by that name, right?"

"Exactly. Tacker was irate. Said some cheeky broad claiming to be with the Cherokee County Sheriff's Department invaded his home and asked a lot of personal questions about his mother's death, while he was still in the throes of heart-wrenching grief for the dear old soul."

"Bull."

"He demanded to know how he could get in touch with you. Fortunately, the new guy never heard of you and told him so."

Molly heaved a sigh. "Good."

"It may not be over. Tacker was still steaming when he hung up."

"What can he do, D.J.?"

"Right off the top of my head, I can think of several things, none of them pleasant."

Molly could think of one in particular. If Tacker found out she was employed by the tribe, he'd lodge a complaint with the council and she'd be called on the carpet. Probably by the principal chief herself, a bright, classy lady whom Molly was very much in awe of. Molly would rather face Tacker again than disappoint the chief.

"I have a legitimate reason to be involved in the investigation," she said, "and it's not my fault he jumped to a wrong conclusion." Instead of complaining to the council Tacker could decide to take matters in his own hands. Molly was more worried about that than she would have D.J. believe. She had seen that look in Tacker's eyes.

"Well, quit rushing headlong into danger without thinking about the consequences."

"I gave it plenty of thought!"

He wasn't listening. "And watch your back, okay?"

* * *

Before going to the office, she emptied a jelly jar and washed it, then drove out Highway 51 to the house where Sherwood Bowman had lived. It was nearly eight; Fred Whillock would be on his way to work about now. Like Sherwood Bowman, Molly had no desire to run into the landlord, either.

She found the faucet easily, filled the jar with water, and headed back to town. No problem, but she was glad to have the chore done. She left the water sample with the county agent on the way to her office.

She was busy all morning and had little time to worry about Buster Tacker or Fred Whillock. She interviewed three tribal members who wanted her to investigate various matters, none of which sounded half as interesting as her current investigation. She agreed to do some preliminary work in all three cases, of course. Since none of the matters were pressing, however, she cautioned that she might not get to them for several days, as she was tied up with an extremely complicated case at present.

A reporter for the tribal newspaper called, wanting to interview Molly for a feature on her and her job, but she put him off for a week.

There were several other phone calls, also, including one from Christine Zucker, who was worried that she'd said too much about Irene Robinson when she talked to Molly on Sunday.

"You didn't tell me anything incriminating," Molly assured her.

"Are you going to talk to Irene?"

"I may, as a routine matter."

"You won't tell her I said anything about her being friendly with Bob Perrone, will you? She could get me fired, Molly."

"I won't tell her we even discussed Perrone."

"I don't want Mr. Darwood to know we talked, either."

"He won't hear it from me."

Christine finally seemed satisfied and ended the call.

Molly spent the time between phone calls bringing the notes in the Country Haven file up to date. She left the office in time to detour by Fred Whillock's house before going to the Oak Hill restaurant to meet Moira for lunch. She wanted a chance to talk to Whillock's wife while he was at work.

Mrs. Whillock was a small, mousy woman. Molly's presence on her doorstep clearly disconcerted her; obviously she recognized Molly from her earlier meeting with Fred. Rather pointedly, she reached out and locked the glass storm door that separated her from Molly as though she feared Molly might force her way in.

Molly stood back several steps from the door and concentrated on appearing nonthreatening. "Mrs. Whillock, I'm Molly Bearpaw."

"I know who you are."

"May I speak to you for a few minutes?"

"My husband says you're a troublemaker. He told me not to talk to you."

"I'm sorry your husband misunderstood, Mrs.—" Molly broke off as the inner door was slammed in her face. Fred clearly ruled the roost around here. Oh, well . . . Molly returned to her car.

* * *

Oak Hill was among Tahlequah's classiest eating establishments. As the name implied, it sat on a hill overlooking the highway, south of the business district, and commanded a scenic view of the town and the surrounding countryside.

Oak Hill's specialties were seafood and prime rib. Since the menu was a bit pricey, at least by local standards, Molly didn't eat there often. In Tulsa or Oklahoma City, the prices would have been considered moderate. Still, a meal at The Shack or a fast-food restaurant cost considerably less. Since

Molly ate out several times a week, she was forced to keep a close eye on her food budget.

She was glad Moira had suggested Oak Hill for their lunch, though. After being rudely dismissed by Mrs. Whillock, she was in the mood for lunch in quiet, welcoming surroundings.

Moira had made a reservation, so they didn't have to wait for a table.

"How's the detecting business?" Moira asked when they were seated. In a figure-hugging bright green dress, she drew several eyes.

"So-so."

"I take it you haven't nabbed a mad poisoner stalking the halls of the nursing home."

"No such luck."

Moira looked at her closely. "You're hiding something, though. You have a suspect, don't you?"

"Not exactly—well, we've found someone who has definitely profited by one of the deaths."

"I guess you can't say who."

"Nope."

"Not even when I remind you, oh so subtly, that you owe me a huge favor?"

"Nope."

The waitress brought water and took their orders. When she left the table, Moira said, "I'm beginning to understand why you like your job. I've been doing some detecting for Felix. Boy, have I had my eyes opened." She reached for her purse, opened it, then snapped it shut again. "Damn, I'm still reaching for a cigarette." She grabbed her water glass and took a long swallow.

"Let's see," Molly said, "it'll soon be two weeks since you had one. I'm proud of you."

"I'm proud of me, too." Moira grinned. "It's the hardest thing I've ever done in my life."

"It has to get easier."

Moira nodded, but not too convincingly.

"You were saying?"

"Oh, yes. Felix wants to cut back on his working hours, take it a little easier—so he's considering bringing in a partner. He placed a notice in a couple of law journals, and more than two dozen applications have already come in, and every mail delivery brings more. It must really be true that the law schools are turning out too many lawyers. Anyway, I started checking some references, to have something to do while Felix is gone, but several cases have turned into wholesale investigations.''

''Oh?''

''I know it sounds boring. That's what I thought, too. But the things people will tell a complete stranger on the telephone.''

''You mean people listed as references by the attorneys wanting to join Felix's firm?''

''That's right,'' Moira said cheerfully. ''Get this. One of the applicants isn't even an attorney.''

''Honestly?'' Molly said with an amused smile. ''What nerve. How did he expect to get away with it?''

''It's a she, my dear, and I suppose she thought it wouldn't occur to us hicks in Tahlequah, Oklahoma, to question her credentials. She said she received her law degree with honors.'' Moira stuck her nose in the air and added, ''from Harvard, no less.''

Her mangled Boston accent made Molly laugh. ''If you're going to fabricate a degree, might as well do it up right.''

Moira grinned. ''She gave one of the Harvard law profs as a reference. Isn't that stupid?''

''This woman has chutzpah.''

''The professor had never heard of her, and he was so incensed that someone would claim to have graduated from Harvard Law when she hadn't, he checked around and called me back. Not only is she no lawyer, she doesn't even have an undergraduate degree. She flunked out of Vassar after two semesters on probation.''

''What was she going to do if Felix actually hired her?''

''Why, wing it, of course.''

''Of course. She probably watches Perry Mason reruns. How hard could it be, right?''

''Another applicant said he had extensive courtroom experience but, according to his former employer, they let the guy handle the defense on what was supposed to be a cut-and-dried property-line case, and he bungled it so badly they lost. Needless to say, they never let *him* set foot in a courtroom again. Furthermore, my contact is sure the man cleaned out the firm's petty-cash drawer when he left."

Moira continued in this vein during lunch: grilled swordfish for Molly, prime rib for Moira. Two other applicants whose references Moira had followed up on had been fired by previous employers for incompetence. A third gave his mother as a professional reference. And two had doctored transcripts to raise their grade averages by more than a full grade-point each.

"This is all very disillusioning," Molly said finally. "Are there no honest people left in the world?"

"If so, they're not looking for work." Moira pushed her empty plate back and shook her head sadly. "Before this experience, I would not have *believed* the lies people tell on employment applications."

As Molly savored the last of her coffee, Moira switched subjects and began talking about the man she'd met recently who "had potential."

Molly listened with half an ear, nodding at appropriate times, but distracted by a faint flicker of conjecture. By the time they left the restaurant, the conjecture had claimed all her attention, and she murmured a distracted "see you" as she parted from Moira in the restaurant's parking lot.

oooooooo

17

At 5:00 P.M., Molly went to Country Haven Nursing Home, only to discover that Irene Robinson wasn't working.

"She had to go out of town on business," said the nurse on duty, whom Molly hadn't seen before.

"When is she due back?"

"This evening, I think. Would you like me to give her a message?"

"No, thanks. It's not important." She hurried away from the station, hoping the nurse didn't recognize her. She didn't want Irene Robinson to be forewarned that Molly was looking for her. Molly intended to confront Robinson with the conjecture—by this time a near certainty—that had lodged in her mind as Moira Pack talked about people lying on their employment applications. She would stop by Robinson's apartment later that evening.

She continued to have the feeling that time was running out, even though there had been no botulism poisonings the past weekend. If anyone had been taken to the hospital, she would surely have heard it by now. If not from D.J., from Mercer Vaughan. If the killer's intended victim was still alive, he'd apparently decided to let things cool off a bit before trying again.

As long as she was on the premises, she decided to look in on Mercer Vaughan. A familiar figure in a wheelchair sat beside a cart containing the dinner trays for A-wing.

"Hello, Mrs. Archer."

She turned her head just sufficiently to glare at Molly out of the corner of her eye. Her white hair looked like a frizzy halo, and the wrinkles on her scrawny neck shifted sideways. Her visible eye glittered slyly, half hidden by a drooping eyelid and thin, white lashes.

"Huh! It's you, up to your tricks again."

"You misjudge me," Molly said, "I'm here to visit Mr. Vaughan." The wheelchair was blocking the closed door to 105.

"Ha! Try to pull the wool over my eyes, will you? Well, you won't get away with it this time. I'm guarding these trays until the last one's carried in."

"That's fine, Mrs. Archer." Molly stepped to one side, and the wheelchair moved until it stood between Molly and the food cart. It still blocked Mercer Vaughan's door.

"You'll have to go over me to shoot the food this time, little lady," the old woman challenged and grinned wickedly at Molly. "I'm fast in this chair, had plenty of practice. And if you try it, I'll holler till they hear me in the next county."

She would do it, too. Molly had heard her. She backed off and a nurse's aide came out of 103. "May I help you, miss?"

"I wanted to visit Mr. Vaughan."

The aide glanced at Mrs. Archer. "Giving you a hard time, is she?" She clucked at the old woman and pushed the chair away from the door to 105. "She's taken it upon herself to escort me today. It's all right, Mrs. Archer. Nobody's going to harm you."

"You're all in this together!" snorted Mrs. Archer and stared threateningly at Molly as she tapped on the door to 105, then opened it a crack.

As on her previous visits, Mercer Vaughan sat in the rocker near the window. He looked quickly toward the door as Molly opened it, squinting.

"It's Molly Bearpaw, Mr. Vaughan. May I come in?"

He lifted one hand from the crook of his cane. "Come."

The nurse's aide followed Molly in. "Ready for your dinner, Mr. Vaughan?" she asked cheerfully.

"Yes'm," he said gravely, but ignored the covered tray after she set it on the bedside table.

The aide left and Mercer said, "Come closer, girl, so I can see you."

Molly moved near to his chair and sat on the edge of the unoccupied bed. "I see you still don't have a roommate."

"No." He watched her intently. "I keep expecting one any day, though."

"How are you feeling?"

"Like I've got a thundercloud over my head."

She smiled. He'd seen those cartoons, too. "I know what you mean."

"Vann Walkingstick came to see me today." Molly knew Walkingstick. He was one of several medicine men who lived in Cherokee County. "He says the Black Man is in this place." He uttered the symbolic words for death with heavy gravity. "But we knew that already, didn't we?"

"Do you know of anybody going to the hospital since Mrs. Tacker?"

"No, and I'd have heard it by now."

"Perhaps it's over, then."

He nodded glumly, unconvinced. "Vann did a *adi': sgahl(v)do dhi':yi* for me." Loosely translated, the Cherokee words referred to a hiding spell, a ceremony to make someone invisible to anyone wishing him harm.

"That's good." She'd meant to cheer him up, but that might not be possible in his morbid mood. To divert him, Molly changed the subject. "Mrs. Archer was blocking your door. If the nurse's aide hadn't come to my rescue, I don't think she'd have let me in."

He smiled faintly. "I heard her. She's been going on about a shooting spree for the last hour."

"She accused me of wanting to shoot the food on the cart. She wasn't about to let me—" Molly halted, struck by a certainty so dazzling that she felt as though her brain were suddenly flooded with light. It had been staring her in the face since the first time she visited the home. Why hadn't she seen it before?

"You all right?"

She jumped off the bed, her thoughts tumbling. "Mr. Vaughan, I just remembered something. I have to go." At the door, she turned back. "Can you hear the food cart when they bring the trays to this wing?"

He nodded, frowning.

"After this, I think you should open your door when you hear it and don't take your eyes off it until all the trays are delivered. Move your chair to the doorway if you have to, to see clearly. Will you do that?"

"I don't understand."

"I haven't quite worked it out, either. Maybe I'm crazy, but please do it."

"All right. If I'm not out of the room, I will. I don't have nothing better to do."

From Mercer Vaughan's room, Molly went straight to David Darwood's office. It was locked; he'd left for the day. She used the pay phone in the lobby to call the sheriff's department. The man who answered said D.J. was off duty. Molly looked up his home number in the book chained to the phone and dialed.

"Thank God, you're there," she said when he answered. "D.J., I think I know how the food was poisoned."

"Molly? Where are you?"

"At the nursing home. We have to talk to Darwood, but he's not here. You have to get hold of him. He'll be more likely to take us seriously if you find him and ask him to meet us."

"Slow down for a sec. What's going on?"

"I can't explain it on the phone. Just find Darwood and both of you meet me at the nursing home."

Her urgency finally got through to him. "Okay. I'll be there as soon as I can. Sit tight."

* * *

"This had better be good," Darwood grumbled as he unlocked his office door. D.J. and Molly followed him inside. He turned on the overhead light and, sitting on a corner of his desk, faced them with his chubby arms folded. "What's so important you had to call me away from my dinner?"

D.J. looked at Molly. "I'll let her explain."

Molly took a deep breath. "I think I know how Mr. Mouse and Mrs. Tacker were poisoned. It was in the food delivered from the kitchen, after all."

Darwood bristled. "Ms. Bearpaw, the health department has given our kitchen a clean bill of health."

"The poison wasn't in the food when it left the kitchen."

"What are you saying? That Mr. Mouse and Mrs. Tacker sat there and watched somebody add something to their food and then ate it?"

Molly glanced at D.J., who shrugged as though to say she was on her own. She'd explained her theory to him before Darwood arrived, but he wasn't completely convinced she was right. "No," Molly said. "The poison was added after the trays left the kitchen and before they reached Mouse and Tacker."

Darwood stared at her disbelievingly. "That's not possible, unless you're saying the aide who delivered the trays added poisoned food to Mr. Mouse's and Mrs. Tacker's meals."

"I don't think it was the aide. I think it was a visitor. Both the victims ate the poisoned food on a Sunday. Isn't that the day when residents receive most of their visitors?"

"Ms. Bearpaw, you can't take two unrelated facts and make them prove anything. Deputy Kennedy, you said this was important. So far I've heard nothing but wild conjecture." He stood, prepared to leave.

D.J. planted himself in a chair, clearly intending to stay awhile. "As long as you're here, Darwood, hear her out," he said shortly.

Darwood returned D.J.'s look, his eyes a little wider than before. Then he walked stiffly around his desk and sat down. He plopped his forearms on the desk and clasped his hands, gazing at Molly as though she were a raving lunatic who had to be humored. "I'm listening," he said, determinedly calm.

"Thank you." Molly was too tense to sit. "While I was waiting, I made a sketch of A-wing." She pulled the drawing from her pocket and laid it on the desk, having shown it to D.J. before Darwood arrived.

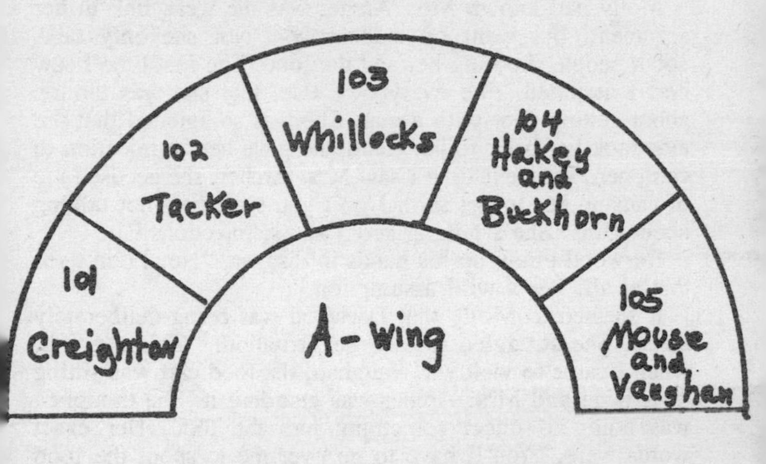

"I've been here twice when the dinner trays were being delivered to the rooms," she went on. "In A-wing, the nurse's aide starts with 101 and delivers them in order, ending with 105. The tray cart is left unattended each time she goes into one of the rooms. That's when the poison was added."

Darwood sighed heavily. "Ms. Bearpaw, this is all very interesting, but where is your proof? In fact, do you have any evidence at all to back you up?"

Molly nodded. "All three times I've been in Country Haven, I've run into Mrs. Archer. Every one of those times she talked about getting shot."

"Mrs. Archer is senile. If not certifiably insane, she

certainly lives in a state of total confusion.'' Darwood's voice had taken on a sneering tone. ''Surely you've suspected that. She's convinced this nursing home is full of people shooting at anything that moves.''

Molly had known Mrs. Archer was the weak link in her argument, but went on stubbornly. ''No, she only talks about people shooting her and the food. The first time I saw her, I assumed, like everybody else, that she was talking about getting shot with a gun. She was so agitated that the aide took her back to her room and gave her an injection to calm her. The next time I saw Mrs. Archer, she accused me of causing her to get shot. Don't you see, she's not talking about guns. She's talking about shots, injections.''

Darwood threw up his hands in disgust. ''No, I don't see that at all. It's a wild assumption.''

It seemed to Molly that Darwood was being deliberately dense. She struggled to hide her irritation. ''This evening, when I came to visit Mr. Vaughan, the food cart was sitting in A-wing and Mrs. Archer was guarding it. She thought I was going to inject something into the food. Her exact words were, 'You'll have to go over me to shoot the food this time.' And then she said, 'You're all in this together.' Look, anybody can buy disposable syringes. Diabetics do it all the time. I think Mrs. Archer saw a visitor inject poison into Mr. Mouse's and Mrs. Tacker's food while the trays were on the cart and the aide was in one of the rooms.''

Darwood pushed back his chair and stood abruptly. ''Ms. Bearpaw, besides being crazy, Mrs. Archer has poor eyesight. She refuses to wear her glasses.''

D.J. stirred. ''Why don't we ask her what she saw, anyway?''

Darwood rolled his eyes. ''Evidently you've never tried to have a conversation with the woman, but if it'll satisfy Ms. Bearpaw, we'll do it right now.'' He marched out of the office, leaving D.J. and Molly to catch up with him.

Mrs. Archer had a private room in C-wing. She was in bed and appeared to be asleep when they entered, but as they approached the bed, her eyes flew open. They held a look of wild panic.

''Good evening, Mrs. Archer,'' Darwood said jovially.

Her eyes flew to D.J., then to Molly, and back to Darwood. "What are you doing here?"

Molly put a hand on Darwood's arm. "Let me." She smiled at the old woman and said in quiet tones of sweet reason, "Mrs. Archer, did you see someone use a hypodermic needle to inject food on a tray while the tray was on the food cart in A-wing?"

Mrs. Archer grabbed hold of the guardrails on either side of the bed with scrawny hands and struggled to get up. "You came to shoot me, didn't you? Get away from me! Help! Help!"

Darwood looked sideways at Molly. "Satisfied?"

"Help! Help!" shrieked Mrs. Archer.

A nurse's aide rushed into the room, coming to a sudden halt when she saw the visitors. "Oh, I'm sorry, Mr. Darwood. I didn't know you were here."

"We're just leaving," Darwood said. "Mrs. Nutter, will you step outside with us for a moment?"

"Everything's all right, Mrs. Archer," the aide said, following the visitors out and closing the door. She appeared nervous, probably because of Darwood's presence.

"Have you met Deputy Kennedy and Ms. Bearpaw?" Darwood asked.

"I've met the deputy," the aide said.

"This is Molly Bearpaw. Ms. Bearpaw, Mary Sue Nutter." Molly recognized the name. Nutter was the nurse's aide who had worked the three-to-eleven shift on the Sundays when Mouse and Tacker ate the food infected with botulism. "Ms. Bearpaw has concocted a theory as to how Abner Mouse and Estelle Tacker were poisoned. Since her theory rather indicts you, Mrs. Nutter, I thought you'd like to hear it."

Nutter shot a frightened look in Molly's direction. "I don't mean to indict anyone," Molly assured her, wanting to strangle Darwood. She went on to explain her theory and ended by asking, "Don't you agree it could have happened that way, Mrs. Nutter?"

Nutter shook her head. "No. I mean, maybe Mr. Mouse could have been poisoned that way, but not Mrs. Tacker."

"Why?" Molly asked.

"Because the Sunday when Mrs. Tacker was poisoned, Zelda Kline and I both had people with us when we delivered all three meals. I know, because Zelda and I have gone over and over everything that happened those two Sundays, trying to figure out how it happened. You see, the weekend of the eighteenth was when the high-school business students spent time observing various businesses around town. Zelda had two girls with her on Sunday when she delivered the breakfast trays and a couple of boys when she delivered lunch."

That eliminated two meals but, based on when the symptoms appeared, Molly and D.J. had already decided the victims were probably poisoned during the late afternoon or evening. "Were there students here at dinner, also?"

"No, but my husband was. When I took the dinner trays around, he was with me." She glanced at Darwood nervously. "One of our children was sick, and he took her to the hospital where our doctor met them. Our daughter had an ear infection. My husband dropped by for a few minutes to tell me what the doctor said. I met him in the hall as I was pushing the tray cart to A-wing, and he went with me and stayed until I took the cart back to the kitchen for the B-wing trays."

Darwood didn't bother trying to hide his smug expression. "Thank you, Mrs. Nutter. You may return to your duties." When the aide was gone, he said, "If you two will excuse me, I'm going home now."

Molly glared after him. "I don't believe it."

D.J. took her arm. "Mrs. Nutter seemed certain of what she was saying, Molly. *I* believed her. Now, let's get out of here."

They walked toward the foyer. "Okay," Molly conceded, "so Tacker's food wasn't injected while it was on the cart. I still say that's how the botulism got in Abner Mouse's food. It's the only explanation for Mrs. Archer's conviction that people have been shooting the food. She may be confused, but not about that. She's talked about it every time I've been here."

"I like your idea that a syringe was used," D.J. admitted. "Everybody says neither Mouse nor Tacker ate anything that didn't come from the kitchen on the days in question, but the kitchen checked out clean both times. Your theory is the only one either of us has come up with that fits the known facts. A hypodermic syringe containing the poison could be carried in a pocket, the botulism injected quickly, and the syringe carried out again without anyone being the wiser." They left the building, stopping beside Molly's car. "It's a neat theory, Molly," D.J. went on, "the only problem is, it apparently doesn't fit Tacker's case."

"If the killer used a syringe the first time, he used it with Tacker, too," Molly insisted. "It worked so well with Abner Mouse, why would he change his method? So, if he didn't inject Tacker's food while the aide was in one of the other rooms, he did it some other time." She drew in a sudden breath. "If it was Buster Tacker, he could have done it after the tray was delivered to his mother's room. Remember, she didn't have a roommate, so only the two of them were in that room. It would have been easy to divert her attention from the food for a moment." She turned to D.J. excitedly. "I know that's how it happened, D.J.!"

"Maybe. Now all we have to do is prove it."

OOOOOOOO

18

Molly drove home, still convinced she was right. As she got out of her car, Florina Fenston bustled out her back door.

"Yoo hoo, Molly!" Obviously, she had been watching for Molly's car.

Molly wondered if Homer had gotten out of his pen and dug up another priceless rosebush in Florina's front flower bed. She was in no mood for more pointed remarks on the responsibility of owners to teach their dogs proper manners. Reluctantly, she walked over to the fence separating Conrad's backyard from Florina's. "Hello, Florina. How is your peace rose?"

"Its system has suffered a severe shock. I've been babying it along, feeding it bone meal. It's had a setback, no doubt about it, but I think it's going to survive, dear."

"I'm happy to hear it."

Florina pulled an index card from the pocket of her dress. "I wanted to share this recipe with you." Puzzled, Molly took the card. The recipe was for something called Glazed Boston Pork Shoulder.

Florina had never felt an urge to share a recipe with Molly before. What was the woman up to? "Uh—thank you, Florina."

"It was my sweet Oscar's favorite." Oscar was Florina's late husband. "Men do love something that sticks to their ribs, don't you agree?"

"I'm sure you're right," Molly said, still at sea.

"Oh, I know all the modern doctors will tell you that pork isn't good for you. Cholesterol, you know. But I shouldn't think an occasional taste would hurt anyone."

"Hmmm," Molly said.

"Perhaps you'll want to prepare that the next time D. J. Kennedy comes to call. I always baked a chocolate cake for Oscar's dessert, when I served Glazed Boston Pork Shoulder. I'll be glad to help you, if you run into any problems. I'm sure you don't do a great deal of cooking, with only yourself to feed. Now that I'm alone, I've learned it's not much fun cooking for one." Florina's bright-green eyes swept Molly's slender form, as though she expected Molly to faint on the spot from lack of nourishment. Then she laughed brightly. "Feel free to call on me if you need me. Why, I made that meal so often for dear Oscar, I could do it in my sleep."

Sounded as though Oscar had had more than an occasional taste of pork, Molly thought. His arteries must have been a mess. Hadn't he died of a stroke? She supposed it would be tacky to bring that up. But all was coming clear now. Florina plainly thought Molly could use some help catching a man. "What makes you think D.J. will come to call?"

"Now, don't you go all coy with me, Molly. I saw D.J. going up your steps Sunday afternoon. He's a fine-looking man. You could do a lot worse, dear."

Molly sighed inwardly. "D.J. and I are working together on a project. He was here to discuss that."

Florina's face fell. "Well, I noticed he didn't stay long. It would have been nice if you'd invited him in, Molly. For something to drink and a good homemade cookie. Regardless of what those wild-eyed feminists will tell you, the way to a man's heart is still through his stomach. When you didn't ask D.J. in, I thought perhaps you'd had a little tiff. You did drive off in quite a hurry after he left."

No doubt she could recall what D.J. and Molly had been wearing, too, down to the last detail, if asked to do so. "It was nothing like that Florina. We exchanged a few words—about business—and then we both had other places we needed to be."

"Oh." Florina pursed her lips, then added, undaunted, "You keep the recipe, anyway. You and D.J. may want to conduct some business in your apartment. If it should happen to be at dinnertime . . ."

"You're too thoughtful, Florina. I'll add it to my recipe file." Molly's recipe file consisted of a shallow cabinet drawer where she kept a basic cookbook, her bread recipes, and a few additional recipes for desserts and main dishes clipped from magazines. She couldn't recall ever making one of the magazine recipes, but they sounded good when she'd read them.

"I have some wonderful cookie recipes, too. My brownies won a blue ribbon at the county fair."

"I'll keep it in mind." Molly went upstairs and tossed Florina's recipe in the drawer with the others. Then she spent more than an hour rereading her notes in the Country Haven file, in the hope that the solution to the mysterious deaths would jump out at her. It didn't.

She pulled out a lined, legal pad and began making a new list of suspects. Making lists was a logical activity, and Molly found logic comforting in times of confusion.

Buster Tacker, motive: Hated his mother and desperately needed his inheritance. Tacker was still number one on Molly's list. The man not only had the best motive and opportunity, she was convinced he was perfectly capable of murder.

Fred Whillock, motive: Inheritance from his parents, killed Mouse and Tacker before parents to throw off investigators? Molly believed Whillock was capable of murder, too, but his motive was less apparent. He didn't seem to be in financial straits. More important, his parents were still alive. Was Whillock biding his time until D.J. and Molly gave up the investigation? Whatever, until an attempt was made on the elder Whillocks, Fred Whillock as murder suspect was pure conjecture.

Ginny, Bowen, and Randy Hulle, motives: None, unless Sally Creighton is still scheduled to die. In which case, Ginny would no longer feel obligated to be at her aunt's beck and call (not that she seems all that resentful of her aunt's demands). Bowen or Randy seem more impatient with Creighton's claims on Ginny than does Ginny herself. Do either of them want to release Ginny from those duty calls strongly enough to murder two strangers and then Creighton? Awfully farfetched. The Hulles weren't exactly prime suspects, unless Molly was missing something.

Bob Perrone, motive: To cause problems for the nursing home, revenge against David Darwood for firing him. (Darwood could conceivably lose his job over the poisonings.) Along with the Hulles, Perrone looked less promising than the first two names on Molly's list. From her one meeting with him, Molly thought he was far more likely to drown his sorrows in drugs then he was to plan revenge. Furthermore no one had reported seeing him at Country Haven on the critical Sundays.

Nellie Mouse, motive: To save Woodrow's contribution to his father's upkeep and to finally be rid of her father-in-law, whom she resented bitterly. When Molly had talked to Nellie, she'd seemed at the end of her emotional rope and had confessed to wanting to "run away." But that was after Abner's death, which had freed her from that particular burden. She remained burdened by the care of her mother, who wasn't in Country Haven. So, Nellie wasn't unburdened in one respect, though she no longer had to part with the money for Abner's care, which had prevented her having such a basic convenience as a dishwasher. Would a woman murder in order to buy a household appliance? Extremely unlikely.

Woodrow Mouse, motive: To save the money he was spending on his father's nursing-home care. Molly didn't really see Woodrow as a suspect. He had truly grieved for his father. And would a guilty man ask her to investigate Abner's death? Not unless he had a compulsion to live on the edge.

Lori Hakey, motive: To retaliate against the nursing home for her boyfriend's firing? To be free of the Sunday visits to her grandmother (which would mean Faye Hakey is scheduled to die next)? An inheritance as yet to be uncovered? Molly was inclined to discount all of the above, as well as Lori Hakey herself as a potential murderer.

Irene Robinson? Would a nurse poison her patients because a friend had been fired by her boss? Too extreme. Of course, if Perrone was much more than a friend . . . Molly left the space next to the nurse's name blank. Perhaps she could fill it in after she talked to Robinson.

When she was satisfied with it, Molly typed the list into the computer, printed it out, and added it to the Country Haven file. While she had the file out of her briefcase, she went over all her notes again. She practically had them memorized now, but she couldn't shake the feeling that the answer was there somewhere, obscured by a mass of unrelated data.

D.J. called at seven to relay the new deputy's report on potential life-insurance policies on the people in the nursing home's A-wing. The deputy had uncovered only two policies in effect.

Lahoma Buckhorn had a ten-thousand-dollar paid-up policy on her life. The Methodist church was named beneficiary of anything left over after Buckhorn's funeral expenses had been paid. Faye Hakey's daughter, who lived in Lawton, had taken out a fifty-thousand-dollar term-life policy on her mother five years ago and kept up the payments herself. The daughter was the beneficiary, with Lori Hakey named as contingency beneficiary, in the event Lori's mother preceded her grandmother in death.

D.J. sounded disappointed. "I was hoping to dig up a whopper on one of those old people, particularly Mouse or Tacker. It would have made a great motive."

"Buster Tacker still has a great motive," Molly reminded him.

Some of the other people on her list had nonfinancial motives, too, which brought Irene Robinson to mind again. At eight that night, she drove to the nurse's house. Robinson was unlocking her front door as Molly parked. Molly got out and called, "Ms. Robinson."

Robinson reached inside and turned on a light and the porch light, then stood in the open doorway, waiting. She was blond, in her late thirties or early forties, dressed in an attractive yellow shirtwaist dress and high-heeled pumps. She looked as though she'd had a long, hard day.

Molly introduced herself and asked if she could come in and talk about the nursing-home deaths. "This isn't a very good time for me," Robinson said. "I've been out of town, and I'm worn to a nub."

"It'll only take a few minutes."

Robinson studied her, frowning. "I know you've been to Country Haven with D. J. Kennedy. After you were there, David Darwood told all the employees not to talk to you alone. What's going on?"

This woman would not be bamboozled by a lot of meaningless words. "I'm an advocate for members of the Cherokee tribe. Woodrow Mouse asked me to look into his father's death. Perhaps Mr. Darwood resents my involvement on that basis."

She smiled faintly. "Racial prejudice isn't Darwood's main problem, if that's what you mean. He's a control freak, a little dictator. He loves calling all the shots for everything that goes on at Country Haven, as well as ordering around the employees. We're supposed to accept his decisions, no questions asked."

"So, if you talk to me and he learns of it, he'll fire you?"

"Maybe, but good nurses are hard to find, and most of them don't want to work in nursing homes. Come on in. I have to get out of these shoes." She kicked off her pumps. "Sit anywhere."

Molly took a chair and Robinson sat on the sofa, tucking her stockinged legs up beneath her skirt. Molly liked her unwillingness to let her boss dictate her behavior away from work, and hated having to drop her bombshell. But if Robinson wasn't convinced Molly had the goods on her, she wouldn't admit anything.

"I can understand why you dislike Mr. Darwood," Molly said, and Robinson raised an eyebrow. "He did dismiss your brother, Bob Perrone, without notice and without recourse."

Molly could practically see Robinson's thought processes. Should she deny everything? Ask Molly to leave? Before she could do either, Molly went on, "I'm aware of the nursing home's antinepotism policy. Obviously, your brother failed to mention the relationship on his employment application."

Her eyes narrowed. "Are you threatening to tell Darwood if I don't cooperate?"

"Not at all," Molly assured her. "I didn't exactly warm to the man myself. Besides, your relationship with a former employee of Country Haven doesn't affect my investigation." She wasn't sure Robinson bought the disclaimer; regardless, if she'd been worried about keeping her job, she wouldn't have let Molly come in. "I have no intention of passing along the information to Mr. Darwood."

Her shoulders sagged a little. Either she was convinced there was no point in going on with the charade, or she didn't see Molly as a threat. "Thank you for that." She studied Molly for an instant and sighed heavily. "When Bob came to Tahlequah, he'd been released from a drug rehab program, his third. He needed to go to work immediately, and it wasn't just the money, either. He needed to keep busy. Otherwise, he'd have been back on drugs within a week." Or a month or two, job or no job. The woman was fighting a losing battle.

"He applied several places around town, but nobody was hiring," Irene Robinson continued. "Then the janitor's job at Country Haven came open . . . It was perfect. He actually seemed to enjoy the work, and I could keep an eye on him. I practically raised him, you see. I'm twelve years older than Bob. Our parents were divorced and we lived with our mother. Bob was only thirteen when she died, and I took him to live with me." She looked wistful for a moment, remembering happier times. "Bob got the job at Country Haven and we pretended we didn't even know each other at first. Then we 'became friends.' "

"Did he meet Lori Hakey at Country Haven?"

"Yes. What do you know about Bob and Lori?"

"I know he's living with her, and she's not too happy about the fact that he's using pot again."

Robinson heaved a sigh of resignation. "That's how it always starts. Smoking pot. But before long, he's using cocaine and other junk, too. Once he reaches that point, he goes downhill fast. Lori called me yesterday and said she wanted him out. I talked him into going back into rehab. I drove him to Topeka today, to the facility where he stayed before."

"What happened to make him start using again?" Almost anything would do, Molly guessed, and Robinson's reply confirmed it.

"Who knows? He gets bored or restless or angry at somebody. He's learned to use drugs to deal with all unpleasantness. And I've learned to recognize the signs right away, so I knew almost to the day when he started this time. I was taking him to N.A. meetings in Tulsa, and he left the pot alone for a while. Then he showed up at work one morning stoned. Probably on a combination of grass and coke."

"And Darwood fired him."

Her expression hardened, and she pressed her lips together. "I begged that bastard to give Bob another chance. I told him I'd gotten to know Bob pretty well, and all he needed was a little understanding and help."

"Darwood doesn't strike me as an understanding sort of guy."

Robinson acknowledged the understatement with a faint smile. "I told him if he fired Bob, it would devastate him."

"Give him an excuse to start using again, you mean."

A chill came into her eyes. Apparently, she preferred blaming Darwood rather than her brother for Bob's relapse. "I know he would have pulled out of it if Darwood had done as I asked. I didn't like the man before—but now—" She broke off and threw Molly a look, as though surprised by what she'd almost said. "Well," she finished lamely, "he had no regard for other people. One of these days, he'll find out what it feels like to be treated like a nonperson, the way he treated Bob."

Molly didn't doubt Robinson's assessment of her boss,

but she thought the woman was less than objective when it came to her brother. Unless she recognized that she was an enabler, she'd spend the rest of her life trying to save Bob from himself.

Having learned what she came for, Molly went through her usual list of questions, for appearance' sake. Irene Robinson had nothing new to add to what others had told her. As she left, Molly assured Robinson again that her secret was safe with Molly. "But I don't imagine you will continue working for David Darwood for long. Will you find a job closer to Topeka?"

"I'm staying here for now," Robinson said flatly, which gave Molly something to think about later. Nurses were in demand almost everywhere. Why would Robinson stay at Country Haven, when she disliked Darwood so intensely for firing her brother? Perhaps because there was something she still wanted to accomplish there?

OOOOOOOO

19

Back at the apartment, Molly filled in the blank space she'd left beside Irene Robinson's name on her list of suspects.

Irene Robinson, motive: In retaliation for her brother's summary dismissal by David Darwood. Robinson was more a mother to Bob Perrone than a sister, and she seemed to have some overprotective maternal instincts. She'd certainly had plenty of opportunity to poison the residents' food, too.

After reading her notes yet again, however, Molly was still inclined to give Tacker and Whillock the number-one and number-two positions on the list.

She went to bed at 10:30, after watching the news. Sometime later, the telephone woke her from a sound sleep.

"Molly Bearpaw?" The voice was husky and low, as though the caller were disguising it by bringing the words from deep in the throat.

Molly's brain was foggy with sleep. "Who's calling?"

"If you want to know how those old people died, be in front of the Park Hill post office at midnight. Come alone."

"Wait a minute. Who—" The caller had hung up, and

Molly wasn't sure whether she'd spoken to a man or a woman.

She switched on the table lamp and looked at her wrist-watch. It was 11:25. She'd been asleep for less than an hour. She got up and put on jeans, shirt, and boots. Should she alert D.J.? She reached for the telephone but hesitated with her hand on the receiver. If she called D.J., he'd insist on going with her. The caller's instructions had been clear: Park Hill post office, midnight, alone. If he suspected she wasn't alone, he wouldn't show himself. She couldn't risk bringing D.J. into it.

A shiver of apprehension ran down her spine. Was she doing what D.J. had accused her of earlier, rushing head-long into danger? But if the caller was on the level, this could break the case wide open.

She'd take Homer, she decided. So he wasn't a terrific guard dog. He was big. His mere presence should give the caller pause, in case he planned to deliver more than information. As an added precaution, she would stay in her car with the doors locked. The caller would have to come to her and say what he had to say through a narrowly opened window.

Having made the decision, she left the apartment before she could talk herself out of it. She arrived in Park Hill with fifteen minutes to spare. Pulling off the road a half block from the post office, she switched off the engine and lights. From where she sat, she had a clear view of the front of the post office, which was illuminated by a bright night-light.

Homer had settled in the passenger seat beside her during the drive, his head on his paws. Now he lifted his head and looked at her questioningly.

She rubbed behind his ears. "Take it easy, boy. We'll just sit here and wait." For the next few minutes, she scanned the shadows beyond the lighted area in front of the post office. No movement caught her eye. Not a single car passed in front of the building. Was the caller already here, hiding, watching her?

The thought caused a prickling at the base of her skull. She had checked the back seat before getting in the car and then she'd locked the doors; but something compelled her to check the back seat again and assure herself, once more, that it was empty. Then she searched the road behind her and the shadowy yards on either side of it, but she saw nothing threatening.

For the first time in her life, she wondered if a gun might not be a comforting thing to have at the moment. But it was only a fleeting thought. She had hated guns since she was six years old, when a gunshot had ended her mother's life. If there hadn't been a gun in the house when Josephine went into her final drunken depression, she might be alive today.

As long as she stayed in her car, Molly told herself, she was safe. She had a sudden image of a gun aimed at her windshield, but forced it away. Why would anyone want to kill *her?*

It was one minute till midnight. She started the engine, drove a half block, and parked across the road from the post office, in plain sight but at the outer edge of the lighted area, where illumination was dimmer.

She sat there for twenty minutes, with Homer beside her, sitting up with his head drooping, half asleep. He'd undoubtedly expected a more exciting outing than this. She saw nothing. Not even an animal or a car passed on the road. It became clear the caller wasn't coming. Had Homer scared him off?

She couldn't have misunderstood the meeting place. Why had the caller chosen Park Hill? Because he or she lived here? She started the engine and drove down the road where Woodrow and Nellie Mouse lived, cutting off the motor several houses away and coasting to a stop. There were no lights on in the house. She restarted her car and backed around the corner at the end of the block and parked where the car would not be visible to anyone approaching or leaving the Mouse home. Leaving Homer in the car, she hiked back down the road and hid behind a clump of forsythia bushes.

She crouched there for fifteen or twenty minutes but saw no sign of life around Nellie and Woodrow's house. She began to feel drowsy, and her legs were going to sleep. If it was Woodrow or Nellie who called her, they'd evidently never left their house, never intended to meet her.

Angry and disappointed, Molly drove home. Maybe it had been nothing more than someone's idea of a practical joke. Whoever it was had known she was investigating Mouse's and Tacker's deaths. But so was D.J., and he had received no call. If he had, he'd have shown up at the post office.

As she reached Tahlequah, she began to think of food. Dinner had been six hours ago and had consisted of a bowl of corn flakes. She remembered the partial loaf of raisin bread in the refrigerator, and a vision of a thick slab, toasted with melted butter and jam dripping off it, and a tall glass of milk, swam in front of her. She headed straight for the refrigerator as soon as she unlocked the door and turned on the light.

Midway, her glance fell on the bed. Lying on top of the rumpled sheets was the lined, yellow page from the legal pad containing the list of suspects, with motives, that she'd made that afternoon. She halted, going very still, listening to her heart beating loudly in her ears. She was sure she had left the list on the table next to the computer. She had definitely not taken it to bed with her.

Later she could not have said how long she stood there, every part of her focused on detecting the sound or scent of a human presence. She could hear her heart thudding and the breath entering and leaving her lungs. She could even hear Homer settling down outside, beneath the stairs. She heard nothing more.

The only sounds Homer made were a few muffled thumps against the garage as he circled in his corner, seeking a comfortable position for sleep. Would he be bedding down if a stranger were in the apartment? Wouldn't he smell an unfamiliar presence and, at least, bark a few times?

She looked around for a weapon, still exquisitely alert. An intruder had been there while she was gone. It wasn't merely the list being in the wrong place. Someone had gone through the Country Haven file, which she'd left on the kitchen table. The folder was still on the table, but her notes had been replaced carelessly, the corners of several pages sticking out of the closed folder. She looked through the folder and found nothing missing.

There were other signs of intrusion. The louvered doors hiding the kitchen were not quite closed. The ballpoint pens on the bedside table had been aligned neatly on top of the memo pad; she had left them beside the pad.

When she pushed back one of the louvered doors, she discovered that a cabinet drawer had been opened and not completely closed again; it stuck out about an inch. The room had been searched. The intruder had tried to put everything back exactly as he'd found it, but several things were slightly off.

Finding nothing better to use as a weapon, Molly took the steam iron from a cabinet and held it, ready to throw, as she moved warily to the closet and opened the door. A jacket hung lopsided on its hanger and a skirtband was pulled loose from one of the clips holding it in place. Evidently the intruder had even gone through her pockets. She straightened the jacket and skirt and closed the door.

Her heartbeat had slowed down. There was no one there now, she told herself, but she didn't fully believe it until she'd looked under the bed and checked the bathroom, including the shower stall.

The door showed no sign of forced entry. He'd probably entered the same way she got into Sally Creighton's house, with a credit card. She made a mental note to have a dead bolt installed the next day.

She was finally convinced that nothing was missing, but the apartment had been thoroughly searched, which was obviously the reason for the late-night phone call sending her to Park Hill on a wild-goose chase. The caller had probably watched her drive away from the apartment. She'd left twenty minutes before midnight, which assured the caller of at least thirty minutes to search the place. Since Molly had spent another twenty minutes watching Woodrow Mouse's house, he'd had close to an hour.

But why?

Since the caller had known about her involvement in the nursing-home investigation, he had to be involved himself somehow. Was the caller the poisoner? Would the murderer know she often worked at home and was likely to have the files relating to the investigation there?

So, Molly reasoned, he was getting worried and had wanted to know how much she knew, if she was focusing in on him (her?) as the prime suspect. Her notes and the Country Haven file had been in plain sight, but he could have searched the kitchen and closet to make it appear he was looking for something else. He'd know D.J. was investigating, too, but he could assume that she and D.J. were sharing information. It was much easier to break into Molly's apartment than to try to get into the sheriff's department files. She'd even taken Homer with her. Homer—she was almost sure—would at least have barked at a stranger going up the stairs.

She'd practically issued the intruder an engraved invitation.

Obviously neither Conrad nor Florina had heard or seen anything, or Conrad would have been waiting up for her, worried sick. In fact, he'd have had the entire Tahlequah Police Department looking for her. The intruder must have left his car some distance away and come to the apartment on foot.

She picked up the list of suspects. The intruder had read it, as well as the notes on all the interrogations in the Country Haven folder. Had he found something that told him she was getting close to identifying him? If so, perhaps it had rattled him so badly that he couldn't remember where he'd found the list and had left it on the bed by mistake.

Or had he deliberately left it in the wrong place as a taunt—or a warning?

Molly shuddered as the last possibility hit home. She undressed and, knowing she wouldn't sleep for a while, got into bed with the Country Haven file and reread every word it contained, picturing the suspects in her mind as she went over what they'd told her. She imagined each suspect as the poisoner, trying to see what she'd written about him from that point of view. What, among all those details, would he feel threatened by?

The motives she'd ascribed to the suspects on her list seemed to her the most potentially damaging words contained in the file. If she'd hit upon the poisoner's motive, he might assume she was close to identifying him.

There was the opposite possibility, too. He might have

felt safer after reading the file, if she'd missed his motive by a mile—or if his name wasn't even on the list. But the intruder had to be one of the people on the list, and the mere fact that his name was there could be threatening enough.

Enough for what? she wondered, as she closed the file. For the poisoner to want to remove her from the case permanently? Oh, now she was being paranoid. D.J. had the same information that she had, and if something happened to her, he wouldn't quit until he got the poisoner.

She felt a little better as she lay down and pulled the sheet up to her chin, but she left the table lamp on for the rest of the night.

OOOOOOOO

20

The next morning, she found an office window broken. Her desk and files had been rifled but, again, nothing was missing. The intruder must have searched the office first. Not finding what he was looking for, he'd lured Molly away from the apartment in order to search there.

Which left her with one of two conclusions. The intruder was now either convinced that she was hot on his trail or that she was looking in all the wrong places. If only she knew which.

She phoned the hardware store and arranged to have the windowpane replaced and a dead bolt and peephole installed on the apartment door. Then she called Conrad and asked him to let the man into the apartment to install the lock and peephole.

"Sounds as though getting into Sally Creighton's house so easily has been bothering you," Conrad observed.

"That's right," Molly said, and let it go at that. No need to worry Conrad by telling him about the break-in. "Better to err on the side of caution." Which was like locking the barn door after the horse escaped.

"Especially with all the craziness going on these days," Conrad agreed.

The new windowpane was installed by ten-thirty, after which she phoned D.J. and asked him to meet her at The Shack for a cup of coffee.

"I really don't have time for a coffee break," he said as he slid into the booth across from her and reached for his cup, Molly having already ordered coffee for both of them.

"But you're here. Thanks."

"Something in your voice worried me. What happened."

"My apartment and the office were searched last night."

A short silence followed, then a soft, "Oh, hell."

"Nothing was taken, but they saw my notes on the nursing-home investigation and a list of suspects with possible motives."

"What time last night?" His voice had hardened.

"Roughly midnight at my apartment. I think they searched the office earlier."

Two lines appeared between his cyebrows, "Are you okay?"

"I'm fine. I wasn't there."

"I assumed that." Something flickered in his eyes. Did he think she'd been out with another man?

"I was sitting in front of the Park Hill post office waiting for somebody who didn't show up." She told him about the phone call and her subsequent actions, ending with her return to the apartment.

His shoulders stiffened, his eyes turned cloudy. "Let me see if I've got this straight. You went out at midnight alone to meet some guy who gives you a cock-and-bull story on the telephone? My God, Molly, what's wrong with you?"

"Not a thing, dammit!" she exploded. "I knew if I didn't go alone, he wouldn't show himself."

"He never intended to show himself, Molly. Holy hell, why don't you think before you act?"

"Why don't you just back off, okay?"

He stared at her, the atmosphere in the booth electric with tension. Gradually, his stiffness eased. He dropped his head and reached for his coffee. He took a swallow and then sighed. When he looked up, his expression had softened. "I'm sorry."

She nodded, biting back another sharp remonstrance. "If nothing else, this proves to me that we're dealing with murder here and, obviously, we're making somebody nervous." She pulled out a copy of the list of suspects with motives and handed it to him. "He could be even more edgy after reading this."

D.J. took several moments to read what she'd written. "What's this about Irene Robinson?"

"I haven't had a chance to tell you. I talked to her last evening. The janitor who was fired by David Darwood is Robinson's brother, Bob Perrone. They kept it a secret because the nursing home doesn't hire relatives. Bob has a history of drug problems and Robinson blames Darwood for his most recent relapse. She took Bob to a rehab facility in Topeka yesterday. Which means, if the poisoner and the person who searched my apartment and office are the same person, we can cross Bob Perrone off that list. Robinson drove back from Topeka and got here at 8:00 P.M., after leaving Bob at the rehab facility. Bob Perrone had no car, so he couldn't have been back in time to search my office and call me at 11:25."

"Unlikely, but not impossible. He could have hitched a ride. I'll get the name of the rehab place from Robinson and call them to make sure he's still there."

"Okay, but if I had to choose between the two, I'd bet on Irene being the one with the nerve to break and enter. That's a strong woman, and it could have been a woman who called me. The voice was blurry and sounded far away, so I couldn't tell for sure. Robinson is like a mother hen protecting her only chick when it comes to her brother, and she just might be vindictive enough to kill a few old people to besmirch the nursing home's reputation."

"And, by extension, Darwood's."

"Right," Molly agreed.

D.J. raked his fingers through his hair. "My money's on Tacker. I'll call that police officer I know in Fort Smith and have him find out where Buster was last night. In the meantime—and don't take my head off, because I'm just asking—do you want me to sleep at your place for a few nights?'' He grinned and ran his fingers through his hair again, leaving it tousled, as though he'd just gotten out of bed. "I'll bring a sleeping bag."

Molly was torn between an urge to put him in his place—again—and a wave of tenderness. But this wasn't the place for either. She shook her head. "I'm having a dead bolt installed today. Besides, I don't think he'll be back. He knows what we have now, and that's what he came for.'' Briefly, she remembered wondering if the misplaced list of suspects had been intended as a warning. But that had been middle-of-the-night paranoia. It seemed improbable in the light of day.

He accepted her decision without comment. "When you left the apartment to go to Park Hill, did you notice any unfamiliar cars in the neighborhood?''

"I've been trying to remember, but I wasn't looking for that.''

"If you did see a car, it's engraved in your unconscious. Maybe it'll come to you.''

Once or twice, she almost thought she could remember a vehicle, like something caught from the corner of the eye that disappears when you look at it straight on. "I'll keep trying.''

They finished their coffee, pondering private thoughts. It was D.J. who broke the silence. "I have to get back. Molly, you will be careful, won't you?"

"Of course.''

He studied her face. "Okay,'' he said finally and left without another word.

* * *

The county agent, Ben Jacks, called Molly at the office Thursday morning.

"I have the test results on your water sample, Molly."

"Find anything unusual?''

"Mostly no, but it did contain a trace of carbon tetrachloride. Did that water come from your own faucet?''

"No, it's not city water."

"Good. If it was, I'd need to report the findings to the water department. Where did it come from, by the way?"

"A water well. No one's using it at the moment."

"Good thing you had it tested. The well needs to be cleaned up before people start drinking from it. Carbon tet's highly toxic."

"I'll see that the owner is notified. Ben, what is carbon tetrachloride?"

"A colorless, nonflammable liquid. If that sample had contained more than a trace, you'd have smelled it. Carbon tet has a distinctive odor. It's an industrial solvent used in the manufacture of fluorocarbons and in fire extinguishers. They used to put it in most household cleaning agents as a spot remover. Some of them still have it, I think."

"How would it get in a water well?"

"Beats me. Maybe somebody spilled some in the well by mistake. Or it could be in the ground water in that area, which might make the source hard to trace."

"Hmmm. Well, thanks, Ben. Would you mail me the test results?"

"You bet."

She'd send Sherwood Bowman a copy of the test results, as promised, Molly mused, as she dropped the phone receiver into its cradle. Would a trace of carbon tetrachloride be enough to make Bowman sick? Would it constitute the grounds for a lawsuit?

She'd let Bowman and his lawyer wrestle with that one. More pressing at the moment was the need to notify Fred Whillock. He would be livid when he learned she'd taken a sample of water from his well, but he had to be told. She looked up Fred Whillock's home phone number and reached for the phone. She would take the easy way out and leave the message with Mrs. Whillock.

* * *

Later that afternoon, she drove out to Country Haven and found Mercer Vaughan sitting on the front porch with another elderly man, whom Mercer introduced as Finn LeMar, his new roommate.

"Howdy, missy," said LeMar, sizing her up. He was small of stature, thin, with big, bony hands that looked misplaced on his skinny arms. He appeared to be in perfect command of his faculties, which should please Mercer, who now had somebody handy to converse with.

Molly settled back against the porch railing as Mercer said, "I been telling Finn about the food poisonings."

LeMar squinted at Molly suspiciously. "They never told my kids a thing about it when they brought me here. If I could afford it, I'd have all my meals delivered from a restaurant." He looked wistful. "Sure would enjoy a good hamburger. The ones they serve here are cooked till they're hard as bricks."

Mercer nodded in agreement. "Maybe the poisonings are over," he said hopefully. "Nobody's been took sick for more'n a week now. And I been watching the food cart like you told me, Molly."

"Have you noticed anybody hanging around it while the nurse's aide was in one of the rooms?"

"Nobody but Mrs. Archer." He cackled suddenly. "She saw me watching it, too, and now she thinks we're partners. Every time she catches my eye, she gives me a big snaggle-toothed grin."

"Maybe she's looking for a fella," suggested LeMar and slapped his leg. "You gotta watch these old ladies."

"No, she ain't," Mercer sputtered, and LeMar cackled.

"Did you have many visitors in your wing last week-end?" Molly asked.

"'Bout the same as usual," Mercer said. "Woodrow and Nellie was here Saturday, brought me some shampoo and deodorant. I sure appreciate them keeping up their visits, even though Abner's gone. 'Course, I knew them all their lives."

"Who else was here?"

"Faye Hakey's granddaughter and all three of the Hulles came on Sunday. So did two ladies, visiting Lahoma Buckhorn. I've seen 'em before. Belong to the church where Lahoma used to go, I think."

"My daughter drove over from Collinsville on Saturday," put in LeMar.

"That's right," Mercer said. "I forgot her. Let me think now. Who else?" He gazed at his hands on the crook of his cane for a moment. "Oh, yes. Fred Whillock and his wife and brother were here, too." He looked at Molly. "That's about it, I guess."

All the people on Molly's suspect list, except for the staff and Buster Tacker. Tacker's absence might explain why there had not been another poisoning, except for the fact that the food cart was being watched. The poisoner could have been there last weekend, intending to inject botulism into food on one of the trays, and been thwarted by Mercer Vaughan's and Mrs. Archer's vigilance. Or, as Mercer had said, maybe it was over.

"We got a new woman in Estelle Tacker's old room," Mercer remarked. "She's got the name of a plant. Fern or Ivy, something like that. She's bedfast. I don't think she's had any visitors since they moved her here from the hospital."

"Moss," said LeMar.

"Huh?"

"Her name's Moss."

"Oh." He squinted at Molly. "You think the food's getting poisoned some way while it's sitting on the cart, don't you?"

"It's only a theory." She glanced at LeMar. "I'd appreciate it if you wouldn't say anything about it, both of you."

"Here I been thinking the kitchen food was safe," Mercer said.

"It may be," Molly said. "I'm not sure of anything right now."

"Did you tell that Deputy Kennedy about this theory of yours?" Mercer asked.

Molly nodded. "He's not convinced that's how it happened, but it won't hurt to keep your eye on the cart for a while, anyway."

"I sure will, and if I happen to be out of the room when they deliver the trays, Mrs. Archer will be there. She follows the nurse's aides to all the wings, not just ours. She's about to drive them crazy."

"I hope they don't stop her," Molly said.

"If they do," LeMar told her, "Mercer and I will keep

on guarding it in A-wing. At least our food will be safe. Don't know about the other wings."

"I don't think the poisoner will switch to another wing," Molly said. "In fact, there's a good chance he won't do it again." She wanted to reassure them, but she wished she felt a little more sure of what she was saying.

She chatted with the two old men for a while longer, then returned to her car. Looking back at the nursing home as she settled behind the wheel, she was relieved that a weekend had passed without another poisoning. But relief quickly gave way to a sense of failure. What new evidence did she have? Only that the killer had let one weekend pass without adding to his list of victims. Which could mean that he'd been prevented by Vaughan and/or Archer. Or he hadn't been at Country Haven last weekend. Or he'd decided to cool it for a while. Or he was finished.

If the latter, he was likely to get away with two murders. No hard evidence tied any one of the suspects to the poisonings. Damn. She couldn't let him go on his way, scot-free. As she drove home, she reviewed her list of suspects, focusing on Buster Tacker. If he was the killer, how would she prove it?

The telephone was ringing as she let herself into the apartment. She grabbed the receiver mid-ring, hoping it was D.J. with information on Tacker's whereabouts the night her apartment had been broken into.

"Molly Bearpaw!" barked a furious male voice.

"Yes."

"You better stay off my property!"

"Hello, Mr. Whillock," Molly said sweetly.

"I could file trespassing charges against you."

"If I were you, I'd be worrying about getting sued. Are you aware that Sherwood Bowman was sick most of the time he lived in your rental house and drank from that well?"

"I only have your word for that, don't I? You're trying to get back at me for running you out of my yard when you came around asking a bunch of nosy questions that were none of your business!"

"Mr. Whillock, I'm doing nothing of the kind. Once the

county agent told me that your well was contaminated, it was my duty to inform you.''

''My wife, you mean,'' he snorted. ''You didn't have the guts to tell me to my face.''

He had her there. ''Would you like me to come by and do that?''

He snorted again. ''How do I know you and Bowman didn't get that water somewhere else?''

''Don't take my word for it. Get another sample and have it tested. Only don't rent the house until the water tests out okay.''

''You stay away from there,'' he snarled. ''If I catch you out there again or anywhere near my wife, you're gonna have more trouble than you can imagine.'' He slammed the receiver in her ear.

OOOOOOOO

21

Molly was eating tuna-fish salad with a cup of chocolate-raspberry decaf when somebody knocked on her door. Peering through the newly installed peephole, she saw D.J.'s drawn face. She threw the bolt and opened the door.

"Hi," he said, walking past her. "Where's your fierce watch dog?"

"I saw Conrad let him in the house a while ago. I saved that dog's life, and he's turning out to be more Conrad's dog than mine."

"You can't trust anybody these days." He glanced around. "You busy?"

"Eating dinner. Have you had yours?"

"No. I just left the station."

"Want a tuna-fish sandwich?"

"Sounds great." He pulled out a chair at the table and dropped into it with a tired sigh. She poured a cup of coffee and handed it to him, then piled tuna salad, lettuce, and tomato slices on a thick slab of oatmeal bread. "You look beat."

"It's been a long day." He finished off half his sandwich

before going on. "Sheriff Hobart's due back next week. It doesn't look like I'll be handing over the poisoner as a welcome-home present."

"Another weekend's coming up."

"The killer didn't strike last weekend."

"Maybe he couldn't. The food cart is now being guarded when the nurse's aide makes her rounds."

D.J. lifted his brows. "Mrs. Archer?"

"Yes."

"Terrific."

She watched him eat the rest of his sandwich. "Mercer Vaughan is helping her."

"At your request, I presume."

"Well—yes."

He gazed at her and a grin tugged at his lips. "One's crazy and the other's half blind and so crippled with arthritis he can barely walk. That oughta scare the crap out of the killer."

She smiled at him. "There's nothing wrong with their vocal chords."

"That's true." He chuckled. "I've heard old lady Archer let loose." He emptied his cup and got up to refill it. "I heard from Fort Smith. Buster Tacker didn't work the night of your break-in, but he claims he was at home from seven o'clock on. My contact questioned a couple of Tacker's neighbors. They both said his lights were on until very late Monday night."

"Which means nothing."

"They didn't see him leave his trailer, but they weren't really looking. As for Bob Perrone, he hasn't left the rehab center since his sister dropped him off."

"Oh." Her voice sagged. "We haven't learned anything new, then."

"Actually, we have. Bob Perrone is no longer a suspect."

Molly poked at the remains of her tuna salad with her fork and frowned. "I never thought he did it, anyway." She tried to shrug off her disappointment. "Do you want some ice cream?"

"What flavor?"

"Chocolate."

"Sure."

She dipped enough ice cream to fill two bowls and they moved to the couch. They discussed the investigation for a few minutes, going over well-trod ground. Nothing new came to Molly, only a cloud of confusion. Finally, she said, "There has to be something we're missing here."

He lifted a shoulder slightly in a small shrug. "I don't know what. I've rolled it over in my mind about a million times. Frankly, I'm tired of thinking about it." He finished his ice cream and set the bowl on the lamp table. Molly was eating hers more slowly, running her spoon around the edge of the bowl. She preferred ice cream half melted. She looked up to find him looking at her solemnly, his eyes very steady and gray.

He cleared his throat. "Do you want to go for a drive or something?"

"Not really," she said awkwardly and found herself unable to meet his gaze.

D.J. was watching her. "Neither do I," he said and wiggled his eyebrows. "Scratch the drive. That leaves something."

She laughed and felt a warm flush creep up her face. She couldn't believe she was twenty-eight years old and blushing over a slightly risqué remark.

His eyes were gentle. "You want me to leave?"

"I didn't say that," came out of her mouth.

He leaned over, took the bowl from her hands, set it beside his on the table, and kissed her. She sat there and let him do it. He tasted of ice cream and, at first, his lips were cool. They warmed up quickly.

After long moments, D.J. lifted his head and said softly, "We're making progress."

She collected herself. "You said you wouldn't hustle me," she reminded him.

He gave her a lopsided grin. "I lied." He kissed her again.

It felt as though she were drowning in warm, thick honey. At length, she managed to surface. "D.J., I'm not ready for this." If only she could say it with more conviction.

He hesitated, then shook his head. "Okay, I'm leaving."

He stood and pulled her to her feet. He held her tight for a moment.

She closed her eyes and buried her face in his warm neck and thought some thoughts that definitely contradicted her claim that she wasn't ready for an involvement. He took a step back, his hands still on her waist, and looked at her intensely for a moment. Then he turned and walked to the door.

Before opening it, he swung around to face her. "When this investigation is over, we're going to have a serious talk." He let himself out.

She gazed at the closed door and resisted an urge to call him back. For the first time she admitted that, between them, something already existed. It was tentative and unclear but, whatever it was, it was growing.

She shook herself and washed the few dirty dishes. Then she took the Country Haven file from her briefcase and read through all her notes one more time, trying to put them together in new ways, looking for discrepancies.

Several of the details she had noted struck a false chord. She shuffled the papers until she found the record of her conversation with the Hulles, laying it alongside the notes she'd made after she and Conrad had visited Sally Creighton's home.

Here it was. Ginny Hulle had said they had hauled off a pile of Coors cans when they cleaned up the house, and, later, Molly made note of several Budweiser cans near the abandoned oil well.

Her brow puckered. It was a small discrepancy, but did it mean anything? Possibly that the teenagers who'd partied in the house were not the same ones who'd gone to the well site. Word would have gotten around long ago that the property was unoccupied, so it was likely that several groups of teens were making use of it. Of course, none of them were apt to admit being there at all. Anyway, it had nothing to do with her investigation.

She sighed and reread the far more troublesome information elicited from Mary Sue Nutter, the nurse's aide, by David Darwood the evening D.J. had called him back to the nursing home. According to Nutter, the food cart containing the dinner trays for A-wing had been left unattended for several moments on Sunday the eleventh, but not on Sunday the eighteenth.

Molly could think of no reason for the aide to lie. In fact, she appeared worried about admitting to Darwood that her husband had accompanied her as she delivered the trays on the eighteenth. Darwood probably frowned upon employees having visitors while on duty. If Nutter had been inclined to lie, she would not have mentioned her husband at all.

Molly put aside her notes and paced back and forth restlessly. When had the food been poisoned on the eighteenth? While it was still in the kitchen? She didn't believe it. Before the trays were placed on the cart, there was no way to know who would receive which tray. It was the aide who arranged them in order of delivery to each wing. In A-wing, she started with room 101 and worked her way around to 105, formerly Abner Mouse's room.

Anyone who was interested could deduce this information from watching the tray-delivery process a time or two, as Molly had, and then know which tray was intended for whom by its position on the cart. Assume, for a moment, that someone had done just that sometime prior to the eleventh, when the first poisoning occurred. Was there a particular reason for choosing Abner Mouse's tray? Perhaps it had been picked only because it was one of the last remaining on the cart. Was that first time a sick experiment?

Moira Pack, for one, had pointed out that there were any number of surer ways to kill someone than with botulism. Fifty percent of those who ingested the poison recovered. And there could have been the additional problem, from the killer's point of view, of where to get the botulism bacilli. If he had cultured it himself and had no access to a laboratory, he couldn't even be sure of what he had.

Moira had been joking, of course, when she'd suggested that Molly seemed to be dealing with a bumbling killer, if indeed she were dealing with murder at all. If the intended victim was still alive, why kill two other old people first? Moira had asked. Were they trial runs?

Molly stopped pacing and gave serious consideration to the question for the first time. All along, she'd suspected that killing Mouse was a smoke screen to make it harder to identify the intended victim, Tacker. Or that the deaths of both Mouse and Tacker were to obscure the motive for killing a third victim, who was still alive. Molly's mind was racing to grasp a new thought. Suppose Moira's remark made in jest was closer to the truth. If the killer cultivated or somehow got his hands on what he suspected was botulism bacilli, but had no access to a laboratory or the expertise to identify the bacilli, how would he confirm his suspicion?

A trial run.

Molly could almost see the shadowy figure, hovering nearby as the nurse's aide delivered the dinner trays to A-wing. He or she had a syringe ready, concealed in a hand or a pocket. When the aide disappeared into one of the rooms, he stepped forward and injected the contents of the syringe into food on Abner Mouse's tray. He may not even have known then whose tray it was. Mouse's and Mercer Vaughan's trays would have been the last to be delivered. Could it as easily have been Mercer's tray?

She imagined the killer, waiting for the moment when he thought he would not be seen, gathering his courage, until there were only one or two trays left on the cart. Mouse could have been a totally random victim, a trial run.

But Mrs. Archer had seen the murderer—seen something, anyway. Perhaps only a glimpse of movement. She had even accused Molly of being the culprit, so it was obvious that she couldn't identify the killer, either because she hadn't seen him that well or because of mental confusion.

Molly felt excitement shiver through her, which she quickly controlled. Don't leap to any conclusions here, she cautioned herself. Even if Abner Mouse's murder had occurred exactly as she imagined, the poisoning of Estelle Tacker remained a question mark. She picked up the thread of her thought and followed it.

After Abner Mouse died, the killer knew that he had possession of the botulism bacilli, and the next Sunday he was prepared to strike again. And that is where Molly ran into a brick wall. When did he inject the poison into Estelle Tacker's food? Could the aide's husband have left the cart momentarily, while his wife was in one of the rooms in A-wing?

It was a possibility she should have pursued before. Mary Sue Nutter worked the three-to-eleven shift; she should be on duty now. Molly grabbed the phone and called Country Haven.

"Mrs. Nutter," she said, when the nurse's aide came on the line, "I've been thinking over what you told us when Mr. Darwood questioned you about delivering the trays on the eleventh and eighteenth." She kept her voice level, with an effort. "You said that on the eighteenth, your husband remained with the cart in A-wing while you delivered the residents' dinner."

"That's right," Nutter said.

"Is it possible he could have left the cart, even for a minute, while you were in one of the rooms?"

"No, I don't think so."

"Would you ask him?"

"Of course. He's at home. I'll call him right now and get back to you."

Molly gave the nurse's aide her phone number and resumed pacing while she waited for Nutter's call. When it came, she jumped and snatched the receiver. "Molly Bearpaw speaking."

"Miss Bearpaw, I talked to my husband. He didn't leave the cart at all that day."

Molly's disappointment was crushing. "He's sure?"

"Yes, he remembers it very well."

"Thank you, Mrs. Nutter."

Frustrated, Molly took a clean cup from the cabinet and half filled it with the last of the coffee in the pot. It was barely lukewarm, but she sipped it, hardly noticing. She stared out a window at darkness. Conrad had sent Homer out into the yard; she heard him under the stairs. She opened the door and called him in.

Homer circled the room, tail-wagging and sniffing the air. She gave him an Oreo cookie, which he ate in one bite. Conrad had probably already given him a treat, so she resisted his pitiful, begging look. He followed her to the couch with a doleful expression and laid his head in her lap. What a manipulator.

She stroked his head absently and went back to her notes, determined not to give up her theory yet. It was the only one she had. She returned to her imagined scenario on August the eleventh: The poisoner waited for his chance to inject the botulism, choosing Abner Mouse's tray, perhaps at random. She could only see him as a black shadow with uncertain outlines. Mrs. Archer may have seen little more—a movement perhaps, a figure hurrying away. Was there any significance in the fact that the old lady had accused Molly of poisoning the food? Even though Archer couldn't identify the person she saw, maybe she'd seen enough to know the figure was a woman.

Mrs. Archer was senile and her eyesight wasn't all that good. Where had she been when Mouse's food was poisoned? If she had been in A-wing or the hall close by, the poisoner would have seen her, and he wouldn't have acted.

She must have been far down the hall, probably approaching A-wing in her wheelchair when the killer turned away from the cart and left the wing. It may not have been the killer at all. It could have been anyone passing the cart, and Archer had built a brief glimpse into a sinister certainty after Abner Mouse died.

Molly stared at her notes, her mind attempting to force its way through some barrier. Forget for a moment that Mrs. Archer may not have seen the killer at all. Blot it out and hang on to the possibility that she had. If Abner Mouse had been a trial run, then there had been no intention to obscure the identity of the intended victim. It had simply turned out that way. Therefore, Estelle Tacker was the intended victim, and the killer was Buster Tacker. He had poisoned his mother's food either right before the tray was delivered to room 102, or after.

Molly was still convinced it hadn't happened before, so she focused on after. Buster Tacker was in his mother's room when the tray was delivered. He had diverted her attention long enough to inject the botulism.

But how would she prove it?

More important, why did she feel dissatisfied with that

conclusion? Was there something else in her notes that she had overlooked?

Something hovered on the other side of the barrier of conscious thought and logical conclusions, a hairsbreadth out of her reach. She stood restlessly, and Homer watched her to see if she were going for another cookie.

When she went to the kitchen table instead, he put his head down and closed his eyes.

Molly spread her notes on the table, placing two sheets containing two separate interviews side by side and examining them for any connection that thus far had eluded her. Then she reached for two more sheets, and two more.

She read what she had recorded of her interviews with Mercer Vaughan, then went on to the interview with Ginny and Bowen Hulle. Something was just beyond grasping, tantalizing, the shape of it almost recognizable. She went back over Ginny Hulle's account of her visit to the nursing home, Sunday the eighteenth, and suddenly a single detail leaped out at her.

If the poisoning on the eleventh was a trial run, the one on the eighteenth was to have been the last, the intended victim finally disposed of. Only it wasn't Estelle Tacker. She had been looking in the wrong place. Now it all made simple and tragic sense.

But then her certainty vanished as quickly as it had come. Where was the motive? If she was right, she had overlooked it completely. If she was right, the murderer would kill again. If she was right, she still didn't know his identity.

Could she prevent a third murder? And how could she prove that she was, at last, on the right trail? There was nothing material—no evidence, not even a credible motive.

She shook off her feelings of despair. She had one last interview to conduct, and she would do it first thing tomorrow morning.

OOOOOOOO

22

Molly arrived at Country Haven the next morning as a nurse's aide was leaving A-wing with the collected breakfast trays. Mrs. Archer followed close behind the aide as she pushed the food cart toward the kitchen, her wheelchair swishing softly on the tile floor.

The door to 105 stood ajar, revealing Mercer Vaughan and Finn LeMar seated in two chairs, talking desultorily. LeMar was picking his teeth with a toothpick, turned away from the door. But Mercer saw Molly and called, "Molly is that you?" She stepped into the room and said hello.

LeMar broke his toothpick and muttered an oath. "They don't make toothpicks worth a damn anymore. Food's always getting stuck between two of my back teeth." He rose from his chair. "I'm going after more toothpicks."

As LeMar passed Molly, Mercer asked. "What're you doing here again so soon? Are you working on a new theory?"

"No," Molly said, glancing at the closed door to 101, "but I thought of a couple of questions I need to ask Mrs. Creighton."

Mercer shook his head as if to imply she was asking for trouble. "Well, get ready to stay a while," he advised, " 'cause you won't get any straight answers. She'll have to preach a sermon first."

Molly feared he spoke the truth. "I better get on with it, then."

"Reckon so," Mercer said, his face falling a little. He had obviously hoped she would stay and chat with him longer. "Think I'll go outside for a walk." He pushed himself slowly out of his chair and reached for his cane. "Looks like we got some rain clouds building up in the east."

"I'll see you later." She went to 101, overcame her reluctance at having to deal with Sally Creighton, and knocked.

"Who is it?"

Molly cracked the door and poked her head in. "Molly Bearpaw, Mrs. Creighton. May I come in and talk to you for a minute?"

Sally Creighton closed the religious tract she'd been reading and laid it on the table beside her chair. Its title was *Signs of the End of the World.*

"Might as well come in." Creighton's bright eyes watched Molly as she stepped inside and closed the door behind her. "You're that young woman who came here with D. J. Kennedy, aren't you?"

"That's right."

"Did you read the tract I gave you?"

Molly swallowed hard and lied, "Yes, ma'am. It was quite interesting."

"Are you ready to face your God in judgment?"

"Yes ma'am." After all, she had never done anything really terrible in her life. A few little lies, maybe, but in a good cause.

Creighton grinned crookedly. "You'd say that, anyway, to keep me from preaching to you." She waved away Molly's attempted protest. "Oh, I've still got all my marbles, and I know what people say about me. Even Bowen and Randy. Ginny is the only one who will discuss religion with me.

Well—'' She eyed Molly with some satisfaction. ''Let it be on their heads. Yours, too, young woman.''

''Yes, ma'am.''

Creighton picked up the tract and offered it to Molly. ''Here. And don't throw this one away before you read it. I have to pay for these tracts. I order them from Reverend Teagarden. Wait.'' She took the tract back and drew a pen from her pocket. She wrote on the back of the tract and gave it back to Molly. ''That's the times when Reverend Teagarden is on TV. It would do you a world of good to listen to him.''

Molly smiled tightly, feeling as though an *S* for sinner were branded in her forehead. Creighton watched her fold the tract and put it in her shirt pocket, apparently willing to let her admonitions go at that.

Molly drew a deep breath of relief. It appeared she might avoid a full-blown sermon, after all. ''Mrs. Creighton, I've been going over my notes on these food poisonings.''

Creighton looked displeased. ''The last day or two, I've stopped worrying so much that every bite I put in my mouth is poisoned. Why do you want to bring all that up again?''

''I'm sorry if I'm upsetting you, but there are one or two points we need clarified.''

Perhaps the *we* caused Creighton to assume that Molly spoke for the sheriff's department. At any rate, she asked without hesitation, ''What points?''

''According to my notes, Estelle Tacker wasn't supposed to eat sweets, but she often sneaked them from the kitchen. I'm told the nursing staff caught her in the act several times.''

''If that's what they told you, it must be true,'' Creighton observed, with a touch of sadness in her eyes. ''But I don't know what that has to do with your investigation. Estelle didn't die from eating sweets, did she?''

''Maybe she did.''

She stared at Molly with some alarm. ''Estelle's son didn't bring her anything to eat the last time he visited her, at least that's what he swears to. I asked one of the nurse's aides about it. Zelda Kline. Zelda probably wasn't supposed to tell me, but Zelda is the talkative type.''

''I know what Mr. Tacker swore to.''

"Are you saying he lied?"

"Not necessarily."

"Then what are you saying, young woman?" Creighton snapped. "Speak up."

"Your niece, Ginny Hulle, says that—"

Creighton's face tightened. "You questioned Ginny?"

"We have questioned everyone who visited the nursing home on August the eleventh and eighteenth, ma'am. Now, Ginny was here on the eighteenth during the dinner hour. Is that right?"

"Of course it's right! Ginny doesn't lie."

"Of course not," Molly said quickly. "Ginny says she left the room a couple of times while you were eating dinner. When she returned from a trip to the rest room, your tray had been taken away."

"This has nothing to do with poor Estelle Tacker." Creighton's voice rose testily.

"Bear with me for another moment," Molly pleaded. "Your niece says that, when she returned from the rest room, your dinner tray was gone, but there was a piece of cake on the bedside table. She thought you had saved your dessert to eat later."

"I still don't see—"

"Mrs. Creighton, did you save your cake and eat it later?"

"How am I supposed to remember a thing like that?" Creighton has assumed a defensive stance. "It was days ago." She stirred in her chair. "But if Ginny said I did, I must have."

"Ginny assumed that's what happened. She didn't see you remove the cake from your tray and put it on the table. She didn't see you eat it."

Creighton flushed in annoyance. "Young woman, what are you suggesting?"

"I'm not implying there was any fault, on anyone's part. But I have to know if that was your cake, or if Estelle Tacker took it from the kitchen and left it here until she could eat it without getting caught."

Creighton's face showed confusion for a moment, as if she couldn't decide whether Molly were attaching guilt to her or not. Then she recollected herself. "Estelle asked the residents of this wing to hide food for her on more than one occasion. She may have left something here that day, I can't remember."

"I think you can," Molly contradicted gently.

Creighton's eyes were sly and then she looked very old, all at once. "It wasn't the first time she'd asked me. I know she wasn't supposed to eat desserts, but if I had refused her, she'd have found someone else. When people get old, Miss Bearpaw, few pleasures are left to them. Estelle was perfectly sane. She had weighed the risk against the pleasure of enjoying a sweet now and then and made her decision. Making decisions is another thing that's often denied people when they get to my age. It makes me mad enough to spit sometimes."

"I understand," Molly told her. "Can you remember when Mrs. Tacker came for the cake that day?"

"After the nurse made her final rounds that night, when she could be assured of enjoying it in private."

"When does the nurse make final rounds?"

"About ten o'clock."

"Thank you, Mrs. Creighton. You've been very helpful."

The age wrinkles in her forehead deepened in bewilderment. "I haven't really." She gave Molly a sharp look. "You're humoring me, aren't you?" she accused, with a lift of huffiness in her voice. "I wish everybody wouldn't think they have to humor old people. It's very tiresome."

"You've got me all wrong."

She sniffed and said with withering disgust, "I suppose now you'll run and tattle on me to the nurses because I hid Estelle's cake for her."

"No, ma'am."

She gripped the arms of her chair combatively. "Let me tell you something, girl. I'm glad I was able to do a favor for Estelle. That cake was the last pleasure she had on this earth."

Molly kept her expression bland. She hoped Creighton and everyone else at Country Haven remained in the dark about what she was thinking, at least until she had something substantial to back her up. She thanked Sally Creighton again and left.

* * *

Molly slept fitfully Friday night. Mostly she lay awake, listening to the rain, hard on the roof. It had started late in the afternoon with claps of thunder that shook the apartment and fierce cracks of lightning. Taking pity on Homer, she let him in for the night. He tried to seek further shelter under the bed, moving about in his sleep as restlessly as Molly did until the thunder and lightning stopped. But the rain continued, a steady drumming on the roof.

The sound should have been restful, but Molly's mind was too active, racing in a circle, like a caged mouse on a wheel. The circle always ended at the same place. There was no credible motive.

Yet she clung fiercely to her instinct that Estelle Tacker's cake had been poisoned while it was in Sally Creighton's room, thus exonerating Buster Tacker, who had not been in Creighton's room and who had left long before ten o'clock, when his mother took the cake to her room.

Molly twisted and turned restlessly in her bed, willing her mind to be still. It would not.

Her list of suspects had been reduced to three names. Insanity had not impelled the killer, so there *had* to be a logical motive, and she must find it.

She slept finally, but it seemed only moments before the telephone woke her.

"Molly, it's Moira."

For a moment Molly could not think where she was. It was chilly in the room and rain battered the windows. In the dull gray light, she saw the tumbled bedclothes and the computer and printer on the table against the wall. Then with a rush, she got her bearings and reached for the blanket that had slipped to the floor during the night. Homer was lying on it, and protested with a yelp and a scornful look when she jerked it out from under him. She ignored him and tucked it around her.

"Hi, Moira." Beyond the kitchen window, the rain-flooded sky was leaden. "What time is it?"

"Almost nine o'clock. Don't tell me you were still asleep."

Molly yawned. "I guess I was."

"I'm sorry I woke you."

"I need to get up, anyway. What's on your mind?"

"Are you busy tonight?"

Was Moira on another matchmaking mission? "Possibly. Why?"

"I told you about the guy I've been seeing—Chuck. Well, his brother is in town for the weekend. He recently started dating again after his divorce, and Chuck asked me to find somebody to make up a foursome tonight. We're going to Muskogee for dinner and dancing. Les is really nice, Molly, and more than presentable. He's a CPA. You'd like him." She paused. "Why don't you say something?"

"I'm waiting for the part where you tell me he's got a great personality."

Moira sighed. "He really does, Molly. Okay, so he's getting pretty thin on top but, personally, I think bald men are sexy and—"

Molly interrupted Moira's sales pitch. "Thanks for thinking of me, Moira, and I have nothing against bald men. But I can't go."

"Oh." She sounded crestfallen. "You don't have to marry the guy, Molly, merely go to dinner with him. Unless you've gotten serious about someone else since last we talked."

"Maybe." Anything to get Moira off her back.

"D.J.?"

"I'd rather not say."

"It is D.J.!"

"I never said that, and don't you dare repeat it," Molly warned.

"Okay, okay, but I'll be checking in for progress reports. Gotta go. I have to find *someone* for Les."

"Before you hang up," Molly said hastily, "when's Felix due back?"

"He got in last night. My nose goes back to the old grindstone first thing Monday morning. I'll probably have to work overtime for a couple of weeks until he clears some of the stuff off his desk."

"I'll call you in a few days," Molly promised and hung up.

A desperate sense of urgency gripped her. Felix Benson would be back in the office Monday and, if she was right, the killer would be under the pressure of time. She threw the bedclothes off and stepped out, shivering a little. She pulled a warm velour robe from the closet and turned on the heater for the first time since April, just to knock the edge off the chill.

It was the last day of August, and they were doubtless in for more warm weather during September, but the extreme heat had been broken. She peered out the kitchen window as she made coffee and oatmeal. No sign of the clouds breaking up anywhere, and rain continued to come down in sheets.

After breakfast, she decided to call D.J. She would have preferred waiting until she had something concrete to offer and not merely another theory. But the urgency brought on by Felix's return would not leave her. A brainstorming session with D.J. might spark a new idea, even if he thought it was an exercise in futility.

When no one answered at his house, she phoned the sheriff's department. D.J. wasn't working today, the deputy on duty informed her. He thought he'd gone out of town—something to do with shopping for ski equipment maybe—although, to tell the truth, he hadn't been listening that closely when D.J. talked about the trip. The deputy was vague about exactly where D.J. had gone. Tulsa, probably, or Muskogee. No, he had no idea how she could reach him or when D.J. might return. He wasn't scheduled to work until Monday.

Molly banged the receiver down in frustration and cautioned herself not to panic. Nothing was going to happen today. If another murder attempt was made, it would probably be tomorrow.

She had to get out of the apartment, though, or go crazy. She folded up the bed and donned sweats and a Gore-tex jacket with a hood. Homer, his snug hidey-hole having disappeared into the sofa, looked up at her accusingly.

"Sorry, pal, but it's time to brave the elements."

Homer didn't move. She didn't much blame him.

Molly lured him outside with the sack of dog food. They raced down the stairs and into the shelter beneath. She filled his food bowl and decided his water didn't need replenishing. She left him to his breakfast and dashed to her car.

She had no particular destination in mind, so she drove to the office and checked the answering machine. She had picked up her messages late Friday afternoon, and no new calls had come in since.

Dropping into a chair, she stared glumly out at the rain. She thought about phoning Felix Benson and telling him what she suspected, but discarded the idea. It would require a long, involved explanation or Felix would think she had lost her mind. He might, anyway. She would have to wait for D.J.'s return. In the meantime, she'd pick up a couple of new mysteries at Computamax, a local book and video store on Muskogee Avenue, and have lunch at The Shack.

The decision gave her a purpose, of sorts, and as she pursued it, her sense of urgency eased a little. She started one of the mysteries while she ate a meatloaf-plate lunch and cherry pie à la mode, and drank three cups of coffee.

An hour later, she drove slowly back to the apartment over rain-slicked streets, wishing she had somewhere else to go, something constructive to do. But she could think of nothing that might aid in the investigation.

Homer was nowhere to be seen. Conrad must have let him in the house. She tried D.J.'s number again, but got no answer. She settled on the couch with the mystery and was soon engrossed once more in the story. It was late afternoon when she finished the book, surprised by the plot twist at the end. She always felt she'd gotten her money's worth if at least part of the outcome was unexpected.

She tried D.J. again, letting the phone ring a dozen times. Still no answer. She brewed a pot of Kona blend and carried a cup to the window. It was still raining, though not as hard as earlier in the day. The heavy cloud cover made it as dark as night at barely 6:00 P.M.

Her restlessness had returned. She desperately needed to talk to D.J. tonight and devise a plan of action. The killer would be forced to make another murder attempt soon. It could be as early as tomorrow, Sunday. She sought to console herself with the thought that the food cart was being watched while in A-wing. When the killer realized this, perhaps he'd conclude he couldn't get away with it again. But that was partly dependent upon how desperate he was. If only she knew his motive, she would have a better idea of how much he might be willing to risk to have his targeted victim out of the way.

Then a new thought struck her like a blow. Sally Creighton was in 101; her tray was the first in A-wing to be delivered. Even if Mrs. Archer and Mercer Vaughan failed to watch the food cart tomorrow, Creighton's tray would not be left unattended. The only time the murderer would have a chance to inject the poison into Creighton's food was after the aide had delivered the tray to 101.

The killer would have only Creighton to deal with then, since she had a private room. It would take but a moment to inject the poison. It wouldn't be difficult to turn her attention elsewhere for that long. After all, he—or she—had done it once before. There could be a problem, though. Only one of the suspects was likely to be alone with Creighton, but if that suspect was the murderer . . .

No, Molly thought, the odds and her instincts were against it. But even if it was one of the others, there was no guarantee the murderer couldn't arrange a few moments alone with the victim.

She could think of no way to protect Sally Creighton except to camp out in her room all day tomorrow. How on earth would she explain *that* to the staff, assuming Creighton would tolerate the instrusion without causing a scene. Which she wouldn't, unless Molly spelled out her growing conviction as to how the poisonings had occurred. Even then, Creighton might not believe her. Without a motive, no one would believe her.

She could not go around pointing the finger of suspicion at people without a shred of evidence. They would be outraged, two of them with good reason. She had not completely scrapped the possibility of a conspiracy, but she thought it was unlikely. They would call someone to throw her out and talk about libel suits, and she would get more than a mild reprimand from the principal chief.

She went to the sink and set down her half-full coffee cup. She'd drunk too much coffee today already. She picked up the second mystery novel, read the back cover, and put it down. She could not concentrate on fiction now. Reality was crowding in on her like the brooding darkness beyond the window.

Maybe a hot shower would relax her. There was nothing more she could do today. She had twisted every fact and supposition, examined them from every possible angle, and she was no closer to an answer than before. She could not find it by more thinking.

Still, she hesitated when she reached in to turn on the shower. Warm water was not going to stop her mind from its incessant circling. She would have to exhaust herself to get any rest tonight. A long walk was a better idea. She would get wet, but that was a small price to pay for a night's sleep.

First, she made another futile phone call to D.J.'s number, unsurprised when there was no answer. D.J. may have decided to stay overnight wherever he had gone.

She still wore the sweats she'd put on that morning. She changed to an old pair of thick-soled hiking boots, pulled a sweater on over the sweat shirt, then grabbed her Gore-tex jacket, pulling up the hood and zipping the jacket all the way to her chin.

She went out into the cold rain. The backyard was a bog; her boots squished with every step. Overcoming an immediate impulse to go back upstairs where it was warm and dry, she bent her head and plunged forward. She got as far as the sidewalk at the front of the house before she changed her mind about the walk. She hesitated, dreading the thought of returning to the apartment to pace.

Retracing her steps, she got in the Civic and backed out of the driveway. Since she was going to get soaked anyway, unless she went back inside, she decided to drive out to

Sally Creighton's place one more time. The answer was there; it had to be.

She clung to that thought as she drove, the rain thrumming on the Civic's roof, the tires throwing out sheets of water. The headlights of the few cars she passed were pale, wavering halos.

When she reached the house, she braked at the head of the long, sloping drive. When she came there with Conrad, she had noticed that the layer of gravel was sparse. It had doubtless not been replenished in years. She would have no trouble going in, but she didn't want to risk getting stuck coming up that steep incline on the way out.

She drove a little farther down the road until she found a place where the blacktop spread out over the shoulder of the highway. She pulled off the road as far as she dared, took the flashlight from the glove compartment, and got out, locking the car behind her.

Briefly, she stood beside the car, wondering what in the world she was doing. What could she possibly discover by trudging through the mud and darkness? But she was there. If nothing else, she would walk off her restlessness.

She dropped her keys into a jacket pocket, ran back up the road, and plunged down the driveway leading to the house.

The wavering beam of the flashlight disclosed deep, fresh tire tracks. Someone, probably a carload of teenagers, had been there since the rain started. There was no car near the house now. They must have come last night.

She walked around the house, shining her light on doors and windows. There was no evidence of a break-in since the broken windows had been boarded up, no discarded litter in any of the rooms that she could see.

She returned to the fresh tire tracks, now noticing that the vehicle had passed the house. The tracks showed no evidence of a car having even stopped there; instead, they continued into the woods. Evidently, the car had been headed for the clearing where she and Conrad had found beer cans on their previous visit. Surprised that anyone would risk getting stuck out there, Molly hesitated at the edge of the trees, raising the flashlight to send a pale arc across the dark, dripping branches.

The woods were black and ominous. Apprehension rippled through her, and she shook it off with difficulty. Don't be ridiculous, she scolded herself. There was nothing here *now*, except perhaps an abandoned car, stuck in the mud.

Wishing she had thought to wear gloves, she tugged her hood close around her face, hunched her shoulders against the chill, and entered the woods. The flashlight beam pierced a blackness that was almost total. Leaf-laden branches sheltered her from some of the rain, while magnifying its sound tenfold.

She walked as fast as she dared in the darkness, eager to be clear of the oppressive, dripping trees, her boots sinking deep into wide tread marks. With every step, she felt more foolish. Of all times to trek across Sally Creighton's acreage, she had to be nuts to have chosen this one. She almost turned back, but the trees were thinning out. She was nearing the edge of the woods, and the clearing was just the other side. At least she could confirm her suspicion that the tracks she was following stopped there.

Before she was completely clear of the trees, however, she heard the sounds of a revving motor and tires spinning in mud. She halted and instinctively turned off the flashlight. Instantly blackness engulfed her.

The vehicle was in the clearing, turned sideways to the woods, having slid half around as the driver buried its tires deeper in mud. Its headlights illuminated a grove of trees to the east of the abandoned well site. An unpleasant and faintly familiar odor hung in the air.

Molly crept off the path, toward the edge of the trees, feeling her way. She didn't dare turn on the flashlight. She stopped beside the thick trunk of an elm and realized for the first time that the vehicle was a truck, not a car. A large tank truck. All she could see of the driver was a dim shadow.

He stopped racing the motor abruptly and the door of the cab flew open. The driver climbed out. He—at least she thought it was a man—wore a dark, hooded slicker. Even when he crossed through his headlight beams, she couldn't see his face. He turned on a flashlight and made a complete circle of the truck, assessing his situation.

If he had to walk out, he would come along the path Molly had so recently walked down. Would he notice her footprints? She couldn't risk returning to the path now.

The driver climbed back into the truck. Molly stayed where she was. He began shifting from forward to reverse and gunning the motor, trying to rock the tires free of the hole they'd dug.

He was occupied in the clearing for the time being. Quickly, Molly made her way to the path and, with her back to the clearing, turned on her flashlight. Slogging and sliding, she ran back the way she had come. If she were concealed beside the road as he came out, she might be able to see his face.

Behind her, the truck's motor whined and stopped, whined and stopped. As she cleared the woods at the back of the house, the whining reached a crescendo as the truck tires spun free. The driver gunned the motor hard—keeping the heavy truck moving fast was the only chance he had of staying unstuck—as the truck headed for the path through the woods. The sound of the motor grew louder as Molly ran toward the driveway. She hadn't reached the house when she realized he was coming so fast the headlights would pick her up any second.

The hard rain had beaten down the tall grass that had concealed the cellar. She caught a glimpse of the door as she switched off her flashlight. The cellar door was the only concealment near enough to reach before the truck came out of the woods and its headlights swept the yard and house. She darted toward it, gasping for breath. With both hands, she grabbed the edge of the cellar door and lifted it high enough to scramble down the steps. She brought the door down on top of her. The dull thud as it hit the facing sounded like the crack of doom. But surely he couldn't hear it over the sound of the motor.

The inky blackness was so thick she felt as though she would choke on it as she huddled on the stairs. The truck roared loudly as it passed close to the cellar. Please God, he hadn't seen her! Her fingers were cold and shaking as she fumbled with the switch of the flashlight, finally succeeding in turning it on.

Gradually the sound of the motor diminished. He hadn't even slowed down at the house. He hadn't seen her, then. But as her heart eased out of her throat, it occurred to her that he couldn't have stopped, even if he had seen her. He wouldn't slow down until he'd reached the paved highway. Then he'd see her car.

Oh, God, what should she do? Stay where she was, or try to hide in the woods? Calm down and think, Molly!

He would see an abandoned Civic parked on the shoulder of the road, but would he recognize it as hers? Chances are, he wouldn't. In which case—if he hadn't seen her duck into the cellar—he would assume that the driver had had car trouble and hiked to the nearest occupied house or been picked up by a passing motorist.

The cellar door was heavy and thick, and she couldn't hear the sound of a motor now. If the parked car made him suspicious enough to leave the truck and walk back, she would be running a bigger risk by leaving the cellar now. He'd spot her for sure.

She turned the flashlight beam on the steps and went all the way down. There was little enough to protect herself with, in case he decided to check the cellar. She tugged at the shelves along the walls, looking for a board that was loose enough to pull out. None of them moved. That left the kerosene lamps and lantern on the top shelf. The lantern looked heavier. It had a metal base and a handle by which it could be swung. If she were waiting on the stairs and hit him in the face, she might be able to get past him while he was stunned. With surprise and luck on her side, she could get away.

She placed the flashlight on a shelf near the top and stood on the bottom shelf to reach the lantern. She lifted it down, grabbed the flashlight, and crept back up the stairs. Bent over with her ear close to the door, she could hear nothing but the steady beat of the rain on the other side.

Within a few minutes, her calves were cramped and her back ached fiercely. If he were coming back, she told herself, he'd have reached the cellar by now. After another moment of strained listening, she moved down far enough to sit on a step, keeping the lantern handle firmly gripped in one hand and the flashlight in the other.

The beam played across the empty, stained shelves, on which Sally Creighton had once kept home-canned vegetables and fruit. Molly's fright had subsided enough so that she was thinking clearly again. As she stared at the shelves, suddenly she knew where the killer had gotten the botulism bacilli. The truth was literally staring her in the face.

For another half hour, she sat on the cellar steps, wet and shivering, before she cracked the door wide enough to peer out. Of course, she could see nothing. But she didn't hear anything, either. Slowly, she opened the door wider and finally stepped out. No one jumped her.

She edged around a back corner of the house and moved forward. She still had the lantern, just in case, as she hurried up the driveway. Again, she smelled the acrid odor that she had noticed when she was watching the well site from the shelter of the woods. What was that smell? It reminded her of a powerful spot remover she had used once or twice to take the stubborn stains from clothing.

As she reached the top of the driveway, it all came together. The tank truck at the abandoned well site after dark. A pile of beer cans, a different brand from those found in the house. Carbon tetrachloride in a water well not a half mile from Sally Creighton's acreage.

She knew why the killer could not afford to let Sally Creighton give the property away.

OOOOOOOO

23

Who had been driving the tank truck? As she drove to town, Molly replayed in her mind the glimpse of the driver she'd had as he left the cab and circled the truck, but she couldn't see his face. The only thing she knew definitely was that he drank Budweiser.

Where was he now? She assumed he'd leave the truck behind the dry cleaners and pick up his car before going home. Maybe she could catch him in the act.

She found Muskogee Avenue virtually deserted and broke the speed limit all the way to her destination, praying there was no police car lying in wait on one of the side streets she passed. She skidded into the alley beside Hulle Dry Cleaners and wheeled into the parking space behind the building. The tank truck was the only vehicle there. She'd stayed in the cellar long enough for him to pick up his car and drive away.

She banged a fist against the steering wheel in frustration. Backing out of the alley, she headed for the nearest gas station, where she asked to use the telephone. It was a long chance, but maybe he hadn't reached home yet.

She looked up Bowen and Ginny Hulle's number and dialed it first. There was no answer. Could there have been two people in the truck? She had been too intent on watching the driver when he opened the cab door to notice if someone was in the passenger seat. The rest of the time it had been too dark to tell.

She hung up and dialed Randy Hulle's number. A woman answered.

"Lucinda?"

"Yes, who's this?" She sounded cross.

"Molly Bearpaw. Remember me?"

"Of course."

"Is Randy there?"

"Not at the moment. He went to the store to pick up some ice cream for me. Randy doesn't know how to say 'I'm sorry,' and the ice cream is his way of apologizing."

"Apologizing?"

"We had a fuss earlier. He's taking me to Tulsa Monday, too. I get to pick out a mink jacket."

"How nice for you. Has Randy been gone long?"

"Only a few minutes this time. He left as soon as he showered and dressed."

"This time?"

"He's been in and out all day."

"What was he doing?"

"Don't ask me. I didn't talk to him. I was giving him the silent treatment. I wanted to go to a movie, but he didn't get back in time. That really got me boiling."

"I see. Thanks a lot, Lucinda."

Molly hung up and wondered what to do next. She drove around town for a few minutes, looking for the elder Hulles' Oldsmobile or Randy Hulle's pickup. She didn't see either vehicle.

Nothing will happen tonight, she kept telling herself, but she was still too shaken by her experience at Sally Creighton's home to take anything for granted. All three of the Hulles had probably visited Creighton last Sunday. Bowen Hulle had said that he and Randy usually went with Ginny every Sunday. But there had been no poisoning last weekend. The murderer may have been prepared to act, but had not been alone with Creighton when a meal was delivered. He probably knew that Sally Creighton had contacted her attorney's office about changing her will, and he might know, also, that Felix would be back at work Monday. It could take a few days to have the will drawn up and witnessed, but could the killer count on that? To be on the safe side, he had to act before Monday.

Even though she was wet and tired and longed for a hot shower and bed, Molly decided to drive out to Country Haven before going home. She had to think of some way to warn Sally Creighton without frightening her half to death or actually spelling out her suspicion.

Two blocks before reaching the nursing home, she noticed the back end of a red pickup truck in an alley, protruding from behind a convenience store. She whipped into the alley. The pickup looked like Randy Hulle's. Evidently he was buying ice cream, as his wife had said. But there could be more than one pickup like that in town, and Molly wanted to see Randy with her own eyes.

She drove around to the front of the convenience store, parked next to an old Ford sedan, and went in. The man behind the counter was reading a magazine and barely glanced at her as she entered. A single customer, a woman, was surveying the candy counter.

"Is that your red pickup parked in the alley?" Molly asked her.

The woman looked up, startled. "No. My car's in front, the Ford."

Molly went to the counter. "Is that your red pickup parked outside?"

The clerk put down his magazine. "Where?"

"In the alley behind the store."

He shrugged. "It's not mine."

"You don't know who it belongs to?"

"No. Probably somebody using the pay phone around the corner there."

Molly ran out. The pickup was still there and no one was anywhere near the pay phone. She wouldn't panic, she told herself. She wasn't even sure the pickup was Randy Hulle's. But if it was, he'd parked and walked wherever he was going, which could mean he didn't want to be seen there. She jumped in the Civic and drove to the nursing home.

There was no Oldsmobile among the few cars parked in front of Country Haven. There were lights in the lobby and in some of the patient rooms, but the building appeared peaceful, slumbering. Molly parked and hurried inside. Hushed silence greeted her. There was no sign of any activity anywhere.

But the feeling of panic was stronger than ever. She started running down the hall toward A-wing, her mud-clogged boots thumping loudly on the tiles. Irene Robinson came out of the area where the nurse's station was located, frowning, and walked toward Molly. "Some of our people are asleep. You'll have to be quiet." Then she recognized Molly. "Miss Bearpaw! You're tracking mud everywhere!"

"I hope mud is the only problem you have to deal with," Molly said as she brushed past Robinson without slowing down. The door to 105 was the only one in A-wing that was open. Mercer Vaughan and his roommate, Finn LeMar, hearing the sound of running feet, had come out of their room and were standing in the hall.

Mercer was squinting fiercely. "Molly, is that you?"

"Have you seen anyone go into Sally Creighton's room?"

Both old men shook their heads, their mouths open. Having already made a spectacle of herself, Molly didn't hesitate to push open the door to 101 and enter the unlighted room.

Muffled sounds came from the bed. Molly switched on the light, revealing Sally Creighton's prone, twisting body with a pillow clamped to her face, held there by the man who was kneeling over her on the bed. He looked at Molly, wild-eyed. It was Randy Hulle.

Molly yelled, "Help!" and grabbed his arm to pull him off Sally Creighton.

He seemed frozen for a moment, and then he leapt off the bed, ran to the window, tried to open it, gave up, and looked around frantically for something to break the glass with.

In the meantime, Irene Robinson had rushed in. "Are you all right, Mrs. Creighton? Can you sit up?"

Sally Creighton was too busy gulping air to speak.

Mercer Vaughan and Finn LeMar hovered in the doorway. Suddenly, Mercer hobbled into the room, shouting, "No, you don't, mister!"

Randy Hulle had picked up a chair and was lifting it to break the window when Mercer began beating him about the head and shoulders with his cane. Hulle let go of the chair and shoved Mercer aside. The old man fell on his backside, his cane clattering to the floor.

Hulle ran for the door, but Mrs. Archer had materialized from somewhere and her wheelchair blocked his exit. Behind the wheelchair, the other residents of A-wing had formed a human barrier.

"We gotcha now!" Mrs. Archer yelled triumphantly.

Hulle was crouched in the doorway, clearly wondering if he could get out by throwing himself at the old people.

"It's over, Randy," Molly said. "Don't make it worse by hurting someone else. Call the sheriff's department, somebody."

Sally Creighton had got her breath back and was sitting up on the side of the bed. Her cotton nightgown was bunched up in her lap, her scrawny, blue-veined legs dangling, but she didn't seem to notice. "I was in bed, reading, when he came," she was saying, glaring at Randy, who was slumped in a chair, his head in his hands. "He said he'd read Reverend Teagarden's tracts and he wanted to discuss them with me. The first thing I knew, the light went out and he had that pillow over my face. I should have known he was up to something. That boy never had a religious bone in his body."

Randy lifted his head and shot her a look of pure hatred.

Creighton shrank back. "Look at his eyes!" she screamed. "He's demon-possessed! Can't you see it?"

OOOOOOOO

24

They were in the nursing home's dining room, seated around a long table. It was almost nine o'clock. One of the two sheriff's deputies who had answered the call from Country Haven had arrested Randy Hulle and taken him to jail. A younger deputy named Crumbley had just finished taking everybody's statements when D.J. showed up.

"I stopped by the station when I got home," he announced. "All the Hulles were there with their lawyer." His eyes roamed the room and settled on Molly. "Good God, Molly, what happened to you?"

"I'm wet and muddy and tired. Aside from that, I'm fine."

"That girl saved my life," Sally Creighton said.

"I had a lot of help from your neighbors," Molly said.

Creighton nodded. "I guess the good Lord wasn't ready to call me home yet."

"I've taken everybody's statements, D.J.," Crumbley said. "You people can go about your business for now."

As the employees and residents of A-wing left the dining

room, D.J. wailed, "Will somebody tell me exactly what happened here?"

"Randy Hulle tried to smother old Mrs. Creighton with her pillow," Crumbley said. "He would have, too, if Molly hadn't arrived when she did."

D.J. pulled out a chair and sat down at the table across from Molly. "You *knew* Randy had come out here to kill Mrs. Creighton?"

She shook her head. "I just had a feeling that somebody might try to kill her this weekend. I tried to reach you all day, D.J."

"I was in Tulsa, buying ski outfits for Courtney and me. God, of all days to pick."

"Well, finally, I gave up and drove out to Sally Creighton's place. It was dark and—"

D.J. raised a hand. "Back up, okay? What made you go to Sally Creighton's place tonight?"

Wearily, Molly pushed her tangled hair off her face. Crumbley said, "Give her a break, D.J. She's already been through this. I've got it all in my notes."

"It's okay," Molly said. "I don't mind telling it again."

"I'm going back to the station," Crumbley decided.

"I'll be by there later," D.J. said, his eyes still on Molly.

Crumbley left as Molly was saying, "Yesterday, I was thinking about the investigation and I remembered that one of the people I talked to said in jest that maybe Abner Mouse's poisoning was a trial run."

"A trial run," D.J. echoed blankly.

"It got me thinking. If the killer had cultivated the botulism himself or had found something that he suspected might contain the bacilli, he had to find out if the food indeed contained the poison. Randy Hulle got it from home-canned green beans, by the way, although I didn't realize that until later. Randy said that much to the deputy who arrested him, before he decided to clam up. When he and his parents cleaned up around Creighton's house, Randy hauled off several pickup loads of trash, which included some jars of home-canned green beans that had been in Creighton's cellar for years. When I went out there the first time, I noticed circular stains on the shelves in the cellar.

Apparently the seals on some of the jars hadn't held, and the contents had leaked out."

"That's what gave him the idea to give Creighton food poisoning?"

"I'm sure that's what happened. He'd been trying to come up with a way to kill her before she had a chance to deed the property to that TV preacher. The green beans were a gift."

"You're saying he put some of the liquid in Abner Mouse's food to see what would happen?"

"That's what I'm saying."

"Holly hell, that's nuts."

"He used a syringe and Mrs. Archer saw him, and that's why she kept raving about the food getting shot. I don't know why she couldn't identify him, but I suspect she got only a glimpse from a distance and her eyesight's not very good. Since she'd been carrying on about people shooting *her* for quite a while, nobody took her seriously."

D.J. looked incredulous. "But why Mouse?"

"I'm not even sure Randy knew whose food he'd injected. Anyone would have done. He didn't try it on Creighton the first time, because her tray is always the first to be delivered by the nurse's aide, so it wasn't left untended on the cart. The aide starts with 101, Creighton's room, and works her way around to 105."

"Mouse's room," D.J. put in.

Molly nodded. "Mouse's and Vaughan's trays were the last to be delivered. Randy had probably been waiting for his chance, and maybe it didn't come until only one or two trays were left."

"So, after Mouse died, he knew he had the botulism," D.J. observed. "Why didn't he use it on Creighton next?"

"He thought he had. When I was reading through my notes yesterday, I noticed something that had escaped me before. Several people mentioned that Estelle Tacker frequently tried to steal desserts from the kitchen. Sometimes the nurses caught her before she ate the food, sometimes they didn't. It never occurred to me to wonder where she hid the food when they didn't find it, until yesterday as I was reading my notes. Ginny Hulle told me that on Sunday the eighteenth, the day that Estelle Tacker was poisoned, she left her aunt's room a couple of times while Creighton was eating dinner. When she came back from the rest room, Creighton's dinner tray had been picked up but Ginny noticed a piece of cake sitting on the bedside table. She assumed Creighton was saving it for later."

D.J.'s eyes lit up. "You wondered if she was saving it for Estelle Tacker?"

"Yes, so I came out here and asked Creighton. She admitted that Estelle Tacker had brought the cake in while she was eating dinner and asked her to keep it until after the nurse's ten-o'clock round. Creighton had no idea what I was getting at, and I didn't tell her. I had no proof. But I realized that if I was right, Buster Tacker wasn't the killer. He'd left the nursing home long before Tacker came after the cake that night. Which meant that Sally Creighton had been the intended victim. I just couldn't figure out what any of the Hulles had to gain by her death."

"I gather it had something to do with the illegal dumping of toxic waste," D.J. said. "I heard some of what Ginny and Bowen Hulle were saying when I was at the station. Apparently it was Randy's job to collect the used cleaning solution from all the Hulle's dry-cleaning plants and deliver it to the waste dump over in Arkansas. I've heard it costs several thousand dollars to dump an entire tank-truck load, and Randy told Bowen they could get a ten-percent discount if they paid in cash. I don't think Ginny Hulle knew anything about it. She was berating Bowen for being gullible. Bowen admitted that he suspected the people at the dump were pocketing the money. Of course it never entered his mind that Randy was keeping the cash. He kept saying, 'But he makes a good living. Why would he steal from us?' "

"He was trying to keep his wife happy," Molly said. "She told me when I questioned her that every time she mentioned getting a job or they had an argument, Randy bought her something. He had promised to take her to Tulsa Monday to get a mink jacket." Molly went on to explain about the abandoned oil-well shaft, into which Randy had pumped the toxic waste, and the Sherwood Bowman investigation, by which she'd discovered there was carbon tetrachloride in a water well near Sally Creighton's property. "The county agent told me that carbon tet is used in cleaning agents, among other things, but I didn't make the connection with the Hulles."

D.J. frowned. "No telling how far it's traveled. The groundwater in that whole area out there could be polluted."

"We have to notify the EPA first thing Monday morning."

"In the meantime," D.J. added, "I better send some deputies to the houses on either side of Creighton's for a mile or two, to tell them not to drink any more water from their wells until they have it tested."

"If there's much carbon tet in the water, they'd have smelled it. Maybe it's not widespread."

D.J. sighed. "The EPA will determine how much damage has been done. The Hulles will be hit with a big fine, too. Lately the EPA has really been cracking down on illegal dumpers. Fines have been running into six figures."

"All the more reason Randy needed to get rid of Creighton before she deeded that property to the TV evangelist. I learned today that Creighton's lawyer is back in town, so I suspected the killer would do something this weekend. I got pretty agitated, and when I couldn't get hold of you, I didn't have anyone to talk to about it. I knew there had to be something that made Sally Creighton's place valuable, at least to the killer. I decided to go out there tonight and see if I could figure out what it was. Randy was at the well site. He'd dumped a load—the smell was so strong it was almost nauseating, and I finally put that together with the carbon tet found in the water well up the road. The tank truck was stuck in the mud at the site when I got there. I saw Randy walking around, but I couldn't tell who it was. I was pretty sure it was a man, though, so it had to be either Bowen or Randy. When I got back to town, I phoned both their houses to see if they were home. Bowen and Ginny didn't answer, but Randy's wife told me he'd gone out to buy ice cream."

"You didn't believe her?"

"I believed that's what *she* believed. But I wanted to check on Sally Creighton. I didn't think he'd act until tomorrow when several visitors would be in A-wing. He must have slipped in tonight without anyone seeing him. Anyway, Creighton's meals are always delivered first—"

"Which meant the killer had to get to it after it was in her room."

"Right. I thought I could at least warn Creighton not to take her eyes off her food tomorrow after it was delivered. It was pure luck that I arrived in time to interrupt Randy in the act of trying to smother her. Irene Robinson was still yelling that I was tracking in mud when I burst into Creighton's room." She laughed tiredly. "You should have seen Creighton's neighbors come to my aid. Mercer Vaughan beat Randy with his cane and got knocked on his rear for his trouble, then Mrs. Archer blocked the door with her wheelchair. All the others closed ranks behind her with blood in their eyes. I'll go into all the details when I can think about something besides a hot shower and bed."

D.J. reached for her hand across the table. "I've kept you here too long. Thanks for giving me the highlights. Can you stay awake long enough to drive home? I can take you and you can pick up your car tomorrow."

"No, I'll make it. Barely." Before anything else, she would have to stop and fill Conrad in on what happened tonight, before he heard a convoluted version on the grapevine. She pushed back her chair. "Don't look so grim. I'll be good as new tomorrow."

"Maybe we can have that talk then," he said, watching her.

She hesitated only briefly. "Come for breakfast. I'll dig out the waffle iron my grandmother gave me." Florina Fenston would be proud of her.

His smile widened. "I thought you'd never ask."

"You caught me in a weak moment." She waved as she left the dining room.

A gleam came into his eyes as he watched her go.

OOOOOOOO

25

Mercer Vaughan couldn't sleep. The sharp pain in his hip persisted no matter which way he turned in his bed. It was the hip that had taken most of his weight when Randy Hulle shoved him down in Sally Creighton's room last night.

After all the commotion was over and the deputies had left, the doctor had come out to examine him. Mercer hadn't asked for the doctor, hadn't needed him. But the nurse wasn't taking any chances. The food-poisoning deaths and Woodrow Mouse's threat to sue the nursing home had the staff on edge, and they were much more attentive to the residents than before. That was about the only good thing that had come out of the events of the past few weeks.

The doctor had said it was a wonder Mercer hadn't broken any bones. It was no wonder to Mercer. He'd been protected by Vann Walkingstick's hiding spell, which had made him invisible to Hulle. Randy had felt the blows of Mercer's cane, though, and had swung his arm out to stop them, grazing Mercer and causing him to lose his balance and fall.

The pain in his hip finally forced him from the bed. The predawn sky beyond his window was the color of lead. It took a few minutes to get his stiff joints limber enough to get dressed, which he did as quietly as he could so as not to wake his roommate, who was snoring. Mercer liked Finn LeMar well enough; it was good to have somebody to talk to. But nobody could take Abner's place.

More minutes were needed for his clumsy fingers to fit buttons to holes and close his pants zipper. He sat in the rocking chair to pull on his socks and shoes. Then he reached for his cane and left the room.

The hallway was dim, and his shuffling steps were loud in the quiet. The nurse wasn't at her station when he passed. Outside, a chilly breeze rustled the trees as he walked across the nursing-home grounds and along the shoulder of the blacktopped road. He was glad for his warm flannel shirt.

He thought about last night. Molly Bearpaw—as full of vinegar as her grandmother had ever been—clomping down the hall in those muddy boots and flinging open Sally Creighton's door. Randy Hulle on top of Sally, trying to smother her with her pillow. It had hit Mercer in a flash that he was watching Abner's killer. Fury boiled up in him, and Molly yelled for help. Without thinking, Mercer had hobbled into the fray and stopped Hulle from breaking a window and getting away. His joints were paying the price today, but it was worth it to feel useful again for a little while.

Reaching the place where he usually turned and started back, he heard a sound—like a murmur of voices—coming from the small grove of trees next to the road. He halted. The sound died away. He waited, hearing nothing now but the moving air.

He wondered if he'd overheard the Little People talking to each other. Even though he'd never seen them himself, Mercer believed without question in the existence of the tiny beings, *Anigûnehiyat'*, the Eternal Ones, who looked exactly like Cherokees, except for size.

As a boy, he had heard many stories about the fun-loving Little People. They were harmless, although his parents had warned him there was a danger of becoming fascinated by them and following them off to unpredictable adventures. That had happened to his father's father when he was young. He had gone fishing in the Illinois River, south of Tahlequah, just below a cliff formation called Standing Rock. The cliff was still there, but since the big dam had been built, it overlooked Tenkiller Lake.

It was getting dark when Mercer's grandfather started home, and he lost his way. After wandering around for a while, he came to a tall rock formation and saw a door in the face of the rock. He went in and found a great number of Little People inside, dancing. They gave him raccoon meat to eat and he lay down by the fire and went to sleep. The Little People danced all night.

The next morning, when he awoke, the fire had died and he was alone. He went out the door and walked a short distance. When he looked back, the door had disappeared. He went up a hill, saw a familiar landmark, and found his way home.

Mercer had loved hearing that story. It had been years, but he could still remember how his grandfather had told it, word for word. He would like to see the Little People himself before he died.

He waited now, leaning against a tree, hoping to hear the voices again. He squinted so hard to clear his vision that his eyes watered. He rubbed his knuckle against his eyes and shook his head because he had begun to feel a little sleepy. When he looked toward the grove again, they were there, a crowd of Little People gathered around an old man with braided hair. They were laughing and moving away from Mercer, deeper into the trees. The old man with them looked over his shoulder, and Mercer saw it was Abner.

"Good-bye, old friend," Abner said. Mercer didn't know if he heard it with his ears or only with his mind.

Mercer gripped his cane and started toward them. "Wait!" But they were gone before he had taken three steps. He called out, "Abner!" But the only sound was the wind in the trees.

Mercer wanted to go after them, but he knew it was no use. They were gone. But he stood there a little longer, and a strange peace descended on him. The pain in his hip lessened as he walked back to the nursing home.

The young nurse was back at her station when he returned, the new one with the deep blue eyes.

She seemed alarmed to see him coming toward her. "Mr. Vaughan, where have you been?"

"Walking. I couldn't sleep."

"There's hardly enough light to see where you're going. You shouldn't be out there at this hour, alone."

Mercer opened his mouth and closed it. He hadn't been alone, he thought. But he didn't say it. It wasn't something she could ever understand.